Praise for

LONELY DOVE

"It has been an absolute joy to journey with Anji in her pursuit of a soulmate. Sonee Singh has written an unputdownable novel that shares the hidden potential of relationships and life through a beautifully told story. Sonee's engaging writing allowed me to easily play the book out in my mind as the conversations placed me there, right in that moment. I fell in love with the characters. I really cared about what happened to them. This is a truly satisfying read, and I'm still smiling."

—Karen McDermott
Award-winning entrepreneur, author, publisher, mentor, and renowned speaker

"Being a true believer in soulmates and twin flames, *Lonely Dove* captured my heart from the opening pages. I enjoyed every stage of this debut novel by Sonee Singh, walking beside the self-doubting, loveable protagonist, Anji, as she bravely stepped forward and embraced her journey of self-discovery and self-worth in her quest to find her soulmate.

"*Lonely Dove* is not just a novel of the search for 'happy ever after' but is filled with empowering messages, relatable, quirky characters, and thought-provoking insight for the reader to consider the importance of self-love and self-acceptance, above any other love.

"*Lonely Dove* is enriched with cultural diversity, and Singh masterfully guided me on a cultural celebration where spices drifted from the pages with her artful descriptions of Indian and Colombian cuisines that had my mouth watering. Peace and purpose were two words that came to me often as I read this novel."

—Mickey Martin
Author of *The Given* Trilogy

"*Lonely Dove* carries a beautiful energy through every page and had me captivated from the first chapter. I found the themes and storyline very relatable, and it evoked strong emotions as I read. It is a universal story that explores complexity in relationships and the importance of trusting our intuition. It is also about universal timing and spiritual growth. Sonee's writing is powerfully descriptive and shows deep spiritual understanding and cultural awareness. This novel effectively communicates the burden of expectations as well as the heartache of breaking traditions. *Lonely Dove* is a timeless love story that has depth and meaning. There are also a few surprises to keep the reader intrigued. This book needs to be on your 'must-read' list."

—Lisa Benson
Author of *Where Have I Been All My Life?*

"We follow Anji's journey through a poetic and metaphysical lens. Singh deliciously presents us with a story that explores Anji's deepest thoughts and hopes, starting in the realm of dreams whilst tiptoeing towards experiences of what love means, unfulfillment, the perils of finding one's soulmate, and the world of spirituality."

—Magali Jeger
Author of *Hanna,* and playwright

Lonely Dove

By Sonee Singh

© Copyright 2022 Sonee Singh

ISBN 978-1-64663-787-4

This is a work of fiction. The characters are both actual and fictitious. With the exception of verified historical events and persons, all incidents, descriptions, dialogue and opinions expressed are the products of the author's imagination and are not to be construed as real.

Published by

⊠ köehlerbooks™

3705 Shore Drive
Virginia Beach, VA 23455
800−435−4811
www.koehlerbooks.com

LONELY DOVE

SONEE SINGH

VIRGINIA BEACH
CAPE CHARLES

To all soulmates—including twin flames—
who make us feel we can be our true selves.

Chapter One

FEBRUARY 1, 2019

ANJI SHOWED UP at the Gray Dog in Union Square fifteen minutes early and loitered outside. She didn't want to be the first one there.

Every few seconds she raised her left hand to her necklace, twirling on the three silver beads for reassurance, as if meditating with her *mala*. Anji pondered on all the terms there were for love in Hindi. She twirled a bead each time a new word came to mind: *pyar, ishq, prem, preeti, mohabbat*. There were many others, but she was too nervous to think of them in that moment.

Anji hoped Danny, a lucid dreaming expert, had answers. She wanted desperately for Danny to help her unravel her vision. Maybe he could help make sense of it all. Had she really seen her soulmate? Under the guise of a professional interview—she was, after all, a journalist—she had hidden her personal interest.

She had long thought love was inextricably linked with finding her soulmate. So far, she hadn't found proof of this. She had experienced different types of love, but what she wanted—the greatest love of all—she hadn't yet. True love had eluded her. And it was what she most yearned for.

Anji wanted to find her soulmate. She had always believed that it was possible. Everything in the Indian culture she hailed from and the Colombian culture she grew up in, confirmed that. Only since she came to America had she begun to doubt that her soulmate would ever show his face. She had been in New York City for twenty-three years, and all indications pointed against the possibility.

That is, until she had that vision while sitting on her rock in Central Park. She had never had a vision before. It took over her meditation; she was no longer in control. What she saw was palpable. It filled her with hope, the same type of hope she had before she reached New York. It filled her with the levity and certainty she felt in her childhood.

Her hand continued to twirl on the silver beads in her necklace as questions popped up in her head. Was it possible? Did she really have a soulmate? Were all her teenage ideations real? Or could they become real? She hoped Danny could shed some light.

Her phone vibrated, indicating it was time for her appointment. At six o'clock on the dot, she walked into the restaurant.

Danny had explained that he was hard to miss, and she spotted him immediately. His six-foot four-inch frame was crammed into a four-top table. He was slender but his bones were wide, filling the chair he sat upon. Anji thought he appeared like a caricature. His wide gray eyes bulged in his face, making his hair appear grayer than it was. He wore a white-and-blue top that contributed to his bland aura. It wasn't a comforting look. Anji noticed that Danny's pants were white and realized she wouldn't have chosen light colors on a snowy day. Or ever.

Anji wore all black. Her hair was down, a curly dark mane that was also hard to miss, but she hadn't pointed that out to Danny. Her hair was thin, wispy, and was typically indecisive about wanting to be defined and curly or a wavy frizzy mane. That evening she'd used styling product and her curls were plump and smooth. As always, she wore a thick layer of *kajal* on her bottom eyelids. She completed the ensemble with ornate silver Indian-style dangling earrings, black nail polish, and deep maroon lipstick.

"Ahn-ha-lee?" he asked, inviting her to sit down.

Anji's full name—Anjali—hadn't been butchered like that since she'd left Colombia twenty-three years ago. In Spanish, *ja* was pronounced "ha" but *Anjali* was meant to be pronounced "ahn-juh-lee." Her last name was easier. Sharma was "Char-ma" in Spanish, which was close enough, in Anji's opinion. She didn't know how Danny had come to that pronunciation of her name. He didn't seem to have one bit of any kind of brown in him.

"Anjali," she corrected, taking a seat at the table.

"What religion are you?" Danny asked.

Anji was taken aback. She was used to asking the questions. She wondered if she'd made the right decision in choosing to interview Danny. When searching for experts on hypnagogic dreams, she found many Christian-only spiritual circles. Danny had stood out because his website didn't overtly mention religion, unless she had missed it. Anji normally scoured reviews and double-checked testimonials to ensure the people she featured in her articles were reputable, but in her urge for answers she hadn't been as diligent with Danny. "Umm . . . Hindu. Why do you ask?"

"I hoped you would be Christian." He paused, as if debating what to say next. "I'm Christian—a Jehovah's Witness. Are you willing to convert?"

Anji pushed back her chair, guessing Danny was part of a religious circle. The interview had not yet started, and she could still back out. "No, I am not. Is that a problem?"

"Oh no. I was curious. It is definitely not a problem."

"Good, I was really hoping to get clarity—" Anji scooted her chair back toward the table.

"I'm happy to provide any clarity I can. After all, I'm not about to lose the opportunity to be featured in *Really Living Magazine*," Danny interrupted, smiling.

Anji smiled back awkwardly, feeling Danny wasn't being completely honest. Then again, neither was she. "It's not going to be a feature article. It's a short piece I'm working on."

The Gray Dog was a small casual place serving smaller plates of sandwiches and tacos, and most of the patrons were young, likely college students. Anji wasn't sure why Danny had chosen the place until he'd told her he was a professor of mathematics at New York University. It must have been a nearby location for him.

"I went to NYU for undergrad," Anji said.

"Has your degree helped your career?" Danny asked.

"I write about alternative therapies and healing, and the pre-med classes I took help me with my research."

"I love the similarities of our schooling." Danny beamed at her, his eyes bigger still.

Anji found it difficult to look at him. She hadn't admitted to Josh—her boss and editor-in-chief at *Really Living Magazine*—that she had created the brief for this article to learn about her own vision. "So . . . let's get to the topic of dreams."

"You've been having strange dreams?"

"I had one." Anji told Danny about the vision she'd had while meditating on her rock in Central Park. It felt odd to speak candidly to a stranger when she hadn't yet told her close friends. It felt stranger still to be asked about a personal matter. In the more than sixteen years she had worked at the magazine, she had been careful not to blur the lines between her professional quest and her personal life. She believed it was one of the reasons she was successful.

"It sounds like a hypnagogic dream," Danny said.

"That's what I guessed, but I wasn't sure."

"Are you a strong believer in Hinduism?" he asked.

"What does that have to do with dreams? Is religion connected in some way?"

"Please, answer the question. I promise I'll explain."

Anji tried to hide her rising irritation. "I'm more spiritual than religious. I participate in major religious festivities, I go to temple once in a blue moon, and I pray on a regular basis."

"I also pray regularly. More than regularly. Daily. Multiple times a day, in fact. Being spiritual matters more than being religious. Does that mean you meditate? I associate being Indian with meditation." Danny spoke fast, rushing to get his words out.

"Yes, although I wouldn't connect meditation with being Indian. The practice may have originated there, but most Indian people I know don't meditate. Just like most Indian people I know don't do yoga. It's a common misconception. Can we get back to the hypnagogic dream?"

"Yes, yes."

Danny explained that it was a state of consciousness between waking and sleeping also known as lucid dreaming. People saw images and visions that allowed them to dive into their subconscious or tap into higher wisdom. "I once asked about Hinduism. I was told it came from a higher consciousness, which I accept. My problem is accepting there is more than one god. What is your take?"

"I'm trusting you'll circle back to how religion is connected to these dreams."

Danny placed his elbows on the table and rested his face on the palms of his hands. He nodded eagerly, like a kid awaiting a story.

Anji sighed loudly. "Despite the many gods, goddesses, and animal deities, Hinduism isn't polytheistic. It is panentheistic. We believe everything is God and God is in everything—all deities stem from the same source."

"What about Jesus Christ?"

"In theory, Hindus accept all divine beings, including Jesus Christ, Allah, and other gods. To us, in theory, it doesn't matter who you pray to. Of course, in practice it is different. That is why there are so many religious conflicts, even between Hindu sects."

"So, you do believe in Jesus Christ." Danny's eyes lit up, and he clapped his hands.

People turned to stare at them. Anji feared Danny's eyes might pop out of his head. "I wouldn't deny he existed."

"Okay, you wouldn't have a problem converting to a Jehovah's Witness?" Danny smiled wide. He seemed giddy.

"I won't convert . . . I still don't understand what my faith has to do with dreaming?"

"Technically, nothing," he admitted.

Anji tried to mask her frustration. "What I want to understand is if we can see things that are destined for us in hypnagogic dreams, like soulmates? Could I have seen my soulmate in the vision I had?"

The first time Anji heard the Spanish word for soulmate, *alma gemela*, her heart went aflutter. Twin soul. She was four, too young to comprehend what it meant. Yet she believed, in the deepest part of her being, that she had one. Her perfect pair—like her mother and father. Her parents and brother, Sid, were all there was—their close family of four. She assumed this was the way it was for everyone. Everyone had a soulmate.

Danny took a deep breath and leaned toward her. "The short answer is yes. You absolutely can. But, I asked about religion because of *me*. *I* could be your soulmate. *I* could be the man in your vision . . . It makes sense. You already believe in Jesus Christ. It wouldn't be a stretch to convert, would it? We clearly have so much to learn from each other. It would be perfect."

The couple next to Danny and her shared a laugh that cut through the air. Anji looked down at the table. She still sensed she had a soulmate. Even now, she hoped, deep inside, he was out there. She didn't dare confess it to anyone—not even Sophie. It seemed a childish notion—so Harlequin romance novel, so cliché. Yet all she wanted was to figure out who he was. And where.

Here was Danny, who so easily claimed he could be her soulmate. It made Anji wonder if her life's quest could be resolved in mere minutes. She gazed down at the wooden table separating them, willing it to give her a clue. It was unpolished, with pieces of bark still attached, as if it had dropped straight from the forest. The intricacy of the wood reminded her that the universe held great possibility. But its liveliness felt incongruent. Out of place.

Anji wanted nothing more than to find her soulmate. Even the vision she had received recently hinted that she was close. But it jarred her that Danny thought finding a soulmate was that easy.

"What if we fell in love? Wouldn't you want to make me happy? Religion is so important to me and you are spiritual. It's a small step from spirituality to religion. It would be the true mark of a soulmate," Danny said.

Anji shook her head in disbelief. The implication that someone called her his soulmate, while simultaneously asking her to change something fundamental about herself stung. "I'm not sure what the point is of talking about what I would or would not do for love. I'm here to interview you. This is my job. That aside, I am not willing to change my religion. No matter what. I accept Jesus Christ existed, but that does not mean I will convert."

"Really? You feel that strongly?" His voice dropped several decibels.

"Yes . . . how about you converting? How would you feel about that?"

"I wouldn't convert," he said flatly.

A smugness settled over Anji. She didn't understand how people could ask others to do something they weren't willing to do themselves.

"See how easily we are speaking to each other and how quickly we got into such an exciting and deep conversation. There aren't many people I can do this with. Can you?" Danny sounded desperate.

"This is a one-of-a-kind exchange. That's because I came here to discuss hypnagogic dreams, and you got into religion and got carried away by the idea of soulmates."

Anji stared at the wooden table again, torn between her need for answers on her own vision and her urge to get away from Danny. She rubbed her sweaty palms together, gathering courage. She pushed back her chair.

Anji had loved all things bright and beautiful, especially her beloved Bollywood movies and Latin American *telenovelas*, where the girl always got the guy of her dreams. Anji had spent her lifetime wishing, with every fiber of her being, for her *happily ever after*, certain it would happen when her soulmate appeared.

Now aged forty-one and still single, she thought of how gullible she had been to be conned by the idea of soulmates, much less to think she would marry the person. She had learned that life was filled with eternal struggles to find her soulmate. Her frustration reached a new level after she'd had that vision a couple of weeks before. That, and this meeting with Danny, felt like unnecessary provocations, the universe daring her to hold onto the childish notion.

Danny put his hand out to stop her from leaving. "We are meant to be. You had your vision and I saw it in one of my dreams." He clapped again, jolting her back to attention.

Anji set her attention back on Danny. She wondered if his dream was similar to her vision. "What did you see?"

"I didn't get a vision per se . . . "

Anji spoke slowly. "What exactly did you see?"

Danny lowered his tone. "I got a general message."

"Did you see anything at all? Did you see me?"

"I didn't see the person and I didn't get images. I haven't dated in over five years and I asked about my dating life. I got a clear message that I would not need to date and I would meet my soulmate soon." Danny didn't appear as tall anymore, and his eyes had shrunk back to their normal size.

Anji leaned in. "There was no indication that I was your soulmate, right? Or that you would be meeting them tonight?"

"Right . . . "

She let out a deep sigh. "Okay, good. I can tell you I am not your soulmate."

"How can you say that? I haven't connected with someone like this in a long time," Danny whined.

"I'm sorry you haven't connected with someone, but we are not soulmates. I connect with strangers for a living. I think we feel comfortable sharing our fears, secrets, or thoughts with someone we don't know, simply because we are not afraid to be judged. We aren't likely to see that person again, so it doesn't matter what we say."

"I can't believe it. You don't think we have something special?"

"Don't get me wrong, Danny. I've enjoyed talking to you, but this is a professional interview. It's clear you've got the wrong idea."

Anji got up, put her coat on, and walked out of the restaurant. Danny rushed to follow her. She tried to get ahead, but his long legs caught up to her.

"Look at your skin. It is a delicious brown—the same as the Kraft caramels I keep in the bottom drawer of my desk. They are my only vice. Are you absolutely sure?" Danny pleaded.

Anji felt it was her life's mission to find her soulmate. For Danny to say nonchalantly that he was sure she was his, without making an effort to know her or ensure true sparks flew between them, irked her. She didn't have time for this—for him. She still needed to pack for her flight to Madrid the next day.

Anji did not have a shred of doubt. "Yes, I am."

Chapter Two

FEBRUARY 4, 2019

ANJI WAITED FOR JOSH to join in for a Skype session. She had landed in Madrid the day before. As a senior journalist at *Really Living Magazine*, she was helping set up their new European headquarters. When Josh's blue eyes popped up on the screen, she took a deep breath and focused on the notes in front of her. They discussed what she needed to get done.

"I am so relieved to have you there. It's an asset to us that you speak Spanish," Josh said.

Anji nodded as she marveled at his complexion. On screen, his cheeks appeared like they were made out of porcelain. Anji had often wondered how he was able to maintain such clear skin, but she hadn't dared to ask. She couldn't believe that her thoughts were running away from her. It was unusual for her to be unfocused, and she wondered if this was related to the vision.

In an effort to focus she said, "This is a new responsibility for me but given the caliber of the team, I'm confident they will fulfill the expectations of the magazine."

Josh flipped his hair, distracting her again. Anji wanted to reach through the monitor and run her fingers through his well-defined curls. It gave him an almost girlish look, making her think of

Bollywood actors who often flipped their hair on screen. Her thoughts drifted to Anil Kapoor, an eighties heartthrob. As a teenager, her concept of soulmates was fueled by visions of him prancing toward her through fields of yellow mustard flowers. She skipped toward him, arms outstretched, as they lip-synced passionate declarations of love to each other. Syncopated rhythms sent their bodies into synchronized and sensuous hip gyrations until they came together in a longing embrace. In true Bollywood flair, an obscenely large flower conveniently blocked their kiss. As Anji grew older, the flower dissipated, and she imagined the wetness of their soft lips coming together, tongues twisting in passion.

"How are you doing on your dreamer's piece?" Josh asked, jolting Anji back to attention.

He had never asked for an update before. She wondered if he knew she was faltering. "The person I interviewed on Friday didn't work out."

"Huh . . . that's unusual. I know I don't need to remind you about deadlines, or that yours is our main story. I know you've got this. You always do."

When Anji had arrived in Madrid the previous morning, there had been three missed calls from Danny and several text messages asking her for a chance to meet again. Anji deleted them. She knew she would never see him again. She had to find someone else to interview to meet her article brief. Hopefully, one of the local journalists knew of a dream expert and Anji could arrange an interview before the end of the week. The article was due at the end of the day on Friday.

"Unless you feel you've got too much on your plate?" Josh asked, sensing her lack of assurance. "We'd discussed that you would have sent in the story before flying to Madrid."

Anji's stomach tightened, as she attempted to push away her doubts. "Josh, you've given me this chance to prove I can take on more responsibility, and I will get it done. I've got this."

Anji had to complete the article, one way or another. She still didn't have a clear answer about her vision and didn't think it was possible to feel worse. She couldn't shake the feeling that something was missing in her life. Love felt elusive. The article brief for *RLM* had created the perfect excuse for her to research vivid dreams, dreams seeming real, dreams coming true, and other dream-related search terms. Most websites covered dream interpretation and didn't offer answers. What she wanted most was to know if she really had a soulmate. Maybe she wouldn't have wasted so many years of futile dating if she had known where to find him. She wondered if there was someone out there who loved her.

The thought stayed with her for most of the day, even though she was busy with the Madrid team. Before getting back to the Hotel Wellington, Anji went for a stroll around the Parque del Buen Retiro to clear her mind. A wintery breeze swept over the lake in the park. Anji circled around the Crystal Palace, surprised by the number of vendors selling trinkets and hand-made items. She couldn't understand how they stayed out in the cold for so long. She walked past them with her head down, shuddering as she pulled her coat tightly.

Anji had not felt lonely all of her life. She had been happy once. She hoped—wished—that she could turn back the clock and soak up some of the feelings from her childhood and pull them into her present. The thought clung to her as she wished she didn't feel so desolate.

A blanket on the ground covered with clear crystals grabbed her attention. She avoided making eye contact with the vendor, but the crystals were so inviting, she couldn't help but kneel down to peer at the pieces more closely.

"They are Lemurian seed crystals," the vendor said.

He explained that most of them were from mines in Colombia. From his accent, it was clear to Anji that he was Colombian. He confirmed that he was from Medellin and had been living in Madrid for two years. Anji picked up a crystal and held it up to the sky. It was nearly translucent and she could almost distinguish the clouds through it.

"That one is from Minas Gerais in Brazil," the vendor said.

"Which ones come from Colombia?" Anji smiled, feeling encouraged by the connection to the country she was raised in.

The vendor pointed to one, and when she held it in her hand, she felt oddly comforted. It was warm and seemed to vibrate under her touch. She decided to buy it.

"Lemurian seed crystals are useful in meditation, healing, opening the heart, and increasing spiritual awareness," the vendor said as he packed the crystal.

Anji felt chills run through her body. She shivered as she placed it in her purse. She thought of it as a talisman.

The scent of frying oil perked her head up. Anji realized she hadn't eaten lunch and bought crispy fried *churros* smothered in cinnamon sugar and a cup of rich hot chocolate, disregarding the knowledge she was overpaying for it in this tourist center. She sat at a nearby bench and was instantly surrounded by a flock of pigeons. She took large bites, fearing the birds would steal her food. When she was done, she sipped the chocolate slowly, allowing the warmth to permeate her. She continued to watch the birds and found that they seemed less aggressive. Her eyes settled on a few white ones and she wondered what the difference was between a pigeon and a dove. Anji searched it on her phone and learned doves had smaller bodies and longer tails. From the descriptions, it seemed that those around her were pigeons.

She couldn't help but to come back to the idea of soulmates. Anji had long let go of her unrealistic teenage dreams but still believed finding her soulmate was the key to her happiness. She remembered how hopeful she'd felt when she first arrived in New York City from her Colombian home in Cali. She had been a bright eighteen-year-old freshman at NYU, eager for her new life and the possibility of love. Although the big city was daunting and intimidating, she hadn't felt more at home anyplace else. She didn't stand out in New York, blending in like all the other immigrants in the city.

Anji didn't encounter other Indians growing up in Colombia, except for her math teacher. He had immigrated from India in the early 1970s after falling in love with a Colombian woman.

"Don't fall for an Indian guy. They won't understand you," he cautioned Anji before she flew out to attend NYU.

Anji wasn't looking for an Indian man. She wasn't *not* looking for an Indian man. She was simply looking for the right man. The hodgepodge of New York matched perfectly with the hodgepodge of her identity. In her naiveté, she thought she would find her soulmate waiting for her on the steps of a brownstone. She hadn't realized she'd still be waiting for him twenty-three years later.

Anji made her way back to the hotel, realizing she longed for the past. For the person she had been. As a little girl, she had felt joy. She twirled and danced and played. Everything seemed easier back then; the world was filled with possibility. Lately, she'd felt she was laboring up a steep hill while wading through a stream of molasses.

She reached the Puerta de Alcalá and stopped to admire it. There was a song from the eighties that Anji used to love called "*La Puerta de Alcalá.*" It brought her chills to be standing in front of it. The gate that watched time go by, as the song said, standing the test of time through changing kings, revolutions, wars, protests, and all sorts of passersby. The gate forced people to bare their truth. Anji felt as if the words had been sung for her in that moment. Shivers ran down her spine.

Just then, someone grabbed her left arm. Anji gasped and stared into the face of an elderly woman. Her eyes were black and she'd lost all her eyelashes and eyebrows. She wore a purple scarf around her head, her white hair visibly thinning underneath. The woman's face had so many wrinkles it was hard to imagine that it had once been supple and smooth.

The woman forcefully spread Anji's fingers open and traced the lines on her left palm as if it were a map. She peered at it diligently, clearly in search of something. It didn't occur to Anji to let go. The act felt familiar. When Anji visited India as a child, a few priests had reacted in a similar way, peering into Anji's hands without asking her permission. One priest had said the lines revealed that Anji would dishonor her parents and live far away from her family. It seemed to Anji she had done just that.

"*Tienes visión espiritual.*" The woman held Anji's gaze.

Anji wondered if the woman knew of her vision or if this was something she told everyone. Anji knew the woman could be duping her into a palm reading, as Romani ladies often did. But there was something intriguing about the way the woman looked at Anji. She felt as if the woman were piercing the depths of her soul.

The woman grabbed Anji's right hand, searching from one palm to the other. The woman could tell that Anji worked with her hands, as an artist, like a painter or writer. Anji's palms were larger than normal and her fingers were slender and long. She said Anji created art with her words. Anji didn't feel her words created art but said nothing.

"*Estas bendecida,*" the Romani lady said, looking into Anji's eyes once again.

Others had told Anji she was blessed. Anji had a clear luck line, a sign that angels and divine beings watched over her. The old woman closed her eyes and said she could see the face of an elephant. Anji felt a flurry of goosebumps and her hairs stood on edge. The elephant was clearly Ganesh, the Hindu god known as the remover of obstacles. Anji had acquired so many Ganesh idols over the years that many of her friends claimed her apartment was a shrine to Ganesh. Anji felt blessed by his strength and nurturing.

"*Necesitas un exorcismo,*" the woman said with a grave tone.

Anji thought an exorcism to be unnecessary, but she let the woman proceed. She told Anji she needed to let go of something that was keeping her stuck. She warned that without fixing what was broken, Anji would never find true love.

It occurred to Anji that she had fallen for the Romani woman's ploy. Anji chided herself for being so gullible. She pulled her hands away and walked off. When Anji turned back, worried that the woman might follow and pester her for money, she was surprised to see that the old woman stood still.

"*Que Dios te bendiga, niña,*" she called out, as if blessing Anji would make it all better.

Anji kept walking, trying to shake off the chills that ran through her. The uncanny precision about the vision, Ganesh, and being a writer shook her more forcefully than she was willing to admit. What if the Romani woman was right?

Chapter Three

SHE STOOD ON THE PLATFORM waiting for a train. The man standing on the opposite platform seemed familiar but she couldn't get a good look. His face was hidden behind a hoodie and he peered down at a book in his hands.

She tried to call out to him. When she opened her mouth, there was no sound. She tried to clear her throat. Even that didn't make a sound. She grasped at her throat, wondering what had happened to her voice.

A train whistled in the distance. She raised her hand to get his attention. He didn't look up. He still didn't notice when she waved. Her hands motioned ever more fervently as she jumped up and down, but to no avail. The train pulled into the platform. He got on the train and took a seat without glancing at her.

As the train chugged away, a pair of dark eyes loomed into sight, blocking her view. A hairless wrinkled face spoke one word, "Exorcismo."

Anji sat with a jolt and opened her eyes. As she focused on the evening sky and the leaves overhead, she realized she was sitting on a bench in the Parque del Retiro. Alone.

Anji had gotten a vision. Again. She had gone back to the Parque del Retiro for a walk. She'd had several long workdays, and Josh had called her a second time to bug her about the piece on dreams. He hadn't been so persistent before, but then again, she hadn't been so resistant to discuss what she was working on.

Anji needed her head to be screwed back onto her body and thought a short meditation would help. It had worked until she got the vision with the taunting face of the Romani woman. Anji was covered in cold sweat.

The first time Anji got a vision was the morning of January 26, and it had come to her in a similar way as it had that afternoon. Instead of lying on a park bench, she'd lain on a rock in Central Park. When she went to her rock in New York she got a sense of peace, and she tried to recreate the same feeling again, that day, in the Parque del Retiro, but it hadn't worked.

Anji wondered if her visions were hypnagogic. The visions were vivid, almost real, which is how Danny described his dreams. Danny told her he entered them easily. He lay still, cleared his mind, and set the intention to go into a hypnagogic state. After a few deep breaths, he found himself in a semi-conscious dream.

On the other hand, Anji didn't intend to enter anything other than calmness. She had meditated and without her awareness, the vision had appeared. She didn't have to try.

The first vision had left her feeling elated. She wished it was real. When her mystery soulmate had whispered, "my lonely dove," a surge had coursed through her. The connection to the man in her dream was unlike any she'd felt before. She had wanted to stay with him. She didn't care that she hadn't been able to see his face. There was something about him that had felt familiar. Most of all, she had felt loved. Despite the weight of her forty-one years, the vision had made her feel she might still have a chance. It had awakened a hope in her that she hadn't felt in a long time. She wondered if it was a sign, a confirmation that she was destined to find her soulmate.

The men in both visions were one and the same. She didn't know how she knew that, but she did. She was certain of it. And she also felt as if she knew him. She wondered how it was possible that he seemed so familiar. She didn't know anyone who could be her soulmate, even though many, like Danny, had labeled her as such. Had she been too quick in dismissing them? She chided herself for rousing too early from her meditation. She was sure that if she had continued the vision for a few more moments, she might have been able to see his face.

She had thought that if she learned more, her dreams would lead her to him. After hours of going down several useless rabbit holes, she had found Danny. He had said he helped anyone seeking answers in their dreams. Clearly, he didn't. And she didn't have an article to present to Josh. She tried to search for other sources but hadn't been able to stop thinking about the Romani woman. She knew an exorcism was not necessary, but she needed to do something.

The second vision—the one she'd just gotten—left her feeling deeply unsettled, dispelling all the magic from the Central Park vision.

Anji walked back to her hotel room. She felt even more jarred after seeing the old woman's face in the second vision. She needed to know more. She had to make sense of it all. Anji had the strange sensation that something bigger than her was pushing her along. What was it trying to tell her?

Anji called Sophie. There was no one better to work this out than with her best friend. The call went to voicemail. She tried Sophie's office number. With the time difference, Sophie was likely eating her lunch at her desk. That call also went to voicemail. Anji texted Sophie, urging to call her back. She stared at her phone. It remained silent.

Anji felt hope slipping away. Maybe it was a sign she was not meant to find her soulmate, the first vision a mere taunt of the life she could have had.

Chapter Four

FEBRUARY 8, 2019

"BIENVENIDA," A PETITE WOMAN with short reddish-brown hair bowed to Anji in namaste, as she welcomed her in.

Anji took a long look at her and was met with an equally penetrating stare. The woman introduced herself as Margarita, the director at Divya. Margarita seemed to be in her sixties and wore a navy-blue wrap dress that showed off her beautiful curves. She had a large rose quartz necklace with ten stones in a cluster. It was so imposing Anji thought it should have weighed her neck down. Yet Margarita held her neck up formidably. The only makeup she wore was burgundy red lipstick. Her lips were thin, almost unnoticeable if it weren't for the lipstick. Anji thought Margarita didn't fit into the all-loving bhakti environment. Most of the people at the center were dressed in earth-colored hemp and cotton clothing. Margarita appeared regal in a goddess-like way.

"Have we met before?" Margarita asked.

"No, we haven't," Anji replied, although she couldn't deny that something about her seemed familiar.

Margarita peered at Anji carefully, the smile not leaving her face. "What is your name?"

"Anjali Sharma, but I go by Anji."

"It's important to know your full name for the work I do. What brings you here today?"

"I'm not here as a client. We spoke on the phone? I'm here to interview you for the article for *Really Living Magazine*."

Anji had found Divya, the bhakti center, after conducting a perfunctory internet search on spiritual dreaming. The journalists in her team had not known of a dream expert, and Anji felt relieved when she found the listing for Divya earlier that morning. The bhakti center was conveniently located a short walk from the Hotel Wellington, and around the corner from the National Library of Spain, where Anji had hoped to sit down to write the article. Anji needed to submit it by midnight. It was four o'clock already.

Margarita looked at Anji carefully. "You should consider working with me."

Anji felt shivers run down her spine. "How about we start with the interview?"

"How about I give you a tour?"

"I am tight on time."

"It will only take a few minutes, and I feel it is important for you to understand what we do, especially if you will be featuring us in your magazine."

Anji didn't clarify that her purpose wasn't to feature Divya but rather to explore lucid dreaming. Still, she agreed, feeling confident that she had enough time to interview Margarita and write the article before the deadline.

Divya looked like a regular wellness center. It had a small café, a couple of yoga studios, and several smaller spaces. What stood out was the temple laden with Hindu deities. Margarita explained the center's philosophy was about expressing devotion through adoration—love for love's sake. Their services helped people connect with the oneness of everything. Light and love were at the heart of their practices. Anji watched a group of twelve people playing drums and chanting in one of the smaller rooms. They sang in meditation with their eyes closed.

"Are they in a trance state?" Anji asked, although what she really wondered was if they were in a hypnagogic state.

"They might be. They might also be enjoying the moment. Would you like to join our *kirtan*? You should try it, my dear. It will help bring light to the darkness that clouds you."

Anji felt the hairs on her neck stand on edge. "Thank you for offering, but not today. What about spiritual dreaming?"

"The avenue of devotion is not what matters. It is devotion itself. The ultimate goal is to reach a state of bliss," Margarita explained.

"Your website mentioned that you offer spiritual dreaming."

"We'll have to update that. We ran a workshop on dreaming for a short while, but we no longer offer it. We explore all avenues of connecting with the divine. Our focus is on releasing fear, worries, and anxiety and replacing them with joy, peace, and ecstasy."

Anji's heart sank. In her rush for answers, she had once again not been diligent. When she saw spiritual dreaming listed on Divya's website, she had booked an interview with Margarita without confirming that it was current. Anji felt she had failed herself professionally.

In that moment, Anji realized she had no choice but to change the focus of the article. She hoped Josh would accept that her source on hypnagogic dreams didn't pan out. She would tell him she would write about bhakti yoga. She could tie-in the European and American issues of the magazine by showcasing Divya in Madrid and the Bhakti Center on the Lower East Side in New York.

"Can I ask you some more questions about your experience with bhakti?" Anji felt slightly encouraged with her new resolve.

"Of course, my dear," Margarita smiled warmly and led Anji to her office.

Margarita's office had large windows and plenty of natural light. It was set up as a living room, and most of the furniture was made out of wood. Splashes of color from large geodes of amethyst, smoky quartz, agate, and jasper offset the sandy upholstery and rugs. They were strewn around the space with some crystals standing up to three feet tall. Anji was drawn to a rose quartz placed on a coffee table and bent down to take a closer look. It was the size of a pineapple and the texture was rough, unlike the smooth, polished stones Margarita wore around her neck.

"That's the unconditional love stone. It opens us to all kinds of love, including family, friends, and relationships. It also brings self-love," Margarita explained.

Anji momentarily considered adding rose quartz into her jewelry repertoire—she could benefit from more love in her life—but decided against it. Anji owned ornate jewelry. They were the most fashionable items she possessed, but she preferred them without stones so she could easily combine them with any outfit. She remembered the Lemurian seed crystal she had purchased and touched her hand to her purse. She would limit herself to admiring the stones on others.

"You have quite a collection of crystals."

"I have selected them purposefully. They are arranged to make the most of the combined energy of the crystals, the space, the healing of my clients, and my intentions."

Anji took a seat on a three-cushion sofa, focusing her attention back to the article. "Tell me about yourself. How did you get into the bhakti culture?"

Margarita sat next to Anji. "I was a gastroenterologist, and the more I treated my patients, the more I realized I knew things about their lives—who they were, what they experienced, and what they were likely to experience—that had nothing to do with medicine. I began to get these messages—let's call them that—from high above to focus on my patients' stories rather than on the symptoms in their bodies.

"I pushed away these messages at first, thinking I might be losing my mind, but the guidance I received was so strong I couldn't ignore them. I studied all I could on spirituality, intuition, and healing, and the more I did, the more I realized I healed my patients from spiritual work rather than purely medicine. After earning a Doctor of Divinity, I left my medical practice. I have worked as an intuitive full-time for twenty years. I set up my space here. I run the center, but what I love the most is the work I do as an intuitive."

"Interesting." Anji felt assured. Being a double doctorate holder gave Margarita an added sense of legitimacy. Even Josh could turn into a believer.

Margarita nodded and smiled, as if she had read Anji's mind. "What happens here stays here. This is a safe space, Anji. Tell me again, what brings you here?"

Anji was confused. "I'm writing an article on bhakti—"

"Yes, my dear, we will get to that. I feel strongly that there is something troubling you. There is a darkness behind your look that doesn't belong."

Anji felt the air drain out of her, as if she were being seen for the first time. She didn't know how to respond.

Margarita put her hand on Anji's leg. "You don't need to worry, Anji. I work with God, Source, the universe—whatever term you feel comfortable with—and I may be able to provide some guidance. I don't want to pressure you. I am offering to help because it feels right. But we will only proceed if this feels right to you too." Margarita's hands motioned around the room as if to imply that it wasn't just about feelings.

Anji glanced at her phone. It was 4:44 p.m. "The deadline for my article is tonight."

"I promise I will answer your questions. But this feels important. It's your choice. We have free will, after all."

Anji hesitated. The pull to finally speak about her visions, the botched interview with Danny, and the encounter with the Romani woman was too great. Anji felt oddly at ease, as if Margarita were an old friend and not someone she had just met. Yet the pressure to finish her article was far greater. Never before had she been this close to a deadline.

"You need to make this decision, my dear."

Anji let out a deep sigh. Here she was again, distracted by something other than the article. "I really need us to get back to the interview."

"Sure, my dear." Margarita's tone was gentle.

"How did you go from working as an intuitive to managing the center?"

"You can read energy too, you know? Right now, you are too blocked to even acknowledge it."

Anji felt shivers run up and down her spine again. "I have been told that but I . . . I need you to get back to answering my questions." She rubbed her arms to dispel the goosebumps.

"Those are God bumps, an indication that you have heard something that rings true." Margarita smiled.

Anji smiled back awkwardly and got back to the interview. Margarita finally answered Anji's questions. When they were done, it was just after five thirty. Anji felt relieved to finally have the information she needed.

"How do you feel right now?" Margarita asked.

"Grateful that I will be able to submit the article on time."

"I mean, how do you feel about your life?"

"That is a broad question." Anji glanced at her phone again.

"What is blocking you from meeting your soulmate?"

Anji felt time stand still. She stared at Margarita in disbelief. "How . . . How did you know to ask me that?"

"I told you I am an intuitive—it's what I do—and it seems I have struck a chord."

"There are strange things happening to me that I can't seem to understand," Anji managed to say.

"Things standing in the way of you and your soulmate?"

"I'm not sure. I don't know what to make of it all . . . "

"What do you feel will happen when you meet your soulmate?"

"My life will be complete. I will finally be happy." Anji couldn't believe the sincerity behind her words.

"You are the key to your own happiness, Anji. It is clear you have darkness to dispel and if you let me, I can guide you in clearing it. You need to surrender to your feelings and intuition, and let them lead the way. It is integral to healing."

Anji felt tears build in the back of her eyes. She faced away from Margarita and didn't speak, willing her tears to be sucked back in.

"What you will learn, my dear, is that our feelings are key. They hold the answers to what is happening in our lives. Most of us are taught to shut off our feelings. My work involves helping people connect with their inner guidance—their intuition—to enable them to do that."

"I've always wanted to connect with my intuition." Anji's voice was barely audible. She let out a deep sigh. "But I also have a deadline to meet."

"It is crucial to follow your gut. We never go wrong when we do."

Anji let out a light snort. "I can tell you countless stories of the many times I've ignored my gut and how awfully wrong it's been. We'll have to leave that for another time."

Margarita smiled. "Are you willing to learn how to follow your intuition?"

Anji was gathering her things and paused to consider the question. "I am."

"Powerful words, you said there, my dear."

"Excuse me?"

"The words 'I am' are two of the most empowering words one can utter. That is how I start all my sessions."

Anji got chills for the third time that afternoon. "What a coincidence."

"There's no such thing as a coincidence. You know where to find me when you are ready."

It was 5:55 pm. It was too late for the library. Anji bought dinner at the café in Divya to take back to the hotel. She had just enough time to complete the article. She vowed never again to use work as a vehicle for her personal exploration. When she left, she noticed a solitary dove perched on a sandwich board placed just outside the entrance to Divya.

Chapter Five

FEBRUARY 10, 2019

IT WAS 10:33 A.M. when Anji got into the cab to Sophie's apartment, which made her three minutes late already. Jet lag had kept her up most of the night after flying back from Madrid the day before. She'd considered Margarita's offer for help, but the more Anji reflected on the conversation, the more she thought Sophie would be a better choice.

Margarita had told Anji she needed to be clear on her emotions, and there was no one who knew her better than Sophie. Sophie had always been there for her. They had been friends—best friends— for twenty-three years. Anji felt more comfortable expressing her feelings to Sophie than to Margarita. For the first time in a long time, there was a lightness within her. Despite the muddle in her head and how perplexed she felt over what had transpired, she felt encouraged. Sophie would be key.

When Anji arrived at Sophie's apartment, she was surprised to see Tony open the door. Sophie and Tony had been married for ten years, but it was rare for him to be at the apartment. Tony ran an investment banking firm in Old Greenwich, Connecticut, and their main residence was a large house in Darien. The apartment where Anji was supposed to meet Sophie that morning was on the Upper

East Side, steps away from The Carlyle. It was where Sophie stayed during the week to be close to the Manhattan-based law firm where she worked. Anji hoped Tony wasn't joining them. Otherwise, she wouldn't be able to have her heart-to-heart with Sophie.

"Tasha and I will be out of your hair soon. It's taken us longer than expected to get ready." It was clear Tony wasn't doing much to get organized. Anji could hear Sophie in the background, likely running after their six-year-old daughter Tasha.

The first time Anji had walked into the apartment nine years ago, after Sophie and Tony bought it, Anji had been surprised to see it filled with European antiques. She imagined similar decor in Sophie's majestic family home in Charleston, South Carolina, where she grew up. Anji had wondered why Sophie tried so hard to get away from her Southern upbringing, yet it infused every element of her environment. Sophie had lost her Southern drawl but not her heritage.

Tony led Anji into the main dining room. Their cook had prepared a brunch spread for ten people. He laid out fresh bagels, plain and chocolate croissants, cinnamon rolls, eggs, bacon, lox, and fresh berries. The hand carved mahogany dining table was set with gold-rimmed china and crystal glasses for four people.

"Are you guys staying for brunch?" Anji asked with trepidation.

"The cook didn't know Tasha and I had other plans."

Anji was relieved. She badly needed Sophie. She also considered it unfair that Tony and Tasha would miss out on all the food. Without thinking she said, "If you haven't eaten, you should stay."

"Tasha woke up grumpy and you know how difficult it can be to make her eat something when she's not in the mood. I'm sure she would calm down if she didn't have to rush out the door." Tony sounded relieved.

Anji nodded knowingly although she regretted offering that they should stay.

Sophie and Tasha came in. As if reading Anji's mind, Sophie said, "Are you sure you're okay with Tasha and Tony joining us? I thought you wanted to speak about something important."

"We can get to it after. Let's eat first." Anji assured her. She didn't have other plans that day and had plenty of time to speak to Sophie.

"You are a gem, sweet pea." Sophie wrapped Anji up in a bear hug, reminding Anji of when they first met.

Anji and Sophie had been roommates freshman year in college. The day they moved in, Sophie had waltzed in as Anji unpacked. "Hi, roomie. I love saying that. You're my first roommate ever." Sophie's slender five-foot eight-inch frame engulfed Anji's five-foot four-inch roundness in what Anji would later call the greatest bear hug of her life. "My name is Sophia but everyone calls me Sophie."

Anji's body tensed at first, her hands rigid at either side. Sophie giggled and tightened her hug. Anji loved Sophie from that moment on. But then again, everyone loved Sophie.

That morning, Anji's body also felt tight. Her hands were cold and clammy. She wanted to tell Sophie about the visions, but she was also worried about how Sophie would react. When Anji had mentioned soulmates in the past, Sophie had scoffed saying they only existed in story books. Now Anji was worried she wouldn't be able to speak to Sophie at all.

Despite willing her knotted stomach to relax, Anji filled every inch of her plate. Brunches at Sophie's were her excuse to indulge, but she wasn't sure how much she could consume.

"I met this guy who told me about spiritual dreaming—" Anji started.

"Was it a date?" Sophie asked.

At the same time as Tony mocked, "Don't tell me . . . he said he saw you in a dream."

Sophie shot him a stern look.

"Sorry, I'll stay out of it," Tony said.

Anji smiled at him. "It's okay. It wasn't a date but, interestingly, he did—"

"Eww, capers! Get them *out!*" Tasha pushed away her plate.

Sophie removed the capers, but Tasha refused to eat, claiming the capers had touched all the food. Sophie prepared a new plate for her, checking with Tasha to make sure there wasn't anything on it she didn't want.

"So this guy—" Anji started again.

"I only want the chocolate," Tasha whined.

Anji took a deep breath, waiting for Sophie to cut out the chocolate from the croissant. She had to remind herself that Tasha was her goddaughter, and she owed it to her and Sophie to be patient. When Tasha was in a good mood, she was fun to play with.

"I want a bacon and egg sandwich," Tasha demanded.

When Sophie got up to make it, Anji decided to wait until after the meal to share more of her experience.

After they ate and Tasha had calmed down, Tony took Tasha out for walk in Central Park. Anji hoped the two of them would drive back to Darien so she could truly have Sophie to herself. Tony called ceaselessly when he was left on his own with Tasha.

She finally told Sophie about the interview with Danny, omitting that she had contacted him to learn about her own vision. "Can you believe he called me his soulmate?" Anji asked.

"I hope you're not going to use that as a reason to see Gandalf again."

Anji nearly choked on a bite of a bagel she was nibbling on. Her stomach hadn't calmed and her plate was still full. "Gandalf? You mean, Danny?"

"Whatever. Tall, white hair, and dwells in the land of dreams. He sounds like Gandalf." Sophie glared at Anji.

"I can't believe you would say that. No, I am not seeing him again. I haven't given him a second thought." Anji refused to believe that one person sensed their soulmate and not the other. She was sure that when she found her soulmate, the invisible cords of their bond were sure to awaken the magic between them.

"You have a soft spot for weirdos."

"No, I don't," Anji said defensively.

"Sweet pea, there's no fooling me. Loners attach to you like leeches. You see the best in people. It's your greatest gift and your biggest flaw."

"Like who?"

"Like monkey owners."

"I wasn't involved with that monkey guy. He followed me around."

"He did more than follow you around . . . "

Anji loved that Sophie was straight with her. No fuss. She came from a place of love. Most people didn't know Sophie was capable of any depth. There was a lightness about her being, as if life breezed past, barely touching her. Only the privileged few who knew Sophie well saw she was a ray of sunlight; bright, dynamic, and transformative if you lingered long enough.

"My sweets, you've had too many *lapsus brutus*." Sophie made up words that became part of their private vocabulary. Lapsus brutus referred to a relationship they got into because of a lapse of judgment. Lapsus came from lapse and brutus from *bruta,* Spanish for dumb. Sophie placed her hand on Anji's arm. "You've got too much to offer. You need a wise and mature soul, but not old. There's a difference."

"I am done dating older men."

"Yes, no more *Older Guy* please."

"Been there, done that." Anji felt a tightening within. That was a person she didn't like remembering, and she took a deep breath and released his memory. She took another deep breath, this time to gain the courage to tell Sophie about the visions. Time wasn't on her side. As if on cue, Tony called. Anji waited patiently as Sophie suggested where to take Tasha in the park.

"Sorry, sweet pea. Let's get back to you."

"I had this vision about a soulmate—"

The phone rang again. "I'm sorry, Tony isn't going to survive. Tasha is insisting she wants to ice skate wearing ballet slippers." Sophie gathered her coat and bag. She asked Anji to join them in the park and Anji declined, putting on her own coat without comment.

"You are meant to pan for gold and not settle until you've found your golden nugget, but don't obsess. Or hide. If you want to meet your soulmate, you need to get out there. He isn't going to pop out of nowhere," Sophie advised.

"Love hasn't come as easily to me as it has for you . . . "

Anji had put herself out there for years and no one stuck. By the time Anji turned thirty, she had begun to lose hope. At thirty-five, she began to worry that something was wrong with her. When she turned forty, she was sure it was irreparable. Anji felt the shriveling of her ovaries, the life seeping out of her womb. She didn't know when, but her life had turned gray, a darker shade with every passing year. Somehow, she accepted it. It was her lot in life. Karma.

Sophie had grown up surrounded by suitors. Since the age of fifteen, she had not gone more than a couple months without dating someone. She met Tony when she was twenty-nine and they married two years later.

"Sweet pea, let's not compare dating lives . . . It *will* happen for you, but you need to see it," Sophie said, as if reading her mind.

Anji walked home. Spending time with Sophie, no matter the interruptions, brought a lightness to Anji. Sophie and Anji tried their best to meet at least once a week. She was grateful that amid the frenzy of life, they were still close. Anji marveled at how they had once managed to find time to hash out minute details of a date, thoroughly examining every action as if on slow motion replay. They no longer had the luxury of spontaneity or freedom from responsibilities. But they were always there for each other.

Sophie inspired Anji to see things with a new perspective. All of a sudden, she felt infused with energy. Anji turned her stroll into a brisk walk, covering the nearly eighty blocks from Sophie's apartment to hers in ninety minutes instead of the usual two hours. Sophie said she was meant to pan for gold and, although Anji felt she had spent her adult-life panning, she hadn't met the right person. That meant she had to do something different.

As she pounded her feet on the concrete, Anji realized what it was. It became clear to her that despite what Sophie or Margarita said, her soulmate was the key to her happiness. She would date as many men as possible. She had not tried that before. It was time to spin that wheel of karma. She would exhaust all her options to find her soulmate.

Chapter Six

JANUARY 26, 2019

IT WAS TWELVE DAYS after her forty-first birthday. She was lying on her rock in Central Park. It was one of many strewn around Central Park. Hers was in the green space between the Pond and Wollman Rink, and she had chosen it because it was away from the trails populated by runners and bikers.

Anji had befriended the rock fifteen years before that, feeling it knew her better than most people. She had never been afraid to share her secrets with it. She went to the rock weekly, unless it was raining or snowing. She would sit for about an hour and walk the sixty blocks back to the East Village. It was her favorite part of the weekend.

She would walk at a leisurely pace, choosing different routes. It made her feel she was a breathing part of the city. She got her best ideas during that walk home, figuring out how to rewrite one of the articles she was working on for the magazine. Or finding a way out of a recent dating debacle.

That morning, like on most Saturdays, she took the subway up to Fifty-Ninth Street and picked up lunch from the Whole Foods at Columbus Circle. She had placed her hand on the rock and said hello as she sat down and, as usual, swore it had said hello back. She had planned to journal and read but ended up meditating instead.

Meditating on the rock was something she had started to do recently. The rock brought her a sense of peace. On some mornings, she listened to guided visions, but that morning she focused on her breath. She didn't know at what point the vision had taken over. She had no conscious awareness of falling asleep, much less of dreaming.

───────────

It was dark out and she was sitting on the beach. It was chilly but not cold. Her skin prickled as the breeze touched her.

His embrace tightened, cocooning her. Their bodies were intertwined, making it hard to distinguish where one ended and the other began. They took shallow breaths, their bellies synchronized in quick, pulsating rhythms. The moonlight shone like a beacon on the beach, casting a pearlescent shadow on their skins.

The grittiness of the sand under her hips forced her to look up. She didn't want to move and instead tried to distinguish the city lights. There was a light haze on the horizon, and if she hadn't known it was New York, it could have been any city.

"My lonely dove," he whispered in her ear.

Her head rested on his chest, and she snuggled in closer, feeling like she never wanted to let go. Warmth radiated to every part of her being, and a tingling sensation spread like wildfire over dry brush. She was glowing from the feeling of loving so deeply and being loved deeply back.

The leaves on the trees chimed in, just then, as if in agreement, their rustling sending ripples into the air. She could hear the murmur of the people around her but couldn't distinguish their words. She listened harder and concentrated on the sounds. She grew confused, thinking they were alone on the beach.

It was cold. Not chilly. She grew conscious of the hard surface she was lying on, the grit gradually disappearing. Then it dawned on her. She wasn't on the beach.

───────────

She was lying on a rock—her rock—the rock she always sat on to meditate. She gingerly opened her eyes, unsure of what she would find. As she focused on the daylight sky and the leaves overhead, she remembered she was in Central Park. Alone.

She sat on the rock trying to collect herself, and if she hadn't had to FaceTime her brother Sid, she would have stayed longer. She had to force herself to get up.

When she parted, she put her hand back on the rock and thanked it, as she always did. She walked away wishing that feeling of elation would stay with her forever.

Chapter Seven

FEBRUARY 14, 2019

ANJI AND SOPHIE were having dinner at Locanda Verde. Sophie and Tony didn't celebrate Valentine's Day. They considered it a commercial celebration and not a truly romantic one. Sophie had told Anji once that she knew she hadn't married her soulmate, but she hadn't intended to. Tony was the best male friend she could ask for and a caring and attentive lover. He kept things interesting. He jetted them off in their private plane to London or Paris, booking separate rooms at the same hotel, and pretended to meet as strangers in the lobby bar. They created different forms of romance and didn't feel the need to celebrate on gimmicky holidays.

Tony was away on a trip and Tasha was at a sleepover. Anji suspected Sophie had arranged it so that Anji wouldn't have to face the evening on her own, but she didn't say anything. She also suspected Sophie felt guilty for having to cut short on brunch.

Sophie looked stunning in a red wrap dress that made Anji feel even frumpier than usual next to her. Sophie always dressed impeccably. She didn't own jeans or understand baggy clothing—even in college. She upgraded from fashionable tracksuits in college to fitted slacks and dresses in law school. Her auburn hair always appeared without a strand out of place, even when she was fresh out of bed, and either cascaded down her back or was held up in a ponytail. That night it was tied back.

Anji's hair was disheveled as usual, and she also wore a dress, but hers hung loosely around her body. It was dark purple. Anji felt her singleness acutely as she dressed for the evening. She struggled to zip the dress and twisted her arms and contorted her torso. No matter how much yoga had improved her flexibility, she resorted to the doorman for assistance, yet again. She often left her apartment with a partially zipped dress, covering the bare parts of her back with a scarf or jacket. Her inability to leave her home with a fully zipped dress highlighted the emptiness she felt within.

"What about this dating marathon you've been on. Any potentials?" Sophie asked.

After brunch with Sophie, Anji had opened accounts on eHarmony, Match, and EliteSingles, and arranged for dates from each site. The first had been on Monday night.

"I didn't know if I was at a noodle shop or having afternoon tea at The Plaza. He managed to hold his chopsticks with his pinky finger held up. Meanwhile I shoved noodles in my mouth, slurping my way down the bowl." A Japanese colleague had told her it was proper to slurp.

"Slurping shouldn't be a thing," Sophie noted.

"Nor raised pinky fingers. We didn't click. He was too dainty."

The next night, Anji went out with a Korean guy. "He looked like he'd jumped out of a Japanese anime. His bangs were center stage, hanging over his right eye. Instead of using his hands to move them off his face, he jerked his entire body in a circular motion. It hardly seemed worth the effort. A few strands moved off his eye for a few seconds before settling back in place."

Sophie laughed. "And?"

"Our fashion clashed. His skinny jeans and fitted button-down shirt contrasted with my boot-legged jeans and *kurti*."

"Sweet pea, aren't you focusing on superficialities?"

Anji shrugged. "He closed his eyes while speaking. I am unnerved by people who can't make eye contact."

"If you didn't like him, you didn't like him," Sophie conceded.

"I didn't connect with any of them."

"You've got to be patient."

"Sophie, I'm forty-one. How much more patient can I be? Had I followed what my parents wanted, I would be raising teenagers by now." Anji felt the disappointment of an unfulfilled dream.

"You technically had a marriage proposal, but, if you ask me, you dodged a bullet when you turned him down," Sophie said.

"Ugh . . . don't remind me of Needy Boy." Anji looked away in disgust.

"I don't know why I brought him up—" Sophie's phone rang.

Anji hoped it wasn't Tony or Tasha. Sophie mouthed that it was the law firm.

"Work is interrupting you on Valentine's Day?" Anji asked after Sophie hung up.

"You know how it is. They don't care if it is a holiday or a weekend . . . So, tell me what happened with the Indian guy last night."

"He's a FOB."

"A what?"

"Fresh-off-the-boat. Some may consider the term offensive—it means he was born in India."

"Wait, what does that make you?"

"No one has called me a FOB because I was born in the West. I'm a coconut." Anji giggled.

"Oh, I get it. Brown on the outside and white on the inside." Sophie laughed.

Anji nodded. "Since Sid and I were born in Colombia, I thought of us as toasted coconuts covered in spice—brown on the outside, tan on the inside, and finished off with a sprinkle of exotic."

"I like the sound of that." Sophie winked.

When Anji first moved to New York City, she had been surprised to learn about these Americanisms. In Colombia, she wasn't identified as different. She felt different and she knew she was different but, at the outset, no one knew. When she graduated high school, the principal had mentioned there was one Indian girl in school. One of her classmates nudged her to ask who it was and was surprised to hear it was her. He'd always thought she was a Colombian with a strange name—many Colombians had strange names.

In New York, people thought she looked like Norah Jones, who was half-Indian although, not in the same way as Anji.

"Being a FOB wasn't the problem. The problem was that I asked all the questions. He waited until we stood outside the restaurant after the meal to ask where in the United States I grew up. When I told him, he suggested we meet again because I was the first Indian he'd met who'd grown up in South America."

"I hope you didn't agree." Sophie gave her a stern look.

"There is no way I could stomach a second date. I don't think I can come up with more questions."

Sophie got a call again. And apologized again. "I need to finish some work."

"I have to tell you about the visions I got. Can't you spare a few minutes?" Anji felt the heat rise into the base of her neck. There was no one other than Sophie who Anji could speak to and it was killing her that Sophie didn't know.

Sophie glanced at her phone. "Just give me the juicy bits."

Anji tried to hide her disappointment and hurriedly relayed the visions, fearing the imminent buzzing of Sophie's phone. "I don't know how the heck Margarita knew there was something going on. She confirmed I had a soulmate. And also said I needed to clear darkness. But I feel I'll be able to figure this out, don't you think? You'll help me, right?"

Sophie nodded. "I will do what I can, my sweets. I feel there will be more."

Anji was relieved to hear the softness in Sophie's tone. "You don't think I'm losing my mind?"

"You've always had a knack for the paranormal. You sense things about people and places the rest of us don't. Remember that party at Josh's where you got bad vibes in the guest bedroom? You said it felt dense, and it turned out his grandmother had died there a few weeks before. I've never doubted your instinct when it comes to these things," Sophie noted.

Anji was surprised to know that Sophie trusted her instinct. Anji didn't always trust herself.

"You really think there will be more visions?" Anji wasn't sure, but in her experience, Sophie was usually right.

"I definitely do. Let them come. Just be careful not to live in a life of dreams rather than real life. I really need to get back to work, sweat pea."

Anji couldn't push away a lingering sinking feeling. She hoped she could speak to Sophie more extensively.

"Can I have my driver drop you off? It'll give us some more time together," Sophie offered in consolation.

Anji agreed.

"Didn't you say it was someone who looked familiar? Let's run through a mental rolodex of the men in your life. Think, my sweets. Who have you felt a deep connection with?" Sophie asked when they were in the car.

"I don't know."

"Say the first name that pops in your head. Quickly. Without thinking." Sophie snapped her fingers.

"Well . . . "

"Quick!" Sophie snapped her fingers again.

"William." Anji was surprised to hear herself say that name. Butterflies in her stomach fluttered so intensely, she felt as if she rose a few inches off the ground.

"Hmmm . . . He is one delicious hunk. I would hook up with him if I weren't already married."

Anji had to admit William was attractive. When she had first met him, she thought he looked like a real-life Ken doll.

"I still swoon over him," Sophie said, biting her lips. She took a deep breath and let it out in a sigh. "And?"

"And nothing." Anji tried to sound nonplussed, but her cheeks were ablaze. William was a constant in her life, but they had never been more than friends.

"Why did you mention him?"

"I guess because I've felt comfortable with him. We could talk about anything—still do." Anji did not want to confess that she had wondered what it would be like to date William. She didn't allow herself to get carried away with these imaginings.

"I can't believe I've never asked you this, but how come you guys didn't date?"

"We don't click that way." William and she were too different— chalk and cheese.

"I find that hard to believe."

"He's dating Natalie anyway, and it is serious."

"They could break up . . . "

"Let's not go there. Natalie is nice and I like her. And William and I are good friends—the best of friends even. In a different way than you, of course." Anji reached for Sophie's hand.

Sophie gave Anji a knowing smile. They had arrived outside of Anji's building. Before Anji got out of the car, Sophie said, "We'll have to keep coming back to this. I know you'll figure it out."

Anji wanted nothing more than to figure it out.

Chapter Eight

JUNE 7, 2008

ANJI NOTICED WILLIAM on the first day of her *Learn Photography the Urban Way* class. Turning thirty made her want to mark the new decade of her life with new experiences. Craigslist advertised the first session as free, and the remaining classes would take place over the next eleven Saturdays. They would learn how to use a DSLR camera—which Anji had gifted herself—while walking around the city.

Harry, the instructor, assembled the fifteen people who had shown up around the fountain across from the Plaza Hotel. Anji decided that if she felt comfortable, she would stay, and if she didn't, she would easily walk away. It was only eight o'clock and the tourist and weekend crowds hadn't yet arrived. William sat at the fountain, staring at his feet. Anji had the impression he didn't want to be there. He looked better suited for the beach carrying a surfboard, not a camera. His hair was messy and he had a casual appearance, although it seemed purposefully disheveled.

Anji was surprised he showed up for the next session. Seven people had enrolled in the course. Despite being a small troupe, they didn't interact much during class, each intent on peering at the world through the lens, captivated by changing light through ISO, along with aperture settings and shutter speeds.

Three weeks into it, Harry suggested they all go for drinks after the session. It was a hot and humid morning in Brooklyn. Sweat dripped down Anji's back and neck. She dabbed her face regularly to prevent sweat from obstructing the viewfinder. She couldn't wait to cool off under an air conditioner, but Harry selected an outdoor beer garden.

To her added dismay, William sat across from her on the park bench they had gathered around. He had the blue eyes that those who did not grow up in the US believed every American had. He oozed athleticism. Anji still felt the same insecurity she had felt in high school. She did not have a single athletic bone in her body. Anji was certain William had never been chosen last for sports teams in school. To her credit, she had not been the absolute last. She had no skill or dexterity, but she had a certain fearlessness that kept her from being the last choice.

"How long have you lived in New York?" William asked.

"I'm coming up on twelve years." Anji was no longer interested in the icy beer bubbles flowing down her throat. She thought of excuses to leave.

"I was born and raised here."

"Interesting . . . you seem like a transplant from California," she said without thinking.

"Why do you say that?"

"You have the quintessential beach-boy persona." Anji regretted the words. She didn't know why she was engaging in conversation with William.

"My parents have a house in Long Island. That's close enough to the beach." William appeared as cool as a fall breeze. He didn't have a single drop of perspiration on him.

Anji was still wiping away sweat from her face. She kept her arms glued to her torso, trying her best to hide the growing sweat stains encircling her armpits. William didn't seem fazed. He told her he had studied economics at Columbia University.

"I attended the Gallatin School of Individualized Study at NYU," she told him. "It's an interdisciplinary program for those of us who want to study a bunch of things but are too lazy to choose a major. Truthfully, I started on one path and later switched to journalism. The program gave me the flexibility to do it. It's akin to getting a liberal arts degree. By the way, what is that? How can arts be liberal? Is there such a thing as a conservative arts degree? And how would you know the difference? Is Renaissance conservative and Impressionism liberal?"

William chuckled. "I'm not sure what you're saying."

When Anji was nervous, she usually got quiet. She wasn't sure why she found herself blabbering. She didn't think someone like William was interested in what she had to say. The heat seemed to have taken over, propelling her to speak. "I don't understand why a liberal arts degree has nothing to do with arts. No other country offers a liberal arts degree. Had I stayed in Colombia, I would need to know exactly what to study."

"What do you mean?" William leaned in, keeping his gaze on her.

"We need to choose a profession and go to a school for that. There is no college. People graduate from high school and go directly to law, medical, engineering, or whatever university."

"What did you want to do?"

The intensity of his blue eyes made Anji feel hotter. She felt as if she had stepped from a sauna onto a rotisserie spit. Sweat cascaded down her back. Yet there was something gentle about his expression that made her feel it was permissible to share her experiences. "Had I stayed in Colombia I would have gone to medical school. As a kid I always wanted to be a doctor—that's not true. When I was in kindergarten, I wanted to be a cashier."

He laughed. "Seriously? You don't seem like the cashier type."

"I couldn't think of anything more thrilling than to punch register keys. Thankfully for my mother, my fascination with buttons did not last. Although I admit I still enjoy pressing buttons."

William leaned closer. "Are you one of those annoying press-all-the-buttons-in-the-elevator people?"

Anji giggled. "I am a love-calculators-with-big-buttons kind of person, which is where my fascination with keyboards started and why I enjoy writing. It involves pressing keys all day. I'm in heaven."

"You're funny . . . and a bit weird." William ordered another round of beers.

Anji wished desperately for the sweating to stop. She would need to peel her shirt off her body when she got home. She didn't expect that he would be entertained by her silly stories and had long forgotten her intention to leave.

"Why did you decide against medical school?" he asked. His tone was more serious, but he still appeared genuinely interested in her.

Anji debated on what version of the story to share with him. She let out a deep sigh. "I almost failed clinical psychology in college. When Professor Newman—can't believe I remember his name— showed the grades from a mid-term exam, I was one of two people who pulled down the curve."

William gave her a sideways glance. "I can't see you failing anything."

"How can you tell?" Anji held her hands around the beer glass, willing its coolness to travel to other areas of her body. This wasn't a topic she was usually open to talking about, but with William she felt safe.

William peered at her as if he had access to her secrets. "You seem to me like someone who has their shit together."

"I did fail. Although, that one exam is the only stain on my record."

"I knew it. You don't have the ability to fail." He sounded pleased with himself.

"I guess you're right. In high school my lowest grade was in physical education, and clearly I am not the fittest person." Anji glanced down at her belly, increasingly conscious of how her top was sticking to her.

"You look good to me," he said. His voice was soft and his expression sincere.

Anji scoffed. She felt heat on her face from the spotlight William had placed on her. "I doubt you had any issues with physical activities."

"I did not. I've always been sporty."

"Like what?"

"Basketball and track."

"I knew it: a jock."

"Yep."

"You are a master of the one-word answers, aren't you?"

William smiled. His blue eyes remained on her.

Anji sensed that he felt at ease with her. "What about now?" she asked.

He shrugged, and after a moment he said, "I run. Daily."

"Like in a gym?"

"Mostly outdoors, but if it rains, yes in a gym."

"Do you like it?"

"I love it." His face lit up.

Anji smiled. "Okay, so now it's three words."

"Hmph." William half-smiled back. "How was it that you recovered from failing psychology?"

"We're coming back to that?"

He nodded, still peering at her.

Anji sighed. She took a moment to collect her thoughts and stared at the beer in front of her. "I didn't fail the class. Just the one exam. Still, it was a wake-up call. I gave up on studying medicine. Studies have always come easily to me and I enjoy learning. I searched for a way to get paid to learn. That's how I became a journalist." When she looked up, William was studying her face, not with the judgment she had expected to find, but rather with genuine warmth.

"It was *that* easy?" he asked.

"Not really . . . "

"Sometimes things are just hard," William said, his gaze hiding a story.

"The hardest part was telling my parents I wasn't going to medical school."

"Why?" He leaned in toward her and was close enough that she could smell the beer on his breath.

"The only three acceptable professions for Indians are doctors, lawyers, or engineers. Anything else is second rate. I think that marked the beginning of their disappointment in me."

"I know the feeling . . . "

"You don't seem like someone who disappoints," Anji pointed out.

"Looks are deceiving," William quipped.

Anji was afraid to ask more.

"It seems to me that you have the makings of a bildungsroman," William said.

"A what?"

"A bildungsroman. It's a coming-of-age story."

"Interesting . . . "

"You like to write and you have an interesting story to tell . . . don't you?"

"Maybe . . . "

"Look who's become a pro at one-word answers."

Anji laughed. "I learned from the best."

FEBRUARY 14, 2019

Back in her apartment, Anji wondered why the name William had slipped out of her mouth when Sophie asked who she had a connection with. He was attentive and caring, and she imagined his girlfriends felt secure walking while holding his arm. It would be nice to have someone like him as a boyfriend or husband. She wouldn't admit it to anyone, but she had always been attracted to William. However, she kept her emotions at bay.

He made her feel all sorts of butterflies and cozy, but the friend kind. She cared for William but she knew they couldn't be soulmates. There was an ease to their friendship despite their many contrasts. Although William and Anji shared a love for reading, William preferred poetry, history, and nonfiction, and Anji read novels. It didn't surprise Anji that his favorite book was *Losing Season* by Jack Ridl. Hers was a tie between *The Namesake* by Jhumpa Lahiri and *The House of Spirits* by Isabel Allende. Once, they couldn't agree on a movie to watch and ended going to two: *Tron: Legacy* was his choice and *Blue Valentine* hers.

William had kept up with photography while Anji had not. Natalie had once told Anji that when they traveled, William was so focused on getting the best shot, he missed experiencing where they were. Anji could imagine William living his life from behind the lens.

Anji heard a knock on the door. When she opened it, there was a large box sitting outside, which she found odd because packages were delivered to the doorman and he didn't bring them up. She had to pick them up from downstairs. There was no trace of the person who had delivered the box.

To her surprise, the box was filled with Agent Provocateur lingerie. There seemed to be countless matching sets of panties and bras, and negligees in every color of the rainbow. When Anji checked the receipt, she saw it was nearly $4,444 worth. She looked at the label and was shocked that it was addressed to her sweet eighty-two-year-old neighbor named Lulu, short for Lucille.

Anji knocked on Lulu's door. Anji's face felt hot from embarrassment. She couldn't decide what was worse: that she had opened a box that wasn't addressed to her or that she knew that it contained sexy underwear.

"Oh, they must be my outfits for Steve," Lulu said sheepishly after Anji dropped it off, apologizing for opening the box without checking the label first.

Anji had expected Lulu to get flustered, but she appeared cool and collected. Anji, on the other hand, felt she had turned every shade of red. She cleared her throat before asking, "Who's Steve?"

"Why, my new boyfriend, Anji. Haven't I told you about him? He's going to be here any moment now. We're experimenting." Lulu winked.

Anji got the sense that Lulu had been eagerly waiting for the shipment of lingerie to arrive. Anji couldn't stop staring at Lulu, who was wearing a robe—not the terry cloth type. It was satin, burgundy colored, and reached down to her mid-thigh.

"Visual pleasure can be deeply intimate," Lulu said, her voice soft, as if sharing a solemn detail. For the first time ever, Lulu closed the door on Anji.

Anji walked away in disbelief. Usually, she struggled to find ways to end conversations with Lulu. If Anji didn't cut off Lulu midconversation, she could get held up for hours. Lulu's mind was surprisingly sharp. She devoured books and the latest in current affairs. A five-minute chat with her was like watching *Headline News*.

Anji wondered what message the universe was sending her. That she needed to get her act together? After all, even her eighty-two-year-old neighbor had a sex life and a date for Valentine's Day.

Chapter Nine

FEBRUARY 17, 2019

AS ANJI OPENED UP to Margarita, words tumbled out of her in an uninterrupted torrent. She felt a whiff of life come back into her. She breathed more easily, having finally been able to express the entirety of what she had experienced in the last few weeks.

The day after Valentine's, Anji had emailed Margarita, who had proposed they meet via Skype on Sunday morning. Margarita's ethereal quality exuded through the screen. Anji couldn't help seeing her as otherworldly. That day, Margarita wore a five-inch oval citrine pendant.

Margarita started the call explaining that the end goal was to ensure Anji had an intimate relationship with herself and that her intuition was so clear Anji would feel she was in dialogue with the universe. Anji had no idea what that meant, but she agreed. They would start with ninety-minute sessions every Sunday and gradually transition to bi-weekly sessions, then monthly sessions, and so on until Anji was self-sufficient.

"Why do you believe the Romani woman?" Margarita asked.

Anji shrugged. "I guess I feel connected to the Romani, especially those in Madrid, because of the Indian/Spanish thing."

"Their Indian origin is not certain. When I embarked on my

spiritual studies, I came to know I have Romani blood. I also learned that the Romani people spread so far and wide it isn't surprising many of us do. That's not why you believe her, is it, my dear?" Margarita's gaze was piercing.

Anji took her time deciding what to say next. "Everything in my life seems to tell me I won't find my soulmate and I will be alone forever. Maybe I'm broken beyond repair, like I lost something along the way, and the pieces no longer fit."

"Why do you feel broken?"

"Circumstances are not on my side. Let me take this week as an example. I went on four dates and none of them worked out. I feel I may have to clear my karma or I won't ever have a relationship."

Anji admitted that the fourth wasn't really a date. The day before, Anji had met an Australian man standing in line at Milk Bar. They chatted and he asked her out to dinner. He suggested an Indian restaurant. Anji claimed restaurant food wasn't real Indian food. When he asked why, she said she didn't want to explain it then. He took back the invitation, saying he didn't want to date someone who didn't feel connected to where they came from.

"I felt he judged me without giving me a chance. I would have liked to show him real Indian food, just not in that moment," Anji said.

"I am confused by your approach, Anji. You say you want to find your soulmate yet you are on a mad rush to meet as many people as you can. Four dates in a week makes it sound like you are on a mission to find a husband as quickly as possible."

Anji took her time to respond. "What I really want—have always wanted—is a soulmate. Yet, from an early age I felt pressure to get married, and sometimes I get caught up in that desperation. But that wasn't my motivation. I thought dating many men would increase my chances of finding my soulmate."

"Why are you seeking your soulmate?"

"I have everything else: a beautiful home, a successful job, great friends, travel. Love is the only thing missing. Even you asked me what was blocking me from meeting my soulmate."

"I was picking up on the energies you were giving off. That doesn't mean I agree this should be your quest. Do you believe that the only type of soulmate is the romantic type? That there is only one person out there for us?"

"In a way, yes. But even I have to admit that I have felt Sophie is a soulmate of a different kind."

Margarita gave her a knowing smile. "Why is that?"

"We have a strong bond and, no matter how busy our lives are—hers in particular—that bond doesn't fade. We've lain in bed together after a crazy night out, holding hands, and looking at each other, wishing we were attracted to women. We had been candid about our attraction to each other, and our friendship was deep and intense. Had it been so, we would have been lovers as well. I feel we know each other inside and out. Many times, we can tell what the other is thinking without saying a word."

"There are many types of soulmates, my dear. Some are romantic and others not. Soulmates are people we have deep connections with. If a romantic soulmate is solely what you are after, I can't help you. I can only help if you are willing to go where the healing takes you. Not the other way around. As I mentioned the last time, opening up to our feelings is vital, and because of this, the work we do together can be intense—especially at the beginning. When we release pent-up emotions, we achieve true and powerful healing."

Anji felt as if she was swimming upstream. She held back tears and looked at Margarita, pleading. "I feel lost. It turns out that the one thing I had been the most sure of in my life—the certainty of having a soulmate—which had become my guiding star, made me feel like a fool. I believed in a dream that is out of reach. None of the men I have had a relationship with are my soulmate. Now I get these visions, and I can't make sense of them. I've always felt there was something wrong with me . . . I need help and I have no idea where to start."

"It could be one of the men in your life or it could be someone else entirely. Dating is complicated for everyone, regardless of culture or upbringing. You need to get clear on what you are seeking. What if you changed your perspective?"

"I don't know what to do. I don't date well. Things might have been different if I'd started dating at an early age, like my friends in Colombia or like Sophie."

In Anji's opinion, Indians and Colombians had a different approach in their search for the one. Colombians panned for gold by dating many candidates until they found their golden nugget. Indians panned for gold by having family, friends, and relatives search for a candidate. The actual person got involved when it was time to decide whether or not to get married.

"When I was eight, I asked my mother when she would allow me to have a boyfriend. She said I could when I was twelve. When I turned twelve, I asked again. 'In a year,' she assured. At the end of that year, she said, 'In another year.' The optimist in me asked year after year. When I turned eighteen, I finally realized it was a lost cause. My mother meant no boys until it was time to marry. Good Indian girls do not have boyfriends. We are expected to focus on school.

"Meanwhile, my friends in Cali had multiple boyfriends or girlfriends by the time we graduated high school. Their parents encouraged them to date from an early age. One of my friend's mothers said, 'The more you date, the more you learn about relationships, and the better chances you have of a lasting marriage.'"

"You feel this has negatively affected your dating experiences?" Margarita asked.

"It confused me for many years. I didn't know if I should follow my own guidance or that of my family and friends. Many times, I thought an arranged marriage was archaic, and I didn't see how it could lead to my soulmate. Then again, that's how my parents met and their marriage is lasting and loving."

"My advice is to take a break from dating until you are in touch with what you want and you are clear on what will make you happy. Let's see where the healing takes you without you directing the course. You will have to face parts of your life you may not want to—the good, bad, ugly, and all the in between. It is how you grow and heal. It requires clearing out the gunk to get to the heart of who we are. Are you prepared to do that kind of work, Anji?"

Anji took a deep breath. It wasn't what she wanted to hear but she was at her wits end. Maybe she would finally heal what was broken within. Seeing Margarita on her screen gave Anji a hint of encouragement for the first time in a long time.

"I am." This time, Anji was aware of the power behind her words.

Margarita nodded in recognition. "I want you to know that our sessions are guided from up above, you see?"

"Not really."

"Do you believe in God? Anji, are you comfortable with me using the term *God*? Because they're all the same: god, goddess, source, universe, lord."

"Yes, I do, and yes I am comfortable with the term."

"Good. Do you believe that there are multiple forces in play in the universe? That we are not alone and that it is not just God as one entity and us as another?"

"Yes, I do. I believe there are multiple manifestations of God. The different forms of the divine are so people have different ways to connect with God. One person has affinity to Kali while someone else feels connected to Shiva."

"Perfect. God has no form, no gender, no personification. It is difficult for us to comprehend God's expansiveness. When I embarked on my spiritual instruction, I attended the University of Metaphysical Sciences. I was most surprised to learn that God works through angels, guides, spirits, and other forms of energetic vibration, and these beings help us make sense of our life and purpose. We each have our own. I learned to call them my high frequency entourage. My HFE connects with your HFE, and through them I get messages for you. But, it only works if you are open to me and I am open to you. If for some reason you don't want them to communicate with me or vice versa, it stops."

"I have always believed I am looked after and there are higher forces at work, but I don't know how to connect with them." Anji felt odd voicing thoughts she hadn't shared before.

"Your homework will be to pay attention to signs from your HFE. When you get them, you will know. Trust me on that. You will simply know."

FEBRUARY 18, 2019

Anji woke up to the sound of a hyena being strangled. It seemed to come from Lulu's apartment. The building had eight units on each floor, and Anji had a corner apartment. She shared a wall with Lulu. Anji wondered if Lulu brought back a pet camel from her recent trip to India. This time, Lulu had talked about silk and spices, and asked Anji if it was possible to add hand railings in the Taj Mahal—it was hazardous for the elderly to walk on so much marble. She hadn't mentioned exotic animals.

The wail came again, urging Anji to get up. The clock read 7:11 a.m. She groaned. She wouldn't forgive herself if something happened to Lulu. Anji pushed back the covers and pulled herself up. She slid down the bed and dragged herself to the wall she shared with Lulu, putting her ear against it. There was silence.

The last time Anji searched for the source of a strange sound was thirteen years before on the first night she had spent in that apartment. Despite the discomfort of sleeping on an air mattress— her new bed wouldn't arrive for a week—she was elated. Anji couldn't believe this space belonged to her.

Back then, she had heard strange creaking noises and ignored them. Wooden floors were known to creak. Then she had heard a voice. Her eyes shot wide open. It sounded like someone was speaking to her. Anji listened at doors and walls but couldn't figure out where the voice came from. Anji still heard the voice from time to time but she had stopped searching for it, reasoning it was just a friendly ghost. After all, it seemed like the same presence she had sensed for most of her life.

That morning, the sound was different. It was clear it came from the hallway. When she opened her apartment door, she noticed a small cardboard box at the end of the hallway. It was shaking, as if something wanted to be let out. Just then, a skinny girl with a face full of pimples who looked around twelve, walked out of the apartment in front of the box. Anji felt a surge of pity as she recalled her own face and back at that age. The girl pulled out a monkey from the box.

"It's kind of loud for a monkey, isn't it?" Lulu asked. Anji hadn't noticed that she too was peering out her door.

"Umm . . . yes. It must be hungry. Sorry." The girl waved her hand in apology and handed the monkey a piece of fruit, which quieted it down.

The girl walked toward the elevator, then paused and asked if they wanted to buy Girl Scout cookies. The monkey sat calmly on the girl's shoulder, chewing at the fruit. Anji agreed to buy Tagalongs and Samoas. The girl convinced Lulu to buy Thin Mints. Anji was sure that if this quintessential American tradition had existed in Colombia, her parents would have had to buy all the cookies themselves.

Anji hadn't always been a quiet kid. She had been a precocious toddler, valiantly approaching strangers, but that stopped when she met people's confused reactions at her mention of words they didn't understand. Anji had unknowingly intermixed Hindi and Spanish back then, but soon grew conscious of her habit and stopped.

She withdrew further when she started getting visits from a blurred white shape. It appeared when she played on her own, never when she was with other people. Even though the shape wasn't flesh and bones, she wasn't scared. It felt kind and benign. When Anji told her mother, she warned Anji not to let her imagination run wild and told her not to speak of it. Anji never spoke of it again, but she was not able to dismiss it. As she grew older, she found it odd that her mother had dismissed it, given the Indian proclivity for the otherworldly. Anji often wondered if the voice in her apartment was the same benign spirit of her childhood. It sounded familiar, and she had heard it at various other times in her life.

Anji reached into her handbag for cash to give the girl for the cookies. Things had a tendency to fall to the bottom of her bag. As she searched, a receipt fell out. She noticed the image of a monkey stamped on the top with a bubble coming out of its mouth saying, "I WIN."

She felt a pit in her stomach and her blood pressure plummeted like a thermostat on an icy winter night. First, Sophie had reminded her of the monkey owner who had once pursued her, then she remembered the conversation with William where they had discussed her failing clinical psychology—she hadn't told William that the same guy was partly to blame for her failing the class. She had just encountered the girl with the monkey, and now this. It was too much of a coincidence. It had to be synchronicity. Margarita had explained that synchronicities were the universe's way of sending us messages. It meant the universe supported and guided Anji. It was Anji's choice whether or not to follow the guidance. That is what it meant to have free will. It was up to her to take action. The universe could only prod and poke.

Anji felt like it was a premonition and the mere thought made her shiver, as if a breeze had just passed through her bedroom. She had only one thought on her mind: Frank.

Chapter Ten

OCTOBER 6, 1996

"WHAT DO YOU THINK about eighteen and twenty-nine?"

It was a crisp fall evening in New York City. Anji was headed back to her dorm. It was her freshman year at NYU and she had just attended a screening of *The Princess Bride* organized by the International Students Association. Sophie had attempted to explain the cult fascination with the perils the main characters, Westley and Buttercup, overcame to be together, but Anji hadn't understood the allure of the movie. She learned she wasn't the only one. ISA organized this screening every year for incoming foreign students to explain the cultural references. Even then, Anji didn't get it, deciding it played to American heartstrings. It wasn't in her to comprehend how fighting kidnappers, attacking pirates, and battling humongous rats were proof of true love.

"What do you think about eighteen and twenty-nine?" he asked again.

"What do you mean?" Anji hadn't been paying attention. She had been remembering her last visit to New York City. She had been eight years old and, at the time, she thought the city was aggressive. Its people were aggressive. Sid had stared at three men who were approaching them.

Upon noticing the unwanted attention, one of them had yelled, "Whatcha lookin at, punk?"

They had walked with a swagger, their pants nearly falling off but for the twist in their hips. Sid and Anji had not seen anyone carry themselves that way in Colombia, India, or anywhere else. The men had stopped in front of Sid, then eleven years old, and stared back. Sid hadn't moved. Anji had willed for Sid to look away, but he was stupefied.

"See something, kid?" came another voice.

Anji's father had stepped between them and Sid, shielding him with his right hand. Anji hadn't been able to hear what her father said, but the men had started to walk away. They had looked back at Sid and yelled, "Careful, kid!"

Anji and her family had stood dumbfounded. Anji had felt her mother's embrace tighten around her. Cali was rife with crime and violence, but they hadn't expected it when they visited the United States.

Anji's father had brought his hands in prayer position and turned to his family. "*Hai Bhagwan*. Nothing happened. We're all good. Let's make the best of our day."

And so they had. They had visited the iconic New York City sights: Times Square, Central Park, the Empire State Building, and Wall Street. Anji wouldn't have remembered much if it weren't for the family photo album. What she did remember was feeling assaulted by the onslaught of traffic, sirens, and flashing lights.

Visits to India were more chaotic. People were everywhere, sometimes appearing in mobs, especially on trains. Four-lane roads turned into seven-and-a-half lanes. Every available inch was jammed with cars, trucks, rickshas, carts, motorcycles, cows, dogs, and the occasional camel or elephant. Yelling, bellringing, and honking were the only means of alerting others of their presence. The non-stop cacophony was intensified by the ambush of odorous spices, incense, frying oil, body odor, open sewage, and diesel fuel. Yet to Anji, India functioned in organized entropy, like a hoarder who could locate a precise item among teeming piles of dust-laden boxes.

In New York City, Anji had only felt peace at the top of the Statue of Liberty, peering onto the large city reduced to miniature, the noise at a safe distance. It was the clearest memory she had from that visit.

Ten years later, Anji did not feel the same menacing sensations. People were nicer, less aggressive. Even this guy had offered to walk Anji back to her dorm.

"Just tell me. What do you think about eighteen and twenty-nine?" he asked for the third time.

Anji couldn't remember his name even though they had just met at the ISA event. She didn't forget a face but names escaped her, forgetting them seconds after a person introduced themselves. "Umm . . . they are two different numbers?"

Anji was grateful he had offered to walk her back. It was after eight o'clock and although the city was no longer menacing, she didn't feel comfortable walking alone after dark. In Cali, walking was an open invitation to get mugged or kidnapped. When Sid and Anji walked the 300 feet from their house to the street corner to get on the school bus, their mother stood outside their walled house to make sure they got on safely. She was waiting for them when the bus dropped them off. These were the only times Anji walked on the street in the eighteen years she lived in Cali.

"Do you think eleven is too much of an age difference?" he asked, bringing Anji back to the present.

"Depends. What are we talking about?"

"I don't think eleven is a big gap when it comes to love." He took a step closer to Anji.

"Interesting . . . " Anji took a step away. They had been walking a couple of feet apart from each other, and she wanted to keep it that way—he could be a murderer. She chided herself for thinking he was safe because he was awkward, as if that made him incapable of hurting her. His face was caught in a tug-of-war between a half-smile and half-smirk. He had stuttered as he asked if he could walk her home.

Anji hoped that being friendly toward him increased the chances he too would be friendly. "My parents are ten years apart, so I guess one more year isn't a big deal. Why do you ask?"

"I'm dating someone eleven years younger than me," he said.

"That's nice." Anji was surprised he was in a relationship. His eyes appeared shrunken behind the bulky lenses of his thick-rimmed glasses. They were too small for the rest of his head. A mess of blonde curls emanated out of his scalp like a halo. He seemed like a mix of the Colombian soccer players Carlos Valderrama and René Higuita.

But not in a cool way. He stood at eye level with Anji. His mane made him appear taller than he really was. He wore white socks under his oversized and too-short jeans. His jeans were ripped but it was clear it wasn't for fashion. They were simply worn out.

"You know? She's the love of my life. She's my soulmate." His face beamed.

"Interesting . . . "

"She's a freshman here."

"I'm impressed you met the love of your life so soon. Unless you knew her from before?" Anji regretted judging him based on his looks. Everyone deserved love. Anji too had struggled with her hair as a child and made a point to keep it tied back. Otherwise, it would hang as crazy as this guy's did. Maybe he had also been made fun of, like she had. Her heart softened. This gave her hope that her teenage dreams fueled by the melancholic ballads of Luis Miguel and Ricardo Montaner would come true. Maybe she would sail the dark seas, taste many lips, and find her soulmate, and they would make passionate love in a blue castle.

"No, I just met her. When you know, you know. Don't you think?"

"I guess . . . I haven't fallen in love like that. I'd like to think it is possible," Anji confessed. There was still hope she would meet the man who would sing "Ek Ladki Ko Dekha To Aisa Laga" when he laid eyes on her, claiming he knew the moment he saw her that she was for him. "How come your girlfriend wasn't at the screening?"

"She was definitely there."

"I didn't see anyone with you."

"You noticed me? That makes me so happy. Can't you picture it? Frank and Anjali. Anjali and Frank." Frank skipped for a step.

Anji was relieved to finally know his name, although she thought it odd she shared names with his girlfriend—Anjali wasn't a common Indian name. "That's wild. My name is Anjali."

"I know your name is Anjali. Didn't you realize I didn't leave your side the entire night?" Frank took another step to narrow the gap between them.

She backed away, but Frank took an additional step toward her. The sleeves of his army jacket touched the blackness of her wool coat. Anji pulled her hand away, pretending to itch a scratch on her face. She picked up her pace. "No, I don't think I did."

"I sat two seats away from you in the movie theater," he said.

A sickness creeped up from the pit of her stomach. "There were a lot of people at the screening."

"I didn't lose sight of you the whole night."

Anji felt a sudden urge to run. It was unlike anything she'd felt before.

"I never lost sight of you," he repeated. His right hand tried to grab hold of her left hand.

Anji swept hair off her face. It was odd that Frank made efforts to get close to her. Then again, she knew little about the ways of men. "Where is your girlfriend?"

"It's you," Frank said softly.

Anji stopped moving, unsure if she'd heard correctly. A person behind swerved out of the way, grunting as he maneuvered to avoid running into her. She was relieved other pedestrians were out that evening. "What are you talking about?"

Frank continued walking for a few steps before realizing she wasn't next to him and made his way back to where she stood. "It's you, Anjali. You are my soulmate."

A chill spread to every inch of her body. She was shocked by the turn of the conversation. "We're not even dating."

"Not yet, but we will," he said with a smile.

Anji rolled her eyes. "Are you crazy? How can you say that? We just met."

"You think it's crazy for us to date?" Frank sounded hurt, but his expression changed into a cheer. "I don't think so. After we go out on a few dates, you'll change your mind."

"We're not going out." Anji walked away quickly.

Frank caught up with her. His tone mellowed out. "I knew from the moment I saw you that we were meant to be together. And then you smiled at me and I knew you liked me. What do you need to know? I'll tell you everything. I am a PhD student in economics. I've been here for twelve years and have a few more to go. This is perfect."

"Look, I smile at everybody. I'm from Colombia and Colombians are friendly. It's in my blood. It doesn't mean I like you."

Frank's smile spread wider. "You're Colombian? I assumed you were Indian. There is so much for us to learn from each other."

Anji didn't clarify her Colombian upbringing and Indian heritage.

She didn't want to give Frank more information. He seemed to use it as ammunition against her, to justify his delusion.

"Pete, my monkey, would approve of you, Anjali," Frank said when they were close to the building.

Anji reached into her backpack for her keys but was having a hard time finding them. Nerves were getting the best of her.

"Pete's like a brother to me." Frank smiled.

Anji continued to fumble for her keys. She placed her backpack on the ground, pulling out books and binders, finally finding her keys at the bottom. The incongruity of his words reeked like day-old fish and the stink invaded her. They were close enough to her dorm building, and after gathering all her belongings, she did the only thing she could think of. She succumbed to her urge and ran inside, leaving Frank out in the cold.

Chapter Eleven

OCTOBER 14, 1996

ANJI COULDN'T SHAKE OFF the feeling that Frank would find a way into the building. She ran up to the fourth floor. People were sitting in the common room watching TV. "Hey guys, if a guy comes in asking for me, please tell him you don't know who I am."

"I'm the doctor for you," said the Operation board game commercial blaring on TV.

"If someone asks about me, please, please say you don't know who I am," Anji repeated.

"Roger that," someone indistinguishable belted out.

Anji was relieved to find Sophie sitting at her desk in the ten-by-ten-foot room they shared. Anji told her that as she had walked back to the dorm after an evening study session in the library, she had sensed someone next to her. She had looked over and, to her dismay, it was Frank. He had said that running into her was a sign they were destined to be together, but eventually confessed that he had seen her enter the library. He had lost sight of her, not knowing where she went inside the library, and had waited outside for her. When he saw her emerge several hours later, he had walked back with her.

"Something tells me the guy is in the building. I have a sick feeling." Anji's heart raced and her pulse throbbed in her forehead.

She felt as if she had jogged back. She hadn't, but she had never walked so fast in her life. Despite Frank's short legs, he'd had no problem keeping up. She made a mental note to strive to get in better shape.

Sophie's big green eyes opened in disbelief. She wore her hair down, and the long, sleek dark brown made her eyes appear greener still.

"Can we keep our door locked? And not answer if someone knocks?" Anji pleaded.

"Of course, sweet pea. Why don't I go out there and make sure? You know those hooligans don't pay attention to anything other than the screen. They're catatonic until someone changes the channel and then they go wild. What if one of them slips up?"

"I don't think Frank would harm me."

"Anji, please. If this dude is giving you the heebie jeebies, trust it."

"What if he does something to you?"

"He has no idea who I am. Stay here. Lock the door. Do not open it under any circumstance—except to me, okay?"

Anji paced, changing direction every few seconds. The door to their room opened in the center, with a wooden wardrobe on either side. In front of the wardrobes, they each had a desk and chair, and behind them were twin beds on wooden frames. There was a single large window at the far end of the room. Two dressers stood against the far wall. The only empty space was the six feet between the two beds.

Anji had butterflies in her stomach, and she broke out in a cold sweat. Even looking at her hands wasn't comforting. Anji liked looking at them because they were the slenderest parts of her body. She sat on her bed for a few seconds but got up and paced again. After the longest twenty-one minutes and thirty-three seconds of her life, there was a quiet knock on the door.

"Anji, it's me, Sophie."

When Anji opened, Sophie exclaimed, "What. A. Creep. It was the short guy with the afro-like hair and thick glasses, right? Between the hair, the glasses, and the beard, you could hardly see his face. He has a horrendous choice of clothing—"

"Yes, yes. That's him. What happened?"

"He asked if we knew you. I answered 'no' before anyone else could. He asked if I was sure and thankfully Leo backed me up. Frank said he had been to all the floors and no one knew you, but he saw you enter the building."

There was a knock on the door. Sophie and Anji jumped out of their skins. They looked at each other with terror, unable to move.

"Sophia? Anjali? It's me Leo."

"Oh, thank goodness. We thought it was that creep," Sophie said as she opened the door. She looked down the hallway to make sure Leo was alone.

"Is that guy bothering you, Anji? What's the deal?" Leo asked.

Leo's dorm room shared a wall with theirs. Anji didn't know him well and didn't know if she should trust him. She looked at Sophie who nodded as if reading Anji's mind. Anji relayed the story, her stomach turning as she did. "He doesn't know how to take no for an answer. He thought walking me home twice meant we had been on two dates. How can he believe we're dating? He won't give up."

"Don't beat yourself up. These kinds of guys don't take hints. My advice is that you engage with him as little as possible. If you speak to him, even for a little bit, he'll think you're into him some way, somehow," Leo counseled.

"What if I told him I'm not into him?" Anji didn't know how to deal with Frank's insistence. She knew she was naïve when it came to men, but Frank didn't feel right.

"Don't do that. Any kind of attention, no matter how small or how negative, is an indication you are interested. They think no means yes or that you're playing hard to get."

"I agree with Leo. I don't think this guy will understand a no," added Sophie.

"Take it from me, Anji. My sister had a guy who didn't leave her alone no matter how many times she asked him to. She had to get a restraining order. It was really tough for her."

"A restraining order . . . goodness, Leo, I hope it doesn't come down to that." Anji had only heard of such things on TV. She shuddered at the thought.

"My sister met her stalker at a party. She chatted with him and he jumped all over it. He thought he had found *the one*, and followed her everywhere, waited for her outside her classes, went to the places she frequented, and called her friends' apartments. If she wasn't at one friend's house, he called the next. If he saw her walking, he followed her in his car at five miles per hour. He dropped off notes and letters, called, and left voicemails—some lasted over an hour. It was intense."

"Sounds like something Frank could do," Sophie observed.

The three of them looked at each other, the gravity of the statement hanging around them like dense fog. Cold shivers ran up and down Anji's body. "How did he find out her schedule or her friends' phone numbers?"

Leo shrugged. "When he saw how upset she was, he apologized yet blamed her. He said she'd forced him to act that way because she wouldn't reply to his calls and notes. It was warped. Once, he called her a slut because he saw her coming out of a male friend's house and thought she had slept with her friend."

"How crazy. Even if she had slept with someone, it was none of his business," Sophie commented.

"Guys like that don't think like the rest of us do. Their imaginations run wild. Make sure you don't give them ammunition to lead them on," Leo explained.

Anji nodded, letting it sink in. She recognized that speaking to Frank egged him on. She thought being friendly would be the best way to appease him. It was clear it hadn't worked. "How did it end?"

"The restraining order I mentioned. She had several witnesses. He was scared of going to jail, so he gave up. But my sister was traumatized. She had to see a therapist. She graduated from college last year, and she's doing fine now. Therapy helped."

"I'm glad your sister is better. I've only seen Frank twice and I already feel traumatized."

"This didn't even happen to me and I also feel traumatized," chimed Sophie.

"Leo, what should I do now? He insisted on walking me to class tomorrow. I told him no repeatedly, but I fear he'll be waiting for me."

"I followed Frank down the stairs to make sure he was gone. I don't think you have to worry about him tonight. Tomorrow morning, go out the side door." There were many entrances to the dorm building. The side door was the best option for Anji to leave without the risk of being seen. Leo suggested she do that for the next few mornings. Leo and Sophie would go out the front door and keep an eye out for Frank.

Anji jumped up to hug Leo. It wasn't like her to be effusive—that was Sophie's specialty—but Anji was touched Leo was helping her.

After Leo left the room, Sophie held Anji's hands in hers. "I'm sorry to say this, sweets, but why did you let him walk you in the first place?"

"I don't know, Sophie. I've been beating myself up over it . . . "

"He is all kinds of wrong."

"In my defense, I haven't had much experience with boys. The closest I came to a relationship in high school was a prank call. All my insights on men are from what I saw on TV." *Telenovelas* were Anji's guides on love. She watched all kinds: Colombian, Mexican, Peruvian, Venezuelan, and Brazilian. She learned about passionate love, forbidden love, tragic love, and unrequited love from *Betty La Fea*, *Café Con Aroma de Mujer*, *Los Ricos También Lloran*, *Marimar*, *Alborada*, and *Cristal*. Stories were exuberant and ridden with tears. There was heartbreak, treason, trauma, and treachery yet, in the end, love conquered all. Even Gabriel García Marquez found love through the plagues of cholera.

"I thought growing up in a country like Colombia would give you better wits. Rule number one: don't trust so easily. Even in sweet old Charleston, where men are gentlemen, we don't pay them attention without the four-one-one."

"What's a four-one-one?"

"Oh sweets, that's right. I forget you didn't grow up here. You dial four-one-one for information. It means you find out every detail on a guy from everyone you know. Rule number two: definitely judge a book by its cover. By Frank's appearance, you should never have let him approach you."

Anji's heart sank. She'd been at NYU a couple of months, and although she'd made friends, they were through Sophie. The ISA was the first opportunity she'd had to make friends on her own. Sophie made friends easily. People hung out in their dorm room just to be around her. Anji wondered if she'd ever get it right.

She tossed and turned in bed that night. At 3:33 a.m. she hadn't gotten a minute of sleep. It occurred to her that this was the first genuine attempt someone had made to have a relationship with her.

NOVEMBER 27, 1996

ANJI OPENED AN EMAIL from Frank that he had sent nearly three weeks earlier. She didn't check email often because she didn't own a computer. She used it at the library, the computer lab, or used Sophie's.

> November 8, 12:43 p.m.
> Dearest Anjali,
> I waited outside your dorm for a few weeks but didn't see you. Did you walk into the wrong building that night? I came in after to make sure you were okay, but no one knew who you were.
> I've searched through the building several times and can't find you. The dorm is too big. I don't think you would deceive me. You couldn't. We're soulmates.
> Please let me take care of you. That is all I want. I can meet you after class. Let's have lunch or dinner.
> I miss you.
> I love you,
> Frank

Anji's spine grew stiff and cold. She was tempted to ask him to stop contacting her, but Leo's words echoed in her head. She looked around the near-empty library to make sure Frank wasn't lurking. Most students had left to celebrate Thanksgiving with their families. Anji didn't think it was worthwhile to fly to Colombia for a long weekend.

She was grateful for the solitary desk she had found amid the stacks of doctoral theses. People hardly went there. She tried her best to read but couldn't get her mind to focus.

"You're safe, *beti*," said a soft gentle voice.

It sounded just like the friendly spirit of her childhood. The sound comforted her but couldn't shake off the sensation she was being watched by someone in flesh and blood. She searched around her to make sure she was alone, peering around bookcases and under desks. She was alone. Still, she collected her items and rushed back to her dorm.

She regretted not accepting Sophie's invitation to spend Thanksgiving in Charleston. She used mounting schoolwork as an excuse to stay behind. Yet, no matter how much she tried, Anji was unable to complete her assignments. She couldn't concentrate. She felt exposed. Anji slept better knowing Sophie was next to her and Leo on the other side of the wall. With everyone away for the holiday, she felt she was at Frank's mercy.

Anji spent most of the weekend in bed. She cried, stared at the walls, and lay with her eyes closed, but hardly slept. She was scared to sit in the common room, fearing Frank would chance upon her. When she stepped out of the room—to use the bathroom or boil water for ramen noodles—she moved quickly, and constantly looked over her shoulder.

Their dorm room never felt so stark. Anji's side was an empty canvas next to Sophie's, whose wall was covered in posters, with Hootie & The Blowfish holding a place of honor. It was surrounded by No Doubt, Ace of Base, Pearl Jam, Metallica, and Goo Goo Dolls. Twenty-two photos of Sophie's friends and family were arranged on her dresser and desk. Anji's wall was empty, and she had two photos on her desk: one of her parents and Sid and a second of her schoolfriends. The most distinctive item was a pencil cup with a Colombian flag and an Indian flag.

Before leaving, Sophie had made sure Anji was properly stocked with snacks, but most of the boxes sat untouched. Anji's stomach didn't cease to churn as she replayed the conversations with Frank, dissecting every moment. She regretted she hadn't acted differently or said something that encouraged him.

She wondered why neither Bollywood nor telenovelas had prepared her for handling a stalker. She vowed never again to rely on them for life advice. She came up with possible escape plans in case Frank found her, replaying those as well to ensure her strategy was solid.

She called her parents every day, which surprised them since she typically called once a week. Calls to Colombia cost her seven dollars and sixty-nine cents per minute. Over the weekend, Anji spent nearly one hundred and fifty dollars on calls home, a near fortune for her college budget. Hearing her parents' voices was the only thing that kept her sane. She wished she could have told them about Frank, sure her father would provide a prayer or mantra to remove the evil-eye, but she didn't want to worry them.

Anji let the Granny Smiths rot and the Chiquita bananas blacken, wishing instead she was at her house in Cali where she could pick tart green *grosellas* in the front yard. Or climb the orange, mango, and avocado trees in the back yard, eating the juicy fruits right from the branches. Her parents also grew limes, figs, lychees, tomatoes, chilies, cucumbers, and a variety of Indian vegetables that weren't found in Colombia.

Anji longed for the comfort of her parents' airy house. Fresh air floated through the open windows. Grates and screens left out intruders, robbers, and insects, but allowed peace and serenity to waft in. Cali smelled of the earth in both of its seasons. When it was dry, Anji felt comforted. It was not the kind of dry that made her sweat, but a cozy heat that made her curl up in a hammock with a good book. When it rained, Anji felt cleansed, as if the skies had washed away all her impurities.

When it rained in India, wetness oozed from the walls. Anji wanted that kind of dampness to seep into her bones so she wouldn't feel so alone. As if in response, an onslaught of smells accosted her just then—dust, spices, dew, humidity, incense, perfume, fragrance, smoke, ash, sewers, and manure—everything India. She opened her window and instead encountered the chaos of New York: pollution, metal, exhaust fumes, rat droppings, burnt oil from food trucks, grease from pizza, and sickly-sweet sugar from nut carts. Anji missed the freedom of walking around the city.

Anji curled up into a ball, wishing for her mother's *kichadi*. Her mother made the dish of lentils and rice for Anji when she wasn't well, along with a cup of warm milk with ginger, turmeric, and honey—the ultimate cure-all. Anji didn't find any kind of cure that weekend. She didn't see the light of day until she had to go back to class on Monday.

———————

DECEMBER 18, 1996

It was the last week of school before the Christmas break, and Anji was working at a computer lab on a final essay. She spotted Frank walk in and froze. There was no way for her to get out of the computer lab without running into him. She ducked, praying he hadn't seen her.

"Are you pretending you didn't see me?" Frank's head appeared behind the monitor.

Anji gasped and jumped out of the chair, dropping the books and binders she held in her lap.

"I'm sorry. I didn't mean to scare you," he said softly. He appeared to have not showered in days. His hair was more unruly than she'd seen it before and his plaid shirt—the same he'd worn the night they met—was unevenly buttoned. His eyes were open wide and shone of instability.

"This is Pete." At the mention of his name, a black capuchin monkey jumped onto Frank's shoulders. His face and underside were grayish beige and he looked like Marcel, Ross's monkey on *Friends*. Frank stepped around the monitor and stood next to the desk.

"Yes . . . " Anji diverted her eyes from Frank's.

"Did you get my email? Did your mother not teach you manners? People are supposed to say hello and reply to emails. 'Yes, please walk me to class. That's very nice of you, Frank. Thank you for taking care of me.'" Frank raised his voice into a mock high-pitch.

People around them watched attentively. Pete imitated the high-pitch. Anji couldn't tell which was more irritating. She shuddered, remembering Leo's sister's stalker who had also gotten upset at manners. Anji felt tears on her cheek that she hadn't known had fallen.

"Aren't you going to say something?" Frank demanded. Pete squealed at his side.

"I . . . I . . . "

"Say something." Frank flailed both arms.

Pete jumped to the ground, forcing Anji to take a couple of steps back. Pete also flailed his arms and screeched. A man got up to say something to Frank and Frank put his hand out toward him. "This is between me and my girlfriend, okay? Butt out."

"I'm not your girlfriend," Anji said quietly, giving the stranger a look of gratitude.

"What was that?" Frank asked.

Anji saw the man nod at her. She said, more confidently, "I'm not your girlfriend."

"So, it's over then." Frank's voice was barely audible over Pete's squeals.

"Frank, I am sorry, but this never began." She hoped Frank could hear her over the raucous Pete was making.

"Do you only want to date jerks? Do you like 'bad boys?' I'm not a 'bad boy.' I'm one of the good ones. You don't deserve me, Anjali." Frank's eyes were the most crazed Anji had seen.

To Anji, it sounded like he was trying to convince himself. "I don't—"

"You're awful, Anjali. Truly, truly awful." Frank stared at her, tears building up. He picked up Pete and secured a leash on his neck as the monkey continued to squeal.

Anji did feel awful. She didn't like seeing other people cry. It made her cry.

Frank walked away slowly. Before getting to the exit, he yelled, "I hate you Anjali . . . and so does Pete."

Chapter Thirteen

JANUARY 28, 1997

ANJI ENTERED THE CLINICAL PSYCHOLOGY CLASSROOM. As she took off her coat, she heard Frank's voice. "Hello, Anjali."

He was seated directly behind her. It was clear he had been there a while, waiting. She wanted to grab her coat and run, but her body wouldn't move. Frank smiled broadly. His eyes looked enormous behind his glasses. Anji was relieved Pete wasn't with him.

"What . . . um . . . what . . . are you doing here?" she heard herself ask, involuntarily.

He seemed more put together than when Anji had seen him in the computer lab. His face beamed. "Pete and my momma asked about you. She was sad I didn't have any pictures of us together—"

"Good morning." Professor Newman walked in.

Anji sat down, sighing deeply. She leaned forward, keeping her back as far away from the back of the chair as possible. Frank tapped on Anji's shoulder. She jumped and dropped her bag. Professor Newman looked up and Anji silently mouthed, "Sorry," as she picked up her belongings.

"Will you go to anthropology next?" Frank whispered.

Every hair on Anji's body stood on edge and her skin prickled with goosebumps. She turned to face Frank, wondering how he knew her next class.

"My love, I know everything about you," Frank said, as if reading her mind.

She shuddered. "What . . . what is that supposed to mean?" she whispered back.

"Momma says clinical psychology, anthropology, biology, and physics are great pre-med choices. She's proud to have a doctor in the family." He looked pleased with himself.

Anji stared in disbelief.

"Your life is my life. Momma asks about you all the time as does Pete—he doesn't ask, but I know he's thinking of you."

Anji continued to sit agog.

"I'm not a fan of Sophia. She's taking advantage of you. She's superficial."

"How do you know Sophia?" Anji managed to ask.

"I don't know why she denied knowing you that night at the dorm." Frank raised his voice.

"Everything okay over there?" Professor Newman asked.

"Yes, yes." Frank waved his hand.

Everything was not okay. Anji's world was falling apart, brick by brick, with every utterance from Frank. It neared implosion. She picked up her things, unconcerned about the disruption she caused, and walked into the cold winter day.

"Why did you walk out of class?" Frank caught up with her and placed his hand on her right shoulder.

Anji shrugged off his hand. "Get away from me, Frank."

Professor Newman followed them. "Do you need help, Anjali?"

She nodded just as Frank said, "No, sir. We're all good here."

Professor Newman looked briefly at Frank and turned to Anji again. "Anjali?"

She looked between them, desperately wanting help but afraid of how Frank would react. Frank's eyes were frantic, as they'd been at the computer lab.

"Anjali, is this man bothering you?" the professor asked. His voice was measured and firm.

Anji stared back at the professor, her eyes pleading, unable to speak.

"Shall I call campus police?" Professor Newman asked.

"No. No. No. She's my girlfriend. This is a lovers' quarrel. Anjali is my girlfriend. There's nothing here. Nothing, nothing." Frank spoke quickly, shaking his head.

"Is this man your boyfriend, Anjali?" the Professor asked.

Anji shook her head slowly.

Frank grabbed hold of his hair and wailed. "She's lying. She's my girlfriend. She is—"

"She is denying it," Professor Newman said, looking at Frank. He looked back at Anji. "Anjali, follow me into my office. We'll call the police from there."

"Not the police. Please, no. Not the police," Frank pleaded. He paced and his face was flushed. Frank reached for Anji's hand and she recoiled, taking a step back.

"Stay away from her." Professor Newman was stern.

Frank looked frantic. His arms flailed and his breath was short and quick. "No. No. No. No. No."

Anji stepped toward the professor. Frank ran off as if chased by a demon.

She followed Professor Newman to his office. "What about class?" she asked.

"I left the teaching assistant in charge."

When campus police arrived, Anji related everything to the officer. He explained that if she wanted a restraining order, she would have to file it with the New York Police Department. He pointed out that Frank hadn't threatened her and she may not have a case. The officer suggested Anji cease to interact with Frank, echoing Leo's words. If Frank did threaten in the future, she shouldn't hesitate to contact them or the NYPD.

MARCH 10, 1997

Anji sat on a bench in Tompkins Square Park resting her eyes with her head leaned back.

"I love watching you sleep." Frank's voice startled her.

She bolted up and her eyes shot open. He was standing in front of her. She grabbed her backpack and sprinted a couple of blocks to

Fifth Street. She had long-ago memorized the location of the Ninth NYPD precinct.

She heard Frank's steps behind her and was certain he exclaimed "No" as she opened the doors. Once inside, she stood still to catch her breath, and looked around her to ensure Frank hadn't been bold enough to follow her in.

A woman in uniform approached her. "Are you alright, hon?"

"I don't know." Anji wiped sweat from her forehead and neck.

"What can I help you with?"

"I need to file a restraining order." Anji felt she was panting.

"Is the person following you, right now?"

Anji nodded.

"Don't worry, they can't hurt you here." The officer walked Anji to a nearby desk. She grabbed a glass of water for Anji and sat opposite her. Her brown eyes were warm and inviting. "Tell me what is going on."

Anji drank the water and took a few deep breaths before explaining all that had happened with Frank, including the time he had approached her three weeks before. She had threatened to call the police then and that was enough for him to scurry away.

"Has he harmed you in any way?" the officer asked. Her voice was kind and gentle.

Anji felt relieved as she answered, "No."

She looked closely at Anji. "Has he threatened to harm you in any way?"

"No." She grew calmer still, her breathing nearly back to normal, and the sweat dissipating.

The officer explained what Anji would need to do to file a restraining order. She reviewed the forms in detail. "It is best if you have evidence of physical injury, certain threat of injury, or harassment. That would make it easier for a judge to grant an order of protection. Don't hesitate to be frank about it and file the report."

Anji's stomach churned. Bile rose to the back of her throat. She broke out in a cold sweat, the momentary calm wiped away. "Can I think about it?"

"Of course, hon." The officer handed Anji a card and encouraged her to come back to the precinct when she was ready.

Before leaving, Anji asked to use the restroom, where she proceeded to throw up her lunch. She didn't know what had made her feel sicker: wondering if she would ever feel safe again or the weight of creating a permanent stain on Frank's record. Yes, he kept on popping up in her life and she wanted nothing more than for him to stop, but she didn't know if she could carry the burden she would eventually feel. Frank frightened her, but she couldn't help but wonder if he posed a true threat. After all, there had been no physical injury and he hadn't threatened her.

She prayed to every god and goddess she could think of for Frank to disappear from her life.

After that, Anji didn't see Frank again. She figured he got scared that the restraining order hadn't been just a threat. She didn't truly know why Frank dropped out of her life or if her prayers had been answered. She was simply grateful he did.

It took a long time before she regained a sense of normalcy. Anji jumped at shadows and strange noises. She quickened her pace and scanned classrooms before taking a seat. She only attended events if someone was with her. She stopped studying in the library, keeping to the safety of her dorm room, and asked her parents to buy her a computer. Anji didn't sleep well, and the only food she could stomach was SnackWell's fat free cookies. Vanilla Creme Sandwich Cookies and Devil's Food Cookie Cake were her only solace.

In the time she lived in New York, this was the only period in which she wished she could move back to Cali. She flipped through her high school yearbook, longing to be cocooned again in a bubble of naiveté. It was a paradox that she had grown up in one of the most dangerous countries in the world, yet she felt safer there than anywhere else.

After that semester, Anji stopped taking pre-med classes and decided instead to become a journalist. She would never admit to anyone else that her decision had something to do with Frank.

OCTOBER 23, 2007

Dear Anjali,

I finally got over you. I never thought I would be able to put my heart back together after what you did to me. You stomped on it and broke it into a billion little pieces. It was hard, but I did it.

Pete hates you. Momma is heartbroken. I can't stand the sight of you.

I found Kaitlin and she has given me what you never could. She loves me. We're married.

I WIN.

And I don't love you anymore,

Frank

The email stung and not because Frank had met someone. Oddly, Anji was content he had found happiness, although she couldn't believe he'd resented her for so many years. She felt sorry for him. For Kaitlin's sake, Anji hoped Frank had healed his obsessive behaviors. Anji prayed for them.

The message stung because Anji didn't know what he had won. And what she had lost.

She had heard the words, "I win," another time and they weren't from Frank. A friend of hers had had a crush on her in college, but Anji didn't like him back. She saw him years later when she was on a work trip to San Francisco. By then, he had married and had two children. He invited Anji to his house for dinner. After they had finished eating, his wife put the children to bed, leaving him and Anji alone. He confessed he felt proud because he was happily married and with kids, and Anji was not.

"I win," he said.

In that instance, Anji clearly understood what her friend had won and what she'd lost.

FEBRUARY 18, 2019

Even though it had been twelve years since Anji had received that email, she knew the words *I WIN* and the monkey on the receipt must somehow be connected to Frank. He was the closest Anji had come to having a relationship in the first twenty years of her life. No matter what he'd said back then, they weren't soulmates. She felt the signs related to Frank came to her now as an admonition of what not to look for in a soulmate. And he had never called her lonely dove.

"Was there any part of you that liked Frank?" Sophie asked over FaceTime, later that evening.

"I thought he was nice when he walked me home the first time, but after he called me his soulmate, I felt sick to my stomach. And then, I felt awful that I couldn't tell him off."

Anji realized she had coasted through life by hiding. Hiding who she was, hiding what she disliked, hiding what hurt her. When she cried as a child, her parents had wiped away her tears and asked her to stop crying, as if that meant the pain went away.

"Why are you still holding on to that?" Sophie asked.

"You know I can't deal with confrontation. I didn't want to hurt his feelings. I felt foolish because everyone told me not to speak to him and I still did. I acted against my better judgment. Growing up in Colombia, I always looked over my shoulder. Everyone did. The country was entrenched in the illicit. When I went to college, I assumed I had left all of that behind. I should have known better. I shouldn't have trusted him in the first place."

"My sweets, you've always believed people are good and trustworthy. Frank broke that."

Anji knew she was right. Frank destroyed her innocence. He had forced her to recognize that obsession didn't equal love. What Frank felt wasn't love. He didn't know her and what he felt had nothing to do with her. She never knew what it was. What Anji did know is that Frank marked the point where she stopped believing and opened up to cynicism. But he wasn't the one who had molded it.

"Besides, back then we didn't have the same sense of empowerment that we do now," Sophie continued. "Let go of the guilt, sweetie. He was the crazy one. You did nothing wrong. There was nothing you needed to change in your behavior. You were being kind and he saw you as his possession."

"You're right. Enough of that. Frank is the one who was out of line. I don't know why I've carried this with me for so long. It's time for me to let it go. Enough of him."

They sat in silence, taking in the significance of the moment.

Sophie was the first to speak. "On another note, do you have more clues on your soulmate?"

"I don't and it bugs me. I don't know if he is in my life or if I am yet to meet him."

"What did Margarita say?"

"I spewed out my life story to her and I'm still no closer to figuring out these visions," Anji said.

"I'm happy that Margarita will help you. I get the sense this is going to be a deep experience for you. Be careful that you don't get so busy trying to prove Margarita wrong that you miss the lesson. Be open to it."

"It?"

"The universe, God, the high above, or whatever you call what is sending you these visions. You're the one who's always talking about higher powers." Sophie motioned her hands above her head.

Anji considered Sophie to be like a sister. They loved each other unconditionally and knew each other so well. Sophie was Anji's confidante, friend, and loyal supporter. True to her name, Sophie also provided wisdom. She had the courage to voice what Anji wished she could and advised her to act in ways Anji wished she could act. Sometimes, Anji felt Sophie held this over her head, judging her.

Despite having resisted at first, Anji was relieved to have found Margarita.

———

FEBRUARY 20, 2019

Anji asked Margarita if they could have an additional call to their regular Sunday Skype session.

"The receipt with the monkey and the words *I WIN* aren't a coincidence, right?"

"As I told you before, there is no such thing as a coincidence, my dear. Everything happens precisely as it's meant to. We don't always have to make sense of why or what it means. I am sensing Frank came up because the universe wants to help you heal. The more you clear and forgive, the more you embody your true self."

"Interesting . . . in those few months Frank stalked me, I felt I lost part of myself—literally. I lost so much hair. Perhaps it's a warning?" Before Frank, Anji could tie a ponytail turning an elastic band once. By the end, she needed to turn it three times.

"A warning of what?"

"Of making sure I choose my soulmate wisely. Like it's asking me to define my boundaries more clearly?" Anji had a hard time saying no, which allowed people to take liberties, as Frank had. It was part and parcel of being a woman, and in particular, an Indian woman. She was more concerned about making sure others felt good. That meant forgetting about her own feelings.

"Do you know why they ask you to put on an oxygen mask first on an airplane, and then assist a child?"

"If we don't, we may pass out before we're able to help the child."

"Exactly. How can you care for others if you're not able to take care of yourself first?"

"Interesting . . . "

"Your HFE is sending you signs that lead to synchronicities. Like the ones you have experienced with Frank. They are nudging you to face your lessons from that relationship. What do you think they are?"

"The lessons? I'm not sure . . . how to stand my own ground. Or how to speak up for myself. I was afraid of hurting Frank and I didn't confront him when I knew I should have."

"What else?"

"Frank was a defining relationship, mostly because I wasn't in a relationship with him. He woke me up from my childhood dreams of what a soulmate is."

"And what is that?"

"Having a soulmate is about safety and being seen. Frank didn't make me feel safe."

"My dear, do you still feel responsible for what Frank did to you?"

"I realized recently that he was the one who was out of line, and although I wished I had acted with more confidence and strength, I didn't do anything wrong."

"That is exactly right. He took a liberty over you that wasn't his to take."

Anji nodded, feeling a sense of strength come back to her. She felt grateful, in that moment, that Frank hadn't deterred her from walking. Anji walked everywhere, feeling the beat of the city as she turned from street to street. She connected with it in every step, feeling herself a free spirit. When she was in college, she experienced the sights she had visited as a child with a renewed perspective. She stood in line for two hours to go up the Empire State Building. When she finally reached the top, she looked upon the vastness of the city, and couldn't help but feel blessed. She was no longer a tourist but a resident of one of the most exciting cities in the world. She cherished the view, and, years later, she would treasure the photo she took back then of the Twin Towers.

She was grateful Frank hadn't affected the magic of those experiences.

Chapter Fourteen

FEBRUARY 23, 2019

IT WAS DARK. Her eyes struggled to focus in the darkness. She was in a large room that appeared to be a warehouse. She slowly moved around, her right hand extended in front of her to make sure she didn't hit something.

As her eyes relaxed, she drew in the little light from the room. She could tell she was in between two stacks of shipping containers.

She heard a click and a whoosh, and in less than a second something hit her hard on the right shoulder, so hard she stumbled backward, slamming into the container. She tried to lean against the container, but the pain was too intense. She couldn't keep her body upright and slid her back down the metal wall. She sat on the floor with her knees bent, feeling her shirt get wet.

Before she could figure out what was happening, there was another click and a whoosh. She was hit on the thigh. It stung as if she had been slapped. Hard. She saw plastic burst against her jeans and paint dripping down her leg. She was being hit by paintballs.

She searched around for a gun. She had to have a gun. Yet she couldn't see anything. She wore a protective vest, but the padding had been removed. She felt a mask on her face and was temporarily relieved. At least she had some kind of protection.

Click, whoosh. A hit to her left arm stunned her. She seemed to be getting used to the pain. She rolled over onto her belly. She dragged herself to the far end of the container in hope of cover.

She heard footsteps.

Click, whoosh, and a hit on her lower back, the ache radiated down her thighs. The steps grew near. She crawled. Click, whoosh, and a hit on her butt. The pain immobilized her.

The footsteps stopped and the hits came fast. Click-whoosh, click-whoosh, click-whoosh, click-whoosh, click-whoosh.

Torturing aches shot up and down the back of her body, so intense she grew numb and still. Her body was heavy and wet.

In a moment of lull, she looked up. A shot fell on the mask, the paint blocking her view. Despite the throbbing, she turned over, and the shooting continued to the front of her body. She curled into a ball, waiting for another pause. But the shooting went on.

When she was fully drenched, there was a pause in the shooting. She waited for another click-whoosh, but all she heard was the sound of dripping paint.

She removed her mask and wiped the paint falling through her eyelashes. She blinked to get a clearer view. Her bald attacker stood in front. He wasn't wearing a mask or any gear. He wore a suit without a tie, and a kerchief was folded in his suit pocket.

Anji shot straight up in bed, covered in sweat, feeling the sheets around her. She hadn't expected to get another vision. She grabbed her phone, and saw it was 10:38 a.m. She was supposed to meet William for brunch in twenty-two minutes at Cookshop in Chelsea. She had no time to make sense of the vision and scrambled into the shower.

"You can't seem to shake the tidsoptimist out of you. I should tell you we are meeting thirty minutes earlier than when I intend to arrive," William said as he hugged her.

"Tidsoma-what?"

"Tidsoptimist. A person who is optimistic about how much time they have and is always late."

"Interesting . . . I operate on IST, Indian Standard Time."

"Is that code for always late?"

"Precisely."

Cookshop was busy as expected. They usually sat at a booth but opted for a table outdoors. It was an unusually warm and sunny February morning.

"You would be impressed at how quickly I got ready," Anji explained as soon as they were seated. "Crosstown traffic was a drag. The taxi took longer than expected."

"Do you need me to teach you how to set an alarm?"

"Ha ha. I set it, but strange things keep happening to me . . . I didn't hear the alarm."

"Strange things are always happening to you. I envy that you are such a heavy sleeper."

"It's different this time. Let's order first." They asked for their usual: huevos rancheros for Anji and a goat cheese scramble for William. Anji told him about the visions, Danny, the gypsy, and Margarita.

"Do you know who your shooter was?" William asked, leaning in.

Anji leaned in as well. The restaurant noise made it hard to have an audible conversation. "I got a sense I knew who it was, but I'm not sure."

William gave her a sideways glance. "I can think of someone . . . "

Anji smiled. She could think of someone too—a couple of people. "You know, I got pranked junior year in high school."

William raised an eyebrow. His beach blond hair had a few grays, making him look more distinguished. His blue eyes appeared intense and a deeper shade of blue.

"Hear me out. It was the closest I came to having a relationship in high school." Anji's tone was forceful.

"Does this have something to do with your visions?"

Anji shrugged. "It could be the shooter."

"Hmph . . . "

Anji ignored William's skepticism. "I was seventeen, and when I picked up the phone, I was surprised to hear a voice I didn't recognize. His name was José and he claimed to be a friend of a friend."

She had picked up the rotary phone, which she loved. Anji was thrilled every time she had to dial "zero" because her finger made one full spin around the dial. There was nothing better than watching the dial make a full spring back into place. It was the first purchase her parents had made as a married couple in the late 1970s, and it sat like an emblem by the main entrance of the house. The day José's call came she regretted not picking up the cordless phone in the kitchen. Everyone would be able to hear the conversation.

José was the first guy to tell Anji she was beautiful and she was so charmed with feeling enamored that she didn't listen to the voice in her head that said this was too good to be true. He said he had seen her at a party but was afraid to approach her. He couldn't stop thinking about her and had finally gained the courage to ask his friend for her number. José didn't want to name this friend.

"Why doesn't José want to name your classmate? Why didn't he approach you at the party?" Sid, who had been eavesdropping, asked later.

William looked at Anji with the same questions in his eyes.

"I was a naïve girl, okay? It was nice to feel liked, even if just for five minutes. That's how long José was able to keep up the farce." Those were the dreamiest five minutes of Anji's high school life. He promised he would call again, and he didn't. He didn't call, nor did any other boy.

"I'm sorry you went through that but, it hardly sounds like José is your shooter. Unless you are saying this prank scarred you that badly?" William pointed out.

"No, it didn't . . . "

"Then what is this really about?"

"I felt out of place for most of high school, and for five minutes someone finally paid attention to me."

"I'm sure it wasn't easy to not hear back from José, but to me it sounds like he did more good than harm. You've always had a good sense about people, Anj . . . a deeper understanding. Like that time with my apartment."

A couple of years back, Anji had visited William at an apartment he had just moved into. She had sensed a dense energy and suggested he do a clearing. She could tell there was a great deal of sadness. William later found out that a previous tenant had taken a bottle of sleeping pills and drowned himself in the bathtub. William didn't do the clearing, but he also didn't renew his lease.

"I can't believe you stayed in that place," Anji observed.

William shrugged. He played with the amber ring on her middle finger. "Have you asked your voices about what's happening?"

A buzzing awoke in Anji's belly. "The voice in the wall doesn't seem to be particularly active these days. And they aren't several voices—it's only one. Although I hear it, I also visualize a shade. It looks to me like a woman wearing a white *sari*, but I can't be sure."

"Have you interacted with it?" William had removed the ring from her finger and was peering at it.

"Not really. I feel at times, the voice and image—the entity— has replied to questions I've asked. Sometimes it sends me words of encouragement. Although it's been with me since I was a child, I don't know if I'm letting my imagination run wild."

"Anj, it's clear to me that you have a skill of some sort. I think you should discuss it with Margarita. She could help you develop it . . . Do you know more about the entity?"

"I'm convinced it's my grandmother on my father's side. She died before my parents got married and I haven't had the courage to tell my father. I'm afraid he'll think I'm crazy."

"You are crazy."

Anji and William laughed. He placed the ring back on her finger.

"Anj, I know you don't want to hear it, but we both know who this vision is about. Maybe you need to do some soul searching there and see what you are resisting."

Anji tried her best not to roll her eyes. It bugged him when she did. She knew he was right. "Enough about me. What's going on with you?"

William worked at Ernst & Young as the head of the advisory division. He wasn't enthusiastic about his job, but he didn't hate it. His father was pressuring him to take over the family real estate investment firm. William's brother and sister were fifteen years younger than him. Anji knew he felt more like a parent to them than a sibling. He had shared with her that he missed out on the joy of growing up with them, the ebb and flow of evolving playmates, co-conspirators, and opponents. He had never fought with his siblings. He only broke up their fights.

No one considered them as possible successors. William's sister had married and moved to Paris where she managed an art gallery. His brother, the youngest, opened a sports therapy center in Los Angeles. Neither of them had what it took to manage the firm. William wasn't sure he did either, but he didn't feel he had a choice.

"What does Natalie say?" Anji asked.

"There's no doubt she wants me to listen to my father. Sometimes I think they're in cahoots."

Anji knew William's sense of responsibility would prevail. He would do what was expected, however unwilling he felt.

As they worked out how much they each owed for brunch, Anji made her calculations out loud.

"You aren't counting in Spanish," William noted.

Her heart sank. "What?"

Anji realized that it was a sign that she had fully transitioned into her American life. No longer counting in Spanish was greater proof of being American than the naturalized blue passport she now carried. It felt like a gut punch. Like she had finally put together all the pieces of her existence into one box. She had been in so many boxes for so long, and she knew she would always be. But for the first time, she felt she could fit perfectly into a tick mark.

As a child, Anji had learned she was different because she heard different languages, and other people didn't pick up on languages in the same way she did. From an early age, Anji knew instinctively which language to speak with a specific person. Her father always spoke to her in English, and she would get upset if he ever deviated. She also used language to her advantage.

When she traveled to India, and she talked with her parents and Sid in Spanish, her Indian family did not understand. When she was in Colombia, she had conversations in Hindi about the guests in her home, whether they were her parents' friends or her own friends, and they had no idea what was being said.

Thinking back, there were many other differences. When they were in India, Sid and Anji didn't always have an appetite for *dal* and *subji*. Instead, they were given rolled up *rotis* filled with *ghee* and sugar. They also got Maggi noodles. Ironically, in Cali, her mother made Anji *parathas* when she got back from school. She remembered the first time one of her friends came over after school. Her friend said the *paratha* was a browner version of pita bread, and when she tasted the flakey buttery deliciousness, she was in heaven. They ate it with honey, which Anji would have never done in India. Or if she was eating it on her own. Anji would have had it with mango *chutney* and plain yogurt.

The biggest contrasts always seemed to center around food.
When Anji went to her friend's house she got fruit juice. Colombians
made a juice out of every kind of fruit, and they made it in water or
milk. Some of the fruits, Anji hadn't easily found elsewhere: lulo,
tomate de arbol, guanábana, curuba, maracuyá, uchuva, pitaya, and
zapote.

In her friends' houses in Colombia, Anji had also been served rice
cooked in oil and onions topped with ketchup. Anji hated ketchup.
She couldn't stomach the rice and ketchup combination that so many
of her friends and classmates seemed to cherish.

Anji stopped seeing food as a defining element of her culture after
she moved to New York City because she could get any type of food.
Her immigrant experience became about defining who she was. When
she first arrived, she had a Hispanic accent, that she lost throughout the
years. Some people thought she was Latina, and others considered her
to be Indian. Some even thought she was Caribbean. She learned for
the first time that Indians had settled in the Caribbean several hundred
years ago as part of the British colony settlements, and communities
of Indians had grown outside of India, just like herself, but had been
disconnected from the country for far longer than she had. Somehow,
this knowledge made her feel more Indian.

She then realized that even the language in her dreams had
morphed. Her whole life, her dreams had been in the languages she
was thinking in and she thought in English and Spanish. When she
spoke Hindi, she thought in Spanish and translated from Spanish.
She hardly ever dreamed in Hindi. It only seemed to come to her
when she thought of her grandmother. When she read in Spanish
and spoke in Spanish she thought in Spanish. When she read in
English and spoke in English, she thought in English.

She recognized now, after living in the United States for so long,
where her predominant language was English, that English had taken
over. Anji felt truly American.

As if reading her mind, William said, "Don't fret, Anj. You are
still as incredibly complex today as on the day we met. Even if you
are truly an American." He winked.

They shared a laugh and Anji felt at peace. Before saying goodbye,
she placed her hand on his forearm and asked, "William, are you
happy?"

He gave her a look and the air turned dense. "If I were to get married, will you be there?"

Anji felt as if he had opened up his soul to her. "You don't have to get married. Especially if it makes you feel the way you look."

"At this point, it's hypothetical . . . Will you come?" William's neck tensed. It is where he expressed every emotion. His veins popped out when he was nervous or tense, as they did then, and lax when he was at ease.

Anji often felt tempted to touch William's neck, as she did that day. But she held back, as she always did. "You want me there?"

"Of course. It'll be nice to see a friendly face, someone who is there for me."

"But aren't your other friends and family there for you?"

He gave her that look again, the one where his eyes pierced into the deepest recess of her soul. She knew it was because they knew each other so well. Yet every time he looked at her like that, she could hear a buzzing in her ear, as if the air around them was charged. As if it carried the unconditional love and support they felt for each other.

The unspoken eloquence only he could master inspired her to say, "I'll be there. I wouldn't dare miss it."

Chapter Fifteen

FEBRUARY 24, 2019

"I AM," ANJI STATED. The energy behind the words felt electric.

"Let's start by connecting within. Close your eyes and imagine you are sitting on a stone bench. Take a few deep breaths and allow the image to come to you." After a few moments, Margarita continued, "Pay attention to the details: what is the bench like, what is around it, and anything else you find interesting. You will find yourself with some members of your HFE."

They were speaking over Skype. That morning, Margarita wore a raw amethyst pendant in a copper setting. She had on a green silk top that made the purple of the pendant appear alive and vibrant, as if it were part of the conversation.

Anji envisioned a gray stone park bench amid a rose bush garden. Two large tree trunks stood on either side of the bench. Climbing ivies twisted around the trunks, and the trees were so tall, their tops were lost in the sky.

"Who do you see?"

"I see three figures." The first was an old Chinese man. He wore a dark brown robe and walked with a cane. He had a thin, long white mustache that dangled down to his chest. He wore a black box-cap on a bald head. Next to him was an older Indian woman in a white chiffon *sari*. She held a crystal staff that had a six-point star engraved on it. Her hair was long and white, cascading down her shoulders, and her expression was kind, with her eyes exuding deep love. Something about her seemed familiar to Anji, as if she were looking at an older version of herself, or as if this woman knew Anji well. For a moment, Anji wondered if this was the same woman of her childhood, the same as the voice in the wall, but she dismissed the thought when she noticed the tiger winding in between the woman's legs. Anji didn't know how but she could tell the large Bengal tiger was female. Her stripes looked as if they were painted on, the orange was bright and the white and black were deep, making the tiger appear as if she were made out of porcelain. Her eyes were brown and green and shone bright like headlights on a dark road. Shimmering gold dust encircled all three guides like a translucent energetic cloud.

"Ask one to come forward," Margarita said.

"Out loud?"

"Yes, Anji. You need to get comfortable voicing your needs."

"Please can only one come forward?" Her voice echoed in her apartment. A few moments later, the tiger stepped forward. The two other figures faded into the background. Anji sat on the bench and the tiger curled up beside her.

"They will be holding something. Ask them to give it to you."

A lacquer box appeared in front of the tiger. She pushed it toward Anji with her paw. Suddenly, the bench and the guides disappeared and the box hung suspended on its own in a black void. The box seemed to Anji like a treasure chest. She felt giddy, as if the contents would reveal a miracle, perhaps the key to what she had been seeking. It spun rapidly. The lid popped open and the box split in two halves, revealing yet another box.

"Ask for the contents to be revealed," Margarita instructed.

Anji wondered if Margarita had access to her vision but didn't ask. She focused on the images appearing in her head. As Anji reached for the box in her mind, butterflies partied in her stomach. Before she could reach it, the smaller box opened into two more halves, with yet another box within. This one refused to open. A ballerina pranced around it. Soon, she was spinning so fast she blasted out of view. In her place, a *torero* appeared. The bullfighter plunged his sword repeatedly into a bull. Anji shivered. She hated bullfighting despite how popular it was in Colombia. She considered it cruel. The image popped like a balloon and showed a couple slow dancing.

They too disappeared and the smaller locked box came back into view. The tiger also reappeared. She stood still and Anji had the impression that she was about to pounce but she remained still. Instead, the tiger's green brown eyes sparkled with intensity. She didn't make a sound, but Anji sensed the tiger was communicating with her. The alertness in the tiger's eyes relayed that the final box would open only when Anji was ready to receive the message.

Anji felt deflated and her heart sank with disappointment. The universe seemed to be confirming that she was blocked. She opened her eyes in frustration and sighed.

"What do these images represent?" Margarita asked after Anji relayed the vision. Margarita assured her she couldn't see the image—she received her own guidance on how to support Anji.

"I'm not sure. They seem incongruent. I don't understand."

"Tell me the first thing that comes to you. Don't judge it."

"Umm . . ."

"Anji, just say it." Margarita was stern but her tone gentle.

"I am the ballerina spinning out of control?"

Margarita smiled reassuringly. "What else?"

"I have a feeling the *torero* represented a bad relationship . . . And I was the bull."

"What about the couple?"

"The dancing couple represents the person I am supposed to be with. The two of us dancing means we come together."

"What do you think it all means, my dear?"

"It's like the gypsy said, I have to put the bad relationship behind me in order to find the person I am supposed to be with?"

"That's a good start, Anji. Yes, it is possible that you allowed whoever the *torero* represents to spin you out of control. Understand he came into your life for your highest good. While he hurt you, it was an opportunity for you to grow. The heart cannot break; it is whole and indestructible. Pain makes it feel broken, but it is not. You let this *torero*—what's his name?"

Anji couldn't bring herself to name Donovan, as if naming him would be some kind of omen. "Sophie and I referred to him as Older Guy."

"It's no matter. You let this man change your perception of yourself. Maybe it doesn't just represent one man, but several. They didn't break you. They hurt you, my dear, but you are whole and complete, like your heart. The universe creates experiences so we learn from them. What do you think your lesson is?"

"I think . . . I think I was meant to learn that I can be loved. Even if this man or men didn't love me, it doesn't mean others will not love me." Anji was surprised to hear herself.

"Let us take a step back for a moment, Anji, because I want you to understand the magnitude of what you have witnessed. You have a gift of vision—spiritual vision. Some call it clairvoyance. The guides who came to you are part of your HFE, and I believe the tiger is your animal spirit guide. She's likely working with you to overcome the challenges in your life."

"You think I have psychic abilities?" Anji felt jittery.

Margarita's look was gentle and compassionate. "Surely this isn't the first time you've heard that?"

Anji felt as if she were caught in a lie. "No, I guess not. I just have a hard time distinguishing if my imagination is leading what I see or if it's real."

"The best way for you to tell the difference is by being aware of how you feel in your body. When a vision is from your inner guidance, you feel open and expansive. When it is your imagination, you feel closed and tight—like you do when you are controlling."

"I definitely feel open." Anji felt nearly capable of anything, like a world of possibility was just within her reach. If only she could open that box.

Margarita leaned toward the camera. The amethyst pendant shimmered in the light of the room. "I could be wrong, Anji, but I am getting a different message about the *torero* than what you have just explained. I feel this *torero* is not a man. I feel this *torero* is you." She peered deeply into Anji's eyes, and asked, "How does that sit with you?"

Anji nodded and tears streamed down her face. She tried to hold them back. Instead, a wail escaped and a dam broke, releasing an uncontrollable torrent of sadness. She folded over her knees and lost herself in sobs.

"That's good, my dear. Let it out. Let it all out. You have held it in for far too long," Margarita soothed.

Anji choked between hiccups, crying harder. She thought she would never stop, but the end came half a tissue box later. Anji sat up. Her eyes were puffy and her nose was red and swollen. A remaining hiccup made its way to the surface. She should have felt embarrassed for crying, yet she had an odd sense of calm.

"Allowing your emotions to arise, whether it be laughter or tears, is important for healing. Crying is a way of letting go of what you no longer need. Don't ever feel embarrassed for crying, my dear. You are a special soul who is worthy of love. You deserve love. You need to stop beating yourself up. The only way for us to heal is connecting with our feelings. Otherwise, they stay bottled within and wreak havoc on our physical and mental health," Margarita said, sensing Anji's discomfort.

"I should work on forgiving myself . . . " The heaviness of the realization sunk to her belly like a ton of bricks.

"Yes, my dear, you need to forgive yourself. Tonight, is only the start. As you assimilate what you experienced, you will heal more and more. Don't hold back on shedding more tears. Allow yourself to clear the density you are holding within."

Anji smiled in earnest. "I feel lighter now. Will this give me insight into the visions I have been getting?"

"We have plenty of time for your clairvoyance to flourish, but don't lose focus. The purpose of this isn't the visions per se, but your healing journey. Don't rush it. Let events unfold naturally."

Anji nodded. "What about the couple at the end of my vision today?"

"I feel it represents a special soul that is meant to be with you, but your pain has blocked you."

"You think I have a soulmate? If I shed some more feelings, will I eventually meet him?" Anji tried to hide her hope.

"It's possible. But as I said, we first need to work on your healing, my dear. If two people are meant to be, the universe will conspire to bring them together."

"I didn't see the face of my attacker in the paintball vision, but I knew who he was. He hurt me more than anyone. There is no way he could be my soulmate. He made me feel small and insignificant. A true soulmate wouldn't have made me feel like that. Why then am I getting visions of him?"

"It takes time to peel the layers but it is necessary. Feelings are the windows into our soul. They indicate what is truly going on and give us clarity to move forward. When I feel sadness, disappointment, or hurt rising, for example, I block out private time to cry, scream, or whatever. I express emotions and I feel lighter, like you said. I recommend that you do it soon. The more you do, the more you will be in touch with your soul. The other side of that is accepting your past and seeing that what happened to you was for your good. Rather than seeing yourself as a victim, consider your lessons. Let go of the past pain that is bogging you down. Claim your past so you can move forward. Accept this Older Guy. Name him. When you do that, it will be easier to release him. Can you start now?"

"Donovan. Older Guy is Donovan."

Anji had met Donovan in 2003 at an annual marketing event sponsored by *Really Living Magazine*. Anji didn't work there yet, and Josh hired her after that night because of Donovan.

Chapter Sixteen

MR. EDWARDS, one of Anji's professors at NYU, had invited her to attend the event hosted by *Really Living Magazine*. Mr. Edwards knew Anji was struggling as a freelance journalist and wanted a stable position. Josh was also an ex-student of Mr. Edwards, and Mr. Edwards wanted to introduce Anji to Josh.

Mr. Edwards had the quintessential university professor look. He was a six-foot tall black man with plastic rimmed glasses and a crew cut. That evening, he wore a navy-blue shirt, a green bow tie, and a dark blue blazer. He and Anji stood at one of the high-top tables near the bar. Anji gazed curiously at the attendees. When she saw Donovan, time seemed to stop, capturing the moment in her memory. Everything blurred except for the sight of him standing twenty feet away. Her heart beat so fast, it reverberated in her head. Her chest rose up and down in rapid succession.

A wave of deep knowing swept over her. She had an intense feeling her life was about to change. Her skin tingled and her hair stood on end. The only other time she had felt that way was the night she made the decision to leave Cali and move to New York City to attend NYU. She had sensed nothing would ever be the same. She felt the same that night.

Donovan towered over the crowd. He was six-feet, four-inches tall and wore a light-gray suit with a light-pink button-down shirt. There was a dark-blue and white polka dot kerchief in his left jacket pocket. His shirt was open to the second button, exposing dark chest hair beneath. It struck her as odd that he had so much chest hair, yet he was bald.

"Do you know Donovan?" Mr. Edwards broke her reverie.

"No . . . no, I don't." She had forgotten Mr. Edwards was there. Her face flushed hot, although her brown skin hid the blushing. She tried to compose herself. She had no idea how long she had been staring at Donovan. "His face seems familiar, but I can't place him."

Mr. Edwards played along. "It's no surprise. He is a bit of a celebrity, if you're into socialite magazines. He's a close friend of Josh's. Josh told me they've gone on numerous trips together—Cyprus, Langkawi, Abu Dhabi, Cinque Terre, and I don't know where else."

"Interesting . . . " Anji tried to sound nonchalant. When she looked back at Donovan, he turned her way, lured by that eerie ability we have to sense when someone is looking at us. She looked away, not wanting Donovan to think that she was overly interested. But he was like a magnet. She stole a glance. They made eye contact. Her stomach summersaulted when she saw him walking toward her. It was too late for her to keep up the pretense.

"Do I know you?" Donovan asked. His smile was electric.

Mr. Edwards extended his hand. "We haven't met. I'm Jeffrey Edwards, a professor of journalism at NYU."

Donovan seemed surprised to see Mr. Edwards. He shook his hand.

"This is Anjali Sharma. She is a student of mine. An ex-student to be precise," Mr. Edwards said.

Donovan gripped Anji's quivering hand. He smiled knowingly, clearly aware of the effect he had on her. He held her hand in both of his in an attempt to calm her. "Do you work at *Really Living Magazine*?"

"No—" Anji squeaked. She cleared her throat. She felt like she needed oxygen. "No, I don't. I've written a few pieces for them, but I'd really like to write for them full time."

"What do you write about?" he asked, still holding her hand.

"Nothing exciting. The latest article was about incorporating essential oils into daily routines."

Donovan nodded politely and released her hand. "You look familiar. Are you sure we haven't met?"

Anji reached for a tissue in her bag. She dabbed the sweat on her upper lip. She hoped keeping her hands busy would make the tremors stop. "We haven't. I'm sorry we were looking your way. Mr. Edwards was telling me about your friendship with Joshua Nolan."

"I told her some of the places you've been to together," Mr. Edwards chimed in.

Donovan smiled and shook his head. "We have some crazy stories to tell. Hopefully he hasn't embarrassed me?" Charm oozed from his every pore.

Mr. Edwards laughed. "No, I sense great respect between you two."

"Yes, that we have. How do you know Josh?"

"Josh was also my student. One of the more successful ones, I would say. Josh is gracious to invite me to events like these. I want to introduce Anjali to him."

"Jeffrey, if you don't mind, I'll take this gracious student of yours and make some introductions: see if we can get her that job she wants. Would you be so kind as to allow me to lead her away?"

"Of course, that's why I invited her. Please, be my guest."

Donovan extended his forearm to Anjali, and she turned to Mr. Edwards for approval.

He smiled encouragingly. "Go on. Get out there and meet people. We can catch up some other time." He turned to Donovan. "Make sure to introduce her to Josh. I want to be sure she makes that connection."

"I certainly will," Donovan said. He turned to Anji and extended his forearm further close to her. "Don't be nervous, Ms. Sharma, I don't bite."

She smiled and hooked her hand around his elbow. "I'll find you later," she said to Mr. Edwards.

"Not to worry, Anjali. Call me to let me know how it goes."

"Thanks, Mr. Edwards. I will."

As Donovan and Anji walked away, Donovan turned to her. "You must be smart, otherwise your professor wouldn't help you get a job."

"I guess," she replied, her voice trembled slightly.

"Confidence, my dear. You need confidence. How do you expect to land this job if you don't believe in yourself? *Really Living Magazine* would be at a loss if they didn't hire you."

Anji knew she needed to feel confident. She was truly desperate for the job. She was tired of living off of her parent's credit cards and she wanted validation. Journalism hadn't been her first choice as a major.

"I have a nose for talent, Ms. Sharma. I can tell you have a bright future."

Anji let out a nervous giggle and turned to him. "How can you tell?"

They stopped walking and he turned to face her. He leaned down and whispered in her ear, "You know what else I know? You are more than meets the eye. You have a soft and sweet exterior, but inside you have a complex life you rarely show others. You are an old soul."

Her heart skipped a beat and her hand tremors acted up again. "How . . . how do you know?"

He tapped her nose with the tip of his finger, flattened the collar on her coat, and continued in a louder tone, "I have a sense about people. I can tell you are hardworking, responsible, and you have conviction. Let's get you that job, shall we?"

Anji felt like a thousand pinballs were released inside her. It was the first time she felt truly seen. "I'm so honored. Thank you."

"Thank me after you get the job."

He let go of her arm. "I know you don't want to let go of me, but we don't want people to believe I'm asking favors for my girlfriend. I want them to see you for who you are."

"This is the second embarrassing thing I've done tonight." Anji released her grip on his arm. She reached for a second tissue to wipe off the sweat on her forehead and upper lip. She couldn't believe he had uttered the word girlfriend like he was stating a fact.

Donovan raised an inquisitive eyebrow.

"First, I stare at you, and then I hold your arm unnecessarily. Please forgive me." Anji sounded mortified.

"No need to apologize. I offered you my arm."

"Right. Sorry." Anji giggled.

"That's enough little girl behavior. Be strong and confident."

She wiped the grin off her face, her heart dipping a little. "Sorry again."

Donovan didn't leave her side. He was methodical, purposefully introducing her to people who were least affiliated to *Really Living Magazine* and progressing to those with closer ties. With each new person, Anji grew less intimidated and more at ease. And finally, when she was ready, Donovan led her to Josh.

Anji was relaxed and spoke to Josh as if they were old friends. He told her he had almost gotten kicked out of immigration in San José because he had arrived still drunk from partying the night before. She shared how the immigration agent at Dubai airport thought her a woman of the night because of the incongruity of having a Colombian passport and an Indian name.

"Ms. Sharma has already written for *Really Living Magazine*." Donovan interrupted the laughter, making them feel like naughty schoolchildren.

"Is that right?" Josh asked.

"Yes, I've published a few pieces." Anji explained that one article was about how she found mindfulness in making her daily *masala chai* in the morning. It was a twenty-minute ritual that involved crushing ginger, cardamom, fennel, clove, and cinnamon, and simmering it with black tea and milk.

Josh was intrigued. He wanted to expand the magazine's coverage on wellness and alternative healing, seeing it as a growing trend. He asked Anji to come into the office the following Monday with writing samples and to meet a few people.

Before leaving the event, Donovan gave her his business card. "Call me with the good news."

"How can you be sure I'll get the job?" she asked, glancing at the card. It didn't have a company or a title. Just his name, email, and phone number.

"How can you not? Look at you. You're perfect."

Anji knew he meant more than just for the job.

AUGUST 4, 2003

Anji showed up at the *Really Living Magazine* offices as requested.

She interviewed with several people and after four hours, she met with Josh. He told her the feedback was positive and Mr. Edwards had given her a glowing reference.

"There is no one I trust more than Mr. Edwards. He believes in you," Josh said earnestly.

"That is nice to hear." Anji tried to give a professional smile and not a girly one.

"After you left on Thursday, Donovan said I would be making a mistake not to hire you," Josh confessed. His blue eyes gazed at Anji intently, trying to decipher the connection between her and Donovan. "I make hiring decisions on merit. You have demonstrated your own merit, but I also don't doubt Donovan. He is an uncannily good judge of character. You made an impression."

"I can't believe Donovan had such positive feedback . . . " Anji looked away.

Her eyes settled on Josh's family photo on his desk. His older daughter was a mini version of his wife. His youngest had inherited Josh's blue eyes and black defined curls. Her hair hung below her shoulders in perfect undulation. Anji thought of her own hair when she was that age.

The girls in elementary school often braided each other's hair during recess, but Anji didn't let them touch hers. Anji's hair was particularly unruly. Her mother struggled every night to undo knots. Despite applying copious amounts of coconut oil to keep Anji's hair silky and supple, it didn't work. Anji offered to braid the other girls' hair while keeping hers pulled into a tight ponytail or a bun, as she had for the interview.

Indian girls were hairy, and Anji wondered if Josh's daughters were as well. Elementary school had marked the last time Anji wore a sleeveless blouse. Around age ten she had reached up to put away her lunchbox in her cubbyhole on the top row.

"Eeewww. You have *underarm* hair! That is *so* gross," a girl had said.

"What are you, fifteen?" asked another girl standing nearby.

The two girls had burst out laughing, pointing it out to the rest of the class. From that moment, Anji had only worn full-sleeved shirts, no matter how hot the day. That is, until Anji's mother started bleaching her facial hair and taking her to a salon to get her arms and legs waxed.

Anji looked at Josh, certain he hadn't struggled with his hair. Yet if he had let it grow out, it would be a crazy mane. She felt relieved to be sitting in the safety of a suit, and that no one seemed to care about her hair.

Josh offered the job to Anji. Her first day at *Really Living Magazine* would be on August 11, 2003.

Chapter Seventeen

AUGUST 5, 2003

THE NEXT MORNING, Anji didn't have the courage to call
Donovan, as he had requested. She emailed him.

> Dear Donovan,
> It was a pleasure to meet you Thursday.
> Thank you for introducing me to so many people, especially Josh.
> I got the job. I'm so excited, and it is all thanks to you!
> Thank you for your time and support.
> Yours kindly,
> Anji

She was shocked when Donovan replied less than thirty minutes
later.

> A,
> Congratulations. I am sure you will do well.
> D

Anji had hoped Donovan would have more to say. She felt like a
schoolgirl again, pranked by the guy on the phone who'd momentarily

convinced her she was pretty. She was sure she wouldn't hear from Donovan again.

She got another email a month later.

A,

Drinks tonight at 8 p.m. Let's celebrate your new job. And my birthday.

D

She broke into a cold sweat. She waited a prudent couple of hours before getting back to him. She didn't want him to think she was too eager. They agreed to meet at The Peninsula Hotel.

She left work early to shower and change before drinks. She also ate a quick samosa. Donovan had not mentioned food, and she wanted to settle the anxiety in her stomach. The potato and pea filled pastry would satiate her for a while. She took a taxi to the hotel. It was two minutes till eight when she stepped into the lobby. Anji exhaled in relief. She was usually late but had managed to get there on time. Donovan was waiting for her, peering down at his BlackBerry when she approached.

She smiled. "Hi, Donovan. Happy birthday!"

He glanced at her but didn't smile back. "Being on time is the same as being late." His tone was curt.

"It's not eight o'clock yet." Her tone was light, yet defensive.

"Let's not focus on trivialities. Promptness is not an option. It is a necessity."

Blood rushed to her face and her heart sank. Her smile faded. "Okay, sorry. I didn't realize it was an appointment. I thought we were having celebratory drinks."

He didn't respond and walked toward the elevator. They went up to the Salon de Ning.

"Good evening. Table for two?" the hostess greeted.

"Yes, on the terrace." Donovan glanced up from his phone to smile at the hostess.

Anji thought it would be chilly, but they sat at a corner table and a partial glass wall protected them. Donovan went back to his BlackBerry and ignored the menus placed in front of them as well as the bowls of Asian-style snacks.

"What will you have?" Anji asked, trying to clear the tension.

"Give me a minute." Donovan was curt and didn't look up.

When the waitress came by, Anji ordered a glass of cabernet, and he asked for a club soda with lemon. They proceeded in silence. Anji drank her wine and Donovan made a call. He didn't look at her. She felt she'd gatecrashed a business meeting. Anji asked for another glass of wine.

Donovan looked at her, his dark brown eyes disapproving. He was still on the phone. Anji entertained herself with the view. It wasn't often that she sat on rooftops, and the view onto Fifth Avenue was breathtaking.

"I left a beautiful woman waiting," Donovan said a few minutes later, finally hanging up the phone. He looked at Anji. "There is nothing more unattractive than a woman with a drinking problem."

Anji took a deep breath. "A drinking problem? That's a bit harsh. This is only my second glass."

He shook his head and stirred his soda and lemon. "How's the job?"

"Good, I think." She wondered if there would be any more interruptions or if Donovan was ready to focus on the two of them.

"What does Josh say?" He looked her up and down a few times, as if trying to read her.

"I haven't seen him since the interview. I'm too far down the totem pole."

Donovan raised his hands momentarily, as if in protest. He rested them on the arms of the chair and leaned forward. "Why are you so dull today? You were full of spunk that night."

Anji froze, drink in hand. "I'm sorry?"

"You heard me."

"I'm not being dull. You are. You've barely looked up from your BlackBerry. It is past nine o'clock and you finally acknowledge I'm here with you. If you were going to be so busy, why did you ask me here?" She still held the wine glass in her hand.

"There's that fire." He sat back in his chair with a sense of smugness that settled over him. His gaze was penetrating.

Anji took a sip of wine before putting the glass down. She felt as if she were in a dream where she was the only naked person in the room and everyone was looking at her. Except it wasn't a dream, she wasn't naked, and there was only one person with his eyes on her.

"Tell me. What do you want out of life?" Donovan's eyes shined like stars.

"Huh?" She still felt annoyed.

"Don't make me repeat myself." His tone was muted, yet playful.

She took a deep breath and softened her tone. "That's a loaded question. What do you mean what do I want out of life?"

"Maybe you should have gone to an Ivy League. Do I really need to ask again?" He leaned forward and repeated slowly, pausing after each word. "What. Do. You. Want. Out. Of. Life."

Anji tried hard not to sound like a schoolgirl. She took a moment to collect her thoughts. "I want a lot of things . . . I want to do well in my career. I want to be a good journalist. I want to be a good writer—"

Donovan waved his hand. "I don't care about your work. I mean personally. You. Out of life. No bullshit."

It sounded like a dare. She gazed down at her hands. "Well . . . "

"I want to gaze at your beautiful black eyes when you answer. Do you know you have a deep, soulful aura?"

Anji looked at him, feeling her insides turn to butter. She tried to sound strong and confident. "My eyes are brown."

"Fine. Beautiful brown eyes. Answer me." His tone was gentle, coaxing.

"I'm sorry . . . no one has ever asked me that." Her voice was barely audible.

Donovan leaned forward again. "Cut the bullshit. Answer me."

Anji sighed, feeling she'd been caught in a lie. She looked at him intently. "I want love, marriage, kids: the happily-ever-after everyone is looking for."

He cracked a half smile and sat back. "Really? That mundane? I thought you would be more mysterious. Why are you holding back?"

"I'm not. And yes, I'm that mundane. If you want mystery, then you tell me. What do you want out of life?"

"Love, marriage, kids: the happily-ever-after everyone is looking for," he mocked.

Anji laughed. "Okay, okay. I get it." She took a deep breath. "I want something I can devote my undivided attention to. Not a thing really, but someone. I want the unconditional love you're meant to feel when you meet the person you are supposed to be with for the rest of your life. I want that feeling of deep love—"

"I don't know about unconditional love. There are always conditions, something that's wanted in exchange—money, affection, protection."

"I haven't felt that kind of love, but I believe it's out there. I can imagine that a parent feels unconditional love for their child. I would like to think that when two people fall in love, they feel unconditional love for each other."

"I don't think it's out there. People are too selfish. When I love, I always want something in return."

"Like what?" Anji asked, surprised at the sincerity in his voice.

"Sex. Security. Image. Status. Something. Always something."

"Interesting . . . " She wondered what he would want from her, or if he would let her off his hook.

"Don't be naïve, angel. It doesn't suit you," Donovan said, as if answering her question.

"I don't think it's naïve to believe in unconditional love. It's about having faith." She didn't know how or why, but she knew it to be true.

Donovan shrugged.

The veil of tension so palpable at the start of the evening, lifted away. Donovan told Anji he was born and raised in New York, an only child. His grandmother had been more of a parent than his actual parents who only had time for each other and their careers. Donovan's grandmother passed away shortly after he graduated college, and he drifted further away from his parents. They exchanged calls on each other's birthdays and Donovan drove out to Scarsdale, where his parents now lived, once a year for Christmas dinner.

Everything Donovan had he'd built on his own. He discerned opportunities from miles away. He had earned a reputation as a savvy investor, and people came to him for advice. He had a long list of friends, associates, and connections, but few who knew him well. He had wondered if perhaps he had been waiting to open up to the right person. "Someone like you, who can really see me."

Anji's breathing stopped. She felt the same wave of knowing from the night they met, a certainty that her life would never be the same.

Donovan continued. He thought there was no such thing as the *right time*. He thought people should travel instead of going to college and that an education was better suited after a few years of work experience. People rarely directly used their college degrees but studying later in life meant people learned subjects useful to their careers. He didn't understand the rush to marry and have children. Donovan had turned forty-six and had no plans to settle down.

Anji admitted to Donovan that she struggled with the expectations of Indian culture. Her Indian-ness was ingrained so deeply that, although she wanted a soulmate, she often felt compelled to find a husband at any cost. Marriage was meant to be her sole duty and she felt the weight of it, even at age twenty-five.

She was caught between cultures. Growing up, her friends had fantasized about white dresses, walking down the aisle, epic parties, and three-tiered cakes. Anji didn't know how to explain that, instead of a white dress, she'd be wearing a red *sari*. Her hands and feet would be covered in *mehndi*, beautiful henna painted designs. There wouldn't be a cake. *Mithai* for sure, but no cake. The bride and groom would sit under a *mandap*, not an altar. There would be ceremonies to last for days. Instead of a walk down the aisle they would have the *Saat Phere*. She would tie her *pallu* to the groom's scarf and, with him mere steps ahead, they would walk around the fire seven times.

They spent the evening talking like confidants until after two in the morning. Anji comfortably shared her struggles and loved that Donovan was equally open to her. She sensed his desolation and wanted to wrap herself around him, snuggling him like a warm blanket.

At the end of the night, Donovan made sure Anji was safely in a taxi. Before closing the car door, he reached inside and kissed her lightly on the lips. "Good night, angel. Thank you for a marvelous birthday."

Chapter Eighteen

DECEMBER 18, 2003

"SOMETHING DOESN'T FIT, sweet pea. Older Guy seems off somehow."

Anji looked down at her plate of food.

Sophie and Anji were celebrating Sophie's birthday at Maialino at the Gramercy Park Hotel.

Sophie watched Anji for a reaction. "Things haven't felt right to me from the get-go. Why would he want to spend his birthday with someone he just met, when he knows so many people?"

"I don't know." Anji didn't admit to Sophie that she had asked herself the same question. She also didn't tell Sophie that she hoped it was because Donovan had fallen in love with her; there was no one other than Anji he wanted to spend his birthday with and every subsequent night since then.

"Have you asked him if you're exclusive?" Sophie looked at her carefully.

"No . . . " Donovan was the center of attention anywhere they went. Anji rarely got a chance to ask him anything. She played with her oxtail tortellini until she could no longer ignore Sophie's searing stare. "Okay, okay . . . I'll ask. But if something is meant to be, it will be."

"Yes, my wise one. And now to juicier topics. What is sex like with Older Guy?"

"Hot." Anji didn't know what compelled her to lie. She hadn't slept with Donovan. Sophie knew the Indian part of Anji was reticent to speak about her sex life. To Anji's relief, Sophie didn't question her further.

"Sweet pea, be sure about him before you get attached, okay?" Sophie cautioned.

Anji couldn't label what she had with Donovan. No matter how hard she tried, she hadn't been able to regain the intimacy they had shared over drinks at The Peninsula. Over the last three months, Donovan had invited Anji to several events. Their twenty-one-year age difference allowed them to be malleable with the roles they played in each other's lives. He introduced her as his friend, his favorite girl, his protégé, or his project. But they always parted ways with Donovan escorting Anji to a taxi.

DECEMBER 19, 2003

Donovan was at *Really Living Magazine*'s Christmas party. Anji didn't know he would be there. He said hello to her and spent the rest of the night by Josh's side. He didn't congratulate her after she was recognized with an award naming her the most promising young journalist. Anji thought he was deliberately avoiding her, too embarrassed to be seen with her. She tried her best to not look his way, and eventually lost sight of him.

She left before the party ended. While she waited to hail a cab, Donovan stepped out of the shadows and offered her a ride home, which she accepted. His car was parked in front of the building, his driver holding the door open. When they reached Anji's building, Donovan's driver left them in the car with the excuse of needing something from a convenience store. Donovan drew Anji to him and kissed her. Anji couldn't believe that at age twenty-five she was finally experiencing her teenage dream of making out in the back seat of a car.

Donovan groped her breasts. The same hand traveled down her body, under her panties, and as his middle finger slipped inside,

Anji tensed up, pushing him away. She didn't want him to know her hymen was still intact. She collected her things and got out of the car with her clothes in disarray.

"Don't be a tease." Donovan was clearly annoyed.

"Another time," she said, and ran into her apartment building.

"Don't forget who helped you get that glorious job you so cherish," he yelled after her.

Sitting in the safety of her apartment, Anji felt like a fraud. She was a virgin at twenty-five, and one of the most influential men in the city wanted to get intimate with her. Anji didn't know what to do or who to turn to. Sophie thought she'd lost her virginity already. Anji had once mumbled something about sleeping with someone but had provided no detail. Meanwhile, Sophie had been having sex since she was a teenager. To her, it was a normal part of life and relationships. To Anji it was forbidden in both talk and action.

Had Anji been honest with Sophie she could have asked her for help. Now, she didn't know how to deal with her virginity. When she was in middle school, a myth had spread that using a tampon would break your hymen, and for a brief second, she considered stuffing her vagina with a few of them. When Anji realized the ridiculousness of her thoughts, she got down on her knees, in front of her altar, and willed for a sign—an indication of how to proceed. She was met with silence.

Anji crawled into bed and curled into a ball.

"Be truthful, *rani.*" Anji heard the same familiar voice that had always accompanied her.

"Not tonight," Anji replied.

She squeezed her eyes shut and covered her ears with her pillow. She held onto it tightly, willing for the world to disappear and swallow her whole. The only thing she felt grateful for in that moment was that the next morning was a Saturday, and sleep didn't matter. The last time Anji had felt this helpless was in third grade.

APRIL 2, 1986

Anji's teacher asked the students to bring their favorite dish for a class potluck. Anji was excited to take her absolute favorite, which was *halwa,* a sweet porridge. Her mother usually made it for her first thing in the morning on her birthday to ensure she had the perfect start to her day. For her classmates, Anji's mother meticulously cooked the *sooji* or cream of wheat in butter and milk. She sweetened it with *gur* or jaggery and spiced it with fennel and cardamom. There was nothing better for Anji than the distinctive flower-like taste of cardamom. Her mother added raisins, cashews, pistachios, and *chironji,* a small tree nut so rare, they brought it in their suitcases from India. Anji hoped her classmates loved it as much as she did.

Not one person touched it.

"It has nuts. That's disgusting," one boy said. Colombian sweets didn't have nuts.

Another boy pointed at the *halwa* and squealed loudly, "It looks like lumps of turd."

Anji tried not to cry in front of the boys and later not to cry in front of her mother. Anji didn't have the heart to tell her mother that the *halwa* had grown dry and stale. She dumped it in the garbage before heading home. When her mother asked, Anji said there wasn't a trace of it left. Anji buried her hurt and never spoke of it.

She stopped taking food from home to school, no matter how Western her lunch was. Instead, Anji asked her mother to give her lunch money, choosing to blend in with a plate of *salchipapa* or a freshly fried *aborrajada* bought at the school cafeteria. A plate of fries with sausages or a large fritter of dough stuffed with plantains and cheese was more appealing than anything spicy and smelly that Anji could have brought from home.

She wished she had someone she could talk to, someone who could help make sense of what it was like to stand out. There was no one. She learned to deal with it herself. After that incident, Anji rarely spoke of her Indian descent. She pretended she was Colombian with a strange name, which was easy to do. After all, it was popular to name Colombian kids George Bush Gomez and Sadam Hussein Perez simply because they appeared in newspaper headlines. Anjali Sharma didn't stand up in comparison.

———————

JANUARY 2, 2004

Anji was having drinks with Donovan at the Mandarin Oriental. Being at a hotel bar, she anticipated the magic of the evening, hoping they would finally rekindle the night of shared stories at The Peninsula. A friend of Donovan's approached them and, to Anji's disappointment, Donovan invited him to join them. Anji distracted herself with the view to Columbus Circle and Central Park while the two men spent the evening catching up.

Afterward, Donovan took Anji back to his apartment. Anji's body trembled from the months of pent-up nerves and Donovan assumed she was cold. He raised the temperature in the room. Donovan lived in a two-story penthouse in Tribeca with floor-to-ceiling windows. Anji felt she had stepped into a curated collection at the Guggenheim, complete with strategically placed security cameras.

"Don't worry, angel, there are none in the bedroom." Donovan winked. He offered her a drink.

"Some water, please." Her throat felt particularly dry.

Donovan watched her empty the glass and, before she could set it down, he took her hand and led her to his bedroom. The dark gray headboard and area rug appeared almost black against the white walls and carpet. The bed was turned down, like they did in hotels, the white linens folded over a gray comforter. The accent pillows in different shades of gray were carefully placed on a white bench at the foot of the bed.

Donovan took his clothes off, piece by piece, and laid each on top of single sofa that seemed to be in place explicitly for this purpose. He stood naked, in front of her. "Now you."

Anji obeyed. Her hands shook as she let each piece of clothing drop on the floor around her. She shivered in her underwear and wrapped her arms around herself.

"Everything," he said, studying her as if she were a piece of art.

She trembled visibly; her eyes settled down at the floor. When her bra dropped, she covered her breasts with her arms. Donovan pulled her arms apart. He watched her carefully, taking in every inch of her body. Donovan led her to the bed.

He pulled her toward him, and rolled on top of her, pulling her legs apart. He entered her immediately, completing the task as a perfunctory act. After he was finished, Donovan rolled back to the left side of the bed, covered himself with a blanket and fell asleep.

Anji lay still, unable to slip under the covers even though her body continued to shake. She felt genuinely cold although adrenaline still pumped through her system. When she was certain he was sound asleep, she got out of bed to go the bathroom, but ended up in Donovan's closet. It seemed to her like the men's section at Barney's. The clothing hung in color-coordinated rows, and the hangers were equally spaced on the racks, as if someone had used a measuring tape to precisely arrange the distance between the hooks. Shoes were meticulously polished, and each contained a wooden shoe tree with a metal pin. Anji's entire shoe collection was smaller than Donovan's collection of black shoes. He had shoes in every color, including pink.

Anji slipped out, careful not to touch a thing. She tried the next door and was relieved to find it was the bathroom. She sat on the toilet and held her head in her hands. Her vagina was sore and her legs felt weak. She wiped off the semen that had dribbled out of her. Everything had happened so quickly that she hadn't thought about him not wearing a condom.

Her body still trembled; her skin felt as cold as the marble beneath her feet. Donovan hadn't kissed her. He'd barely touched her other than pounding in and out of her. She heard him snore through the bathroom wall. She got up and cupped her hands under the faucet and drank water, spilling some down her throat and chest. She cupped some more water and wiped her vagina, drying herself off with toilet paper.

She considered leaving but the prospect of knocking into a museum-like piece, opening the wrong door again, or setting off an alarm was too much for her to bear. She put on her underwear and blouse before getting back into bed. This time, she made sure she was under the covers. She lay face up and didn't dare move in case she woke Donovan. She stared at the ceiling for most of the night. The last time she remembered looking at the clock it read 3:21 a.m.

The next morning Anji awoke to Donovan reading the newspaper, still in bed. He'd already showered and dressed and had a pot of coffee on a tray draped over his legs.

"Was it good for you?" he asked, glancing her way.

"Last night? Or my sleep?"

"Don't be a smart ass. Last night, of course."

"Yes," she whispered, her voice barely audible.

He looked at her.

She cleared her throat. "Yes," she repeated with certainty.

"Good." Donovan poured her coffee and after she had finished the cup, offered to have his driver take her home. Anji dressed and left, as indicated.

Chapter Nineteen

AFTER THAT NIGHT, Anji was more inclined to believe they were in a relationship. Donovan was devoted to his BlackBerry, while she read, wrote, stared into space, and drank. He knew she was there. "Can you get *her* tea?" or "Bring *her* food," or "Make sure to get *her* what she wants," were a constant part of the exchanges with his staff. He even arranged for someone on his staff to make an appointment for Anji with his family doctor so that she could get on birth control.

Anji loved it when he called her *angel*, not just because of its significance, but also because it was the closest he got to using her name.

"Why don't you call me by my name?" she once dared to ask.

"Stop acting like a child, angel." His voice was stern.

"You know my name doesn't mean angel, right? Anjali means *divine gift*." She tried to sound strong.

Donovan raised his eyebrows and went back to his device.

Once again, as she often did with Donovan, she felt like a child. She didn't raise the subject again, not wanting to vex him.

They weren't always together. Days and weeks went by when she didn't hear from him.

When he summoned her after weeks of not communicating, she ran to his side, no questions asked. It didn't matter. Only he mattered. He mattered to her. And he mattered to him. Donovan's driver picked her up and dropped her off, and when he wasn't able to, Anji took a cab to make sure she arrived early. She rarely walked anymore, as she had once cherished doing. The precision of keeping time was more important. She tried with all of her strength not to be needy, yet she felt like a leech desperate for any sip of blood.

APRIL 3, 2004

Anji was spending the weekend with Donovan at his apartment. She wondered why they didn't take a trip somewhere but then felt grateful she was spending any time with him at all. They'd had a quiet dinner the night before and a light breakfast by the pool that morning. The pool had a clear retractable roof, and space heaters were interspersed among the lounge chairs. The sunlight shimmered through, making it feel like a warm summer day. The pool itself was heated.

The housekeeper, Cynthia, brought over a second pot of tea for Anji. Cynthia wore her customary black dress and white apron. Anji couldn't understand why Donovan asked Cynthia to wear a uniform. Sophie didn't do it with her staff.

"I read your article in *Really Living Magazine* on cupping therapy. It was really interesting Ms. Anjali."

Anji was surprised to hear Cynthia say her name. Most people Donovan employed addressed her as ma'am. "Thank you, Cynthia. Call me Anji, please."

Cynthia's eyes quickly darted to Donovan.

Donovan was immersed in sunlight. His laptop was next to him, but he was reading the newspaper. He didn't look up. Anji sat under a parasol. It was strange to need a parasol in April, but the sunlight was sharp and stinging.

"Fine. Ms. Anji, if you please," Anji suggested, smiling.

Cynthia gave a slight giggle and said, "Ms. Anji, then."

Donovan cleared his throat. Cynthia nodded and walked away.

"Why did you drive her away?" Anji asked.

He glanced at the book Anji was reading. "Why do you have to read that shit?"

She yawned and went back to reading *Mr. Maybe*. Anji enjoyed the mindless reading. It was entertaining and it helped her unplug. Donovan didn't understand how stories could provide entertainment.

Donovan seemed to take her silence as a sign to proceed. "You should at least choose better quality literature, something you can learn from."

"We can learn from everything, including Jane Green. She makes the challenges of love and adulthood seem approachable." Anji tried to sound nonchalant and lighten the mood.

"It is beneath your intellect to read chick lit." His tone was tight.

"Are you suggesting what I should read?"

"I'm not suggesting anything, angel. I wouldn't dare."

"You are a perpetual source of suggestions." Anji air-quoted "suggestions."

"Do not do that. It is also beneath you," he chided.

"See. There you go with your suggestions. And this time I didn't air quote, although it would've been appropriate." Anji sounded pleased with herself, certain she was winning the argument.

"They are for your own good."

"For my good?"

"Yes, angel. For your own good. Just like losing a few kilos would be for your own good."

Anji felt her heart sink and blood rushed to her face. "In this country it's pounds—not kilos. You should know that. You're American," Anji managed to say, her un-toned torso staring her in the face.

"If you could lose just five kilos you would have a great body."

"You don't like my body?" Anji asked quietly. She wanted to cover up in a towel as she had done in high school when she stood next to her classmates' svelte bodies. Anji never felt she looked good in a bikini. She had long legs but a short upper body. Her family said her thighs were like Sri Devi's, a Bollywood actress from the 1980s famously known as Thunder Thighs.

"I tolerate it."

Now, Anji wanted to dig a hole in the ground and hide. Ironically, when she was with Donovan, she was the smallest she had ever been: a size six. She had been a size ten most of her life. She went through a mental rolodex of all the women Donovan had introduced her to.

It occurred to her that most were a minuscule size zero. Anji may have been at her thinnest, but she felt like she was six times their body size. In that moment, she wished she did yoga more than once a week, or that she had found a way to get rid of the stubborn baby fat that hadn't left her in twenty-five years. She had a full and curvy frame that gave her a permanent chunky look. Anji tried to get back to reading but kept going over the same lines.

Lunch was set up at 12:30 p.m.

"The beet salad you requested, Mr. Donovan," Cynthia declared excitedly.

Anji tried to hold back tears. She didn't like beets, and Donovan knew it.

"Do you not like beets?" Cynthia inquired, noticing Anji's sullen expression.

"She will like them. We will make sure of that." Donovan answered on Anji's behalf and turned to Cynthia with a naughty smile. "Thank you, Cynthia. It looks splendid."

After Cynthia left, Anji asked, voice trembling, "Did you do this on purpose?"

"Angel, beets are full of antioxidants. Any reputable wellness expert would know that. Isn't that your expertise in that little magazine of yours?"

"It's not my magazine. And, it's not little." Anji sat down putting her hands underneath her butt.

"Please don't sit on your hands," he admonished.

The words echoed of Anji's mother, who scolded her repeatedly. "It's not ladylike, *beta*. Women should keep their hands on their lap."

"It's not about the health benefits of beets. It's about me not liking them. We talked about this. Last night." Anji's voice was as forceful as she could muster. She kept her hands underneath her butt.

"Stop acting like a spoiled child," he said sternly.

Anji attempted to eat a few beets, but after gagging she gave up. Thankfully, Cynthia had added tomatoes, herbs, pine nuts, and cranberries to the salad. Anji ate those.

Donovan watched Anji. "Please don't tell me you want fatty Indian food. I won't have any of that. Salads are light and healthy."

Anji ate as much of the salad as she could. Afterward, she went back to reading. At some point, she fell asleep. When she woke up, Donovan wasn't there. She went into the kitchen and asked Cynthia for a latte. Her stomach was growling and she felt a latte would fill her up without hurting her pride. Anji asked Cynthia to bring the latte to the study.

Anji found a comfortable pale gray chaise longue to lay on. She hadn't changed out of her bathing suit and felt a slight chill. She covered herself with a white blanket that had been placed at the foot of the chaise and waited for Cynthia to bring the latte.

Without intending to, she fell asleep again. After some time— Anji wasn't sure how long—she woke up to the sounds of heavy objects falling on the floor. She opened her eyes and saw Donovan standing ten feet away in front of the bookshelf. She sat up slowly, noticing six books sprawled on the ground. She also saw that her now cold latte had been served on a side table.

Donovan picked up a seventh book from the shelf, his eyes on Anji. She watched the book leave his hand, fall four feet, and pound unceremoniously onto the marble tile. By the time she looked up at his face, he had picked up another book. His face was bright red, his veins protruded, as if he were lifting a ton of bricks instead of a two-pound book.

As that book hit the floor, he turned to her again. They made eye contact, and Donovan paused briefly before picking up a ninth book. They stared at each other. He let that book slam to the floor. His countenance was daring, challenging her to gain the courage to ask him to stop. She was frozen in place.

"I. Hate. People. Who. Are. Lazy." He enunciated every word, his lips twisting like a marionette. "No one who sleeps as much as you do *ever* gets *anywhere*!" he shouted.

Her silence fueled him.

"Do you think I got where I am by sleeping?" He paused as if waiting for an answer. "Do you think I became who I am by lounging around in other people's houses? Do you think I want to be with someone who sleeps all day? Do you think that is why I brought you here?"

Anji could barely breathe. She couldn't make sense of what was happening.

"ANSWER ME!" Donovan roared.

"No." Anji's voice was barely audible.

"What is *wrong* with you?"

"I'm tired," her voice quivered.

"If you want to feel energized, go for a run. Get on a treadmill. *Move!* Didn't you hear me when I told you to lose a few kilos?"

He picked up another book, glanced at its cover, and hurled it in her direction. The book hit her on her right shoulder and cheek, and the impact combined with her reflex to move away, knocked her backward. She let out a loud yelp.

She lay on her back, her face up toward the ceiling. Another book slammed the same way. His aim was impeccable. She stared at the book sprawled by her face, until the slam of the next book against the floor propelled her to crawl under the chaise. She heard the next book fall.

Donovan paced in front of the bookshelf. "Do you know how many women I've been with?" He stopped in his tracks, picked up another book, and dropped it.

"How many *beautiful* women?" He dropped another book.

"*Smart* women?" Another.

"I thought you would be *different!*" One more.

"But you are such a disappointment. Such a *nobody!*" And another.

"A NOBODY!" Again.

"A FAT AND STUPID NOBODY!" Another book pounded the floor.

Anji lost count of the scattered web of spines and pages covering the marble tiles. Donovan continued to shout and drop books, throwing one every once in a while toward the chaise lounge. A few hit Anji as she continued to cower under the chair, praying it would stop.

Donovan screamed vehemently. His voice grew hoarse and the shouting threw him into a coughing fit. He left the study, presumably to get water.

Anji heard him open the door to the toilet down the hall. When she heard the faucet run, she scrambled to her feet. She started toward the bedroom, but Cynthia pulled her into the kitchen.

"Forget it. Forget your things. Forget everything," she whispered.

She pushed Anji into the pantry, and before closing the door, said, "Do not make a sound, you hear me? Not a sound."

It was the largest pantry Anji had ever seen. It was half the size of her apartment. She heard Donovan screaming her name throughout the house. Anji crawled underneath the lowest shelf, next to a case of sparkling water. She remained as still as she could, with her head between her knees. Tears streamed onto her thighs.

Cynthia said something to Donovan but Anji couldn't hear. Donovan continued to yell. Anji prayed that he wouldn't hurt Cynthia. The shouting went on for a while.

All of a sudden, everything got quiet. Anji didn't have the courage to leave until Cynthia came to get her. Anji's body was so tight she could barely move. Cynthia helped her up, and they stumbled out of the pantry, out of the apartment, and down the elevator. There was a cab waiting, and the doorman was holding the door open for Anji.

She slid into the back seat and, before closing the door, Cynthia handed her cash for the ride. Anji didn't know at what point Cynthia had draped a towel around her.

"I will make sure you get your things," Cynthia assured. She held on to the cab door. "You don't have to put up with this, you know."

Tears welled up in Anji's eyes. "Neither do you . . . "

"Oh, child, I've taken care of him since he was a little boy. I'm the only family he has."

Anji felt a pull toward the man she loved—a forty-six-year-old man in need of being held. She was sure that if she held Donovan for long enough—if he let her—she could ease some of his pain.

Cynthia looked at Anji to make sure she was listening. "You're young. Find someone who deserves you."

Chapter Twenty

APRIL 4, 2004

THE NEXT MORNING, Anji woke up to intense pain in her shoulder. She had fallen asleep on the sofa, still draped in the towel. There was dry caked-on blood, and she could barely lift her arm. The sight was revolting. She knew she needed stitches, and suspected the dry blood held the wound together.

Anji cut off her bathing suit and got into the shower. She watched a streak of blood run continuously down the drain and considered how much easier it would be if she bled out. She thought she heard the words, "Mount Sinai," but dismissed it with the other resounding thoughts in her head. Yet she heard the words again. And again. That familiar sound of her childhood. It prodded her to move. She got out of the shower, put on pants, and draped a button shirt around her as best she could.

Anji took a cab to the emergency room in Mount Sinai. She needed four stitches. When the doctor asked what happened, she mumbled something about being at a rowdy book party. He put her arm in a sling.

Anji called in sick to work and didn't go out. Days merged into nights and nights into days. She sat catatonic in her apartment. No one knew she had been with Donovan that weekend. Sophie was in Charleston, visiting her family, and Anji hadn't spoken to her.

Anji hid in her apartment, lights off, watching an endless stream of images on the screen. She couldn't tell what she was watching. She stacked empty plates in the sink and collected wine bottles on the floor. The pile of dishes and rows of empty bottles were the only orderly parts of her life. The rest of the time, she drifted.

After a week, Anji went back to work. She sat at her desk and wrote, went home, ate, drank, and stumbled into bed. She didn't bother turning the lights on. The light from the screen provided her the only illumination necessary. On weekends, it was simpler. She didn't have to go to work.

A box was delivered to Anji's apartment with all her belongings, including Jane Green's *Mr. Maybe*. She didn't know if Cynthia had surreptitiously gathered her things or if Donovan had asked for them to be taken away. The only thing she was sure of was that Cynthia had packed the box. Donovan wouldn't have done it.

MAY 5, 2004

Anji found Donovan sitting at her desk when she arrived at the office in the morning. He was peering down at his BlackBerry, as usual. She stood, paralyzed, just outside the door, feeling the world had sucked her into a void. He sensed her presence and looked up.

"Hello, angel." He stood up from the chair and walked over. He kissed her, lightly, on the cheek.

His touch prodded her to move. Anji entered her office and sat down at her desk, watching him carefully. Donovan returned to the chair he had just occupied. He was smiling and there was light in his eyes. "I was meeting Josh and couldn't pass up the chance to see you."

Anji noticed her hands were trembling and placed them on her lap, away from view.

"What are you doing this weekend?" His voice was soft and gentle.

"Not much," she answered casually, trying to keep herself busy. She powered on her computer. The levity in his being felt promising.

Donovan leaned in. "How about Bermuda?"

"What about it?" Her hands were shaking so much she wanted to sit on them. She stopped herself, placing them back on her lap.

"Come away with me," he whispered.

Her head whipped to face him. "What?"

"Come away with me." His eyes were soft, and the light in them burned brighter.

"I can't just get away like that."

"Yes, you can." He pulled an envelope out of his breast pocket and slid it across her desk. "It's all done. Be at the hangar at six o'clock on Friday."

He didn't wait for an answer and stood up. When he reached the door, he turned and said, "I'm looking forward to being with you, angel."

Anji stared at the emptiness of the doorway. She picked up the envelope, holding it with both hands. She stared at her name printed on the outside. Somehow, it surprised her that Donovan still knew her full name—he never used it. Hands still shaking, she retrieved a confirmation that a private jet would fly them to Bermuda. She wasn't sure why he had given her a copy of it. Her name wasn't listed.

She didn't know if she should go. The scar on her shoulder looked vicious. A contorted redness remained etched on her skin. And she hadn't lost any kilos. She had moved much less in the last few weeks than she had at any other point in her life. She was sure she had gained kilos. But she sensed a change in Donovan. He was kinder. She hoped the light in his eyes indicated he was repentant. Maybe he had come to terms with how much he loved her.

She folded the confirmation and put it back in the envelope. Friday was two days away. She tried to focus on work, but all she could do was run through her wardrobe mentally. She resolved to go shopping after work.

Two days later she was on the plane to Bermuda. Donovan didn't say much on the flight. He promised to focus on her exclusively once they landed, and the time on the plane would be the last he would be on his laptop and BlackBerry. Anji took that as a sign that he was truly repentant. Maybe this weekend away from work, social engagements, and other people would give them the chance to get back to how they had been at The Peninsula. They would finally be themselves.

Donovan booked them at the Fairmont Southampton. They arrived late and Donovan said he preferred to order room service for dinner. Anji saw samosas on the menu but Donovan said, "Indian food is heavy."

He ordered steaks and salads instead. Anji didn't mention that she considered beef to be heavy.

The next morning, they went for a stroll on the pink coral sand beach, holding hands. Afterward, they had a couples' treatment at the Willow Stream Spa.

The massage therapist gasped when she worked on Anji's shoulders. "Does it hurt?"

"It's nothing," Anji whispered, hoping Donovan hadn't heard.

That afternoon, they sat by the pool. Anji didn't remove her coverup, even though she had applied several layers of concealer and foundation over the scar. She hadn't brought a book with her. She lay on a lounge chair, staring up at the sky. Donovan ordered a glass of cabernet for her, without asking. Her heart melted. She felt change in the air.

The waiter presented the wine, and next to it was an olive-green gift bag. He had a twinkle in his smile. "For you, Mrs. Miller."

Anji warmed at the slight of name, and looked over at Donovan, who pretended not to notice. She opened the gift bag and found a matching jewelry box inside. Her heart beat out of her chest and her hands shook as she pulled out the box. This was the moment she'd longed for. She had waited for this her whole life and it was finally here. The butterflies in her stomach were running wild.

She looked over at Donovan again. He smiled. She opened the box slowly, wanting to savor every moment. When she opened the box, she stared at the contents, no words came to her. The anticipation and jitters suddenly fell flat and cold. She tried to keep her smile in place as she stared back at a pair of Van Cleef & Arpels white coral earrings set in gold in a classic Alhambra design.

"They're vintage," Donovan said softly, as if that made it better.

"They're beautiful." Anji exclaimed, noticing her voice was several pitches too high.

"When I saw them, I immediately thought of you, angel. Put them on." Donovan sounded pleased.

Anji obliged. Donovan turned her face from side to side. Smugly, he sat back on his lounge chair and went back to reading *The Economist*. Anji regretted not bringing a book to hide behind. She lay with a nervous smile on her face—the same one that she had plastered on since she had opened the box. Her cheeks felt tight from the effort and she was afraid she was smirking Joker-like. She also knew that if she let go of the smile, tears would come.

She touched her hands to her ears, feeling the dangling earrings. Her breathing became more difficult. Her breaths got shallow and breathing with her mouth open didn't help. She got up to go to the restroom, mumbling something about wanting to get a closer look. The minute she closed the door, she put her hands on her chest, hoping that it would somehow ease her breathing. It didn't.

She sat on the toilet and held her head in her lap for a while. Her body was covered in cold sweat, and she hugged her knees, feeling her knuckles turn pale from the effort. She didn't know how long she remained in that position, but she did until her breathing eased. When she had calmed, she splashed her face with water and walked back out to lie on the lounge chair.

"Everything okay?" Donovan inquired. "You were gone for a while."

"Yes, great." After a few moments, she said, "I had to admire the earrings. They're lovely. Thank you so much."

"Anything for you, angel."

Anji didn't sleep much that night. She didn't want to ruin their beautiful getaway with unfulfilled expectations. He hadn't given her a diamond ring, but she was sure their relationship was back on track. The swim out to the coves, their stroll on Horseshoe Bay Beach, and the dip in the warm turquoise water were all good signs. This had been his way of making it up to her.

JUNE 12, 2004

Anji arrived at her office and was surprised to find a voicemail from Josh. It had been left at 6:54 a.m. Josh rarely communicated with her. She braced herself as she heard the recording, hoping she hadn't done anything wrong.

"Anji, I was calling to check if you wanted to ride with us to the wedding. Stop by my office and let me know," Josh's message said.

Anji was relieved she wasn't getting reprimanded. She wandered over to Josh's office. "The wedding?"

"Donovan and Helen's," Josh said matter-of-factly.

Anji stared at him, flabbergasted. She couldn't have heard correctly. "Donovan?"

"He was here last month to hand-deliver the invitation, and he said he would stop to see you. I thought it strange they left the invites until the last moment. One would think it was a shotgun wedding if Helen hadn't been talking about it for so long." Josh spoke as if it were the most obvious of statements.

"Right . . . yes." Anji felt hot and the buzzing of a thousand bees had taken refuge in her head. She felt disoriented, wondering who on earth Helen was.

"It's quite a hike to Scarsdale. You can ride with us."

"A wedding," she managed to say.

Josh gave Anji a confused look. He continued awkwardly, "Donovan and Helen are all class—personally hand delivering all their invitations for a June wedding at his parents' garden."

"Interesting. . . Josh, I'm sorry." Anji cleared her throat, attempting to dispel the weakening in her voice. "Did you say you got yours last month?"

"Yes. Didn't Donovan come see you that day, too? He was here first thing."

"Yes, yes he did." Anji said, fighting hard to keep herself together. She cleared her throat again, hoping Josh would assume she needed a drink of water.

"You'll be there, right?"

Anji cleared her throat. "No." She cleared it again. Anji's envelope hadn't included an invite. "No, I won't."

"I'm sorry if I put my foot in it. Donovan speaks so highly of you." Josh sounded surprised.

"We're not that close, I guess," Anji said quietly.

Josh tried to defuse the tension and smiled. "The wedding is going to be epic. Donovan is never seen without Helen. Those two are inseparable."

Anji mustered a smile back and ambled back to her office. The word "inseparable" reverberated like an echo in a canyon, making the buzzing in her head harder to bear. Her body moved slowly yet her thoughts were ablaze as she finally realized what had kept Donovan busy all those weeks when he didn't contact her. It dawned on her then that what she had wanted so desperately from Donovan he had given to someone else.

Chapter Twenty-One

JUNE 12, 2004

ANJI SAT IN THE SAFETY of her apartment. Her eyes settled on the small olive-colored bag she'd left on the coffee table. The box screamed out what was now so clear. The trip to Bermuda hadn't been an apology. It was a goodbye.

Anji felt herself sink to the depths of the ocean. Barnacles had already begun to build their home around her broken hull. She wondered if Helen had scars or if that had been a special treatment Donovan had reserved for Anji.

For the first time in months, she sobbed, curling into a ball. She remained that way for hours. It took great effort to stretch her legs. And it hurt. She cried out, the sound of her voice echoed against the four walls, reminding her she was still alive. She thought how much easier it would be if that weren't so. Then she need not worry about what to do next.

Anji didn't go to work the rest of the week. She didn't change out of the clothes she'd worn to work on Wednesday. She didn't care. She spent the weekend on the sofa.

When she got up on Monday morning, she noticed several missed calls and messages from people at work. She decided to rip off the band aid. She would go to work to get fired. It was easier if it were all over at once.

She threw her outfit into the trash, knowing she'd never wear it again. Her hair was plastered to her head, a thick sheen of oil clung to it. She reeked and wondered if this was how she would be if she were homeless. She showered but didn't bother applying makeup. She tied her hair in a ponytail and put on fresh clothing. That alone seemed like a feat.

When Anji got to work, she was surprised she wasn't fired on the spot. Instead, her boss expressed concern over how ill she looked. Anji blabbered something about intolerable migraines, and her boss gave her the rest of the week off. Anji promised to be back at work the following Monday. She didn't know whether to feel disappointed or relieved.

Anji's stomach growled as she left the *Really Living Magazine* offices. She couldn't remember the last time she had eaten. She ordered a thin-crust vegetarian pizza from East Village Pizza and bought a bottle of wine from the nearby deli. She ate three slices and left the rest. The next night she did it again. She ate three slices and left the rest in the box, which she piled on top of the box from the night before. Something about the process made Anji feel like she was having her own kind of slumber party. This one was filling up with odors of decay.

Sophie called several times, eager for their regular catch-up. Anji didn't call her back. On Friday evening, Sophie showed up with a bag of food from Dean & Deluca. After her knocks went unanswered, Sophie let herself in—she had a key. Anji was on the sofa, pizza boxes piled at end of the couch, and a row of wine bottles arranged next to them.

Anji barely noticed Sophie come in. She didn't greet her and didn't move from her horizontal position. Sophie got rid of the trash right away. As she gathered the pizza boxes, she said, "There are handwritten messages on the tops of these boxes. One says, 'Smile. You'll feel beautiful. Another says, 'Cheer up! This too shall pass.' A third says, 'Today is a new day. It's an opportunity to begin again.' You should see these messages."

Anji continued to stare blankly at the TV screen.

Sophie sighed. "I feel bad getting rid of them, but the stench is so awful I have to."

JULY 23, 2004

Relaxing into calm. The words popped into Anji's head. She felt anything but relaxed, which meant the elusive calmness was even further from reach. She wasn't even sure if the words popped into her head or if she'd heard them somewhere. She had gotten used to hearing voices that didn't seem her own.

The thought of calmness weighed on her as she stretched in bed. She'd never been one to rise quickly, as her mother did, jumping out like a jack-in-the-box at the first ding of the alarm. Her mother was the Energizer bunny, but not Anji. She remained still for a few moments, feeling the ache in her back radiate up to her neck. Her shoulder spasmed as if on cue. She wondered if this was what it would feel like when she was older. She wished she could sleep more but that wasn't an option. Not if she wanted to stay employed. She still wasn't sure if she was disappointed or relived that she still had a job. She did it without thinking.

Anji had worked diligently for the past few weeks. She hadn't missed a day of work since she had pretended to have suffered from migraines. She let out a deep sigh and slid down the mattress, placing both feet firmly on the floor. She loved sleeping on a high-top mattress even if it meant that getting on it required her to climb on, and every morning required her to slide down.

Anji steadied herself before she dragged her feet to the kitchen, the creaking of the floorboards echoing the creaking within her joints. Black coffee was her fuel. She tried to remember how long she had been drinking her coffee black. Ironically, she didn't drink coffee when she had lived in Colombia. She started drinking it in college, but back then, it was mostly milk and had six packets of sugar. The thought of it made her stomach turn.

She fantasized about going back to a time when the thought of facing the light wasn't so daunting. Despite the daily effort to get to work, writing for *Really Living Magazine* was the only thing that kept Anji moving on a path she recognized. It was her only certainty. Everything else was dark. She moved by inertia, once she got herself going in the morning. Life was a nuance of blurs, and days passed as shadows. She saw couples together and turned away, certain she would never have that. It wasn't destined for her.

Anji couldn't bring herself to talk about how she felt, even with Sophie. When Sophie asked, Anji resorted to silence or one-word answers. When Donovan and Helen's wedding was featured in the social pages, Anji seemingly had no reaction. She looked at the images listlessly, as if she hadn't known the protagonist. She did finally understand that she had never been Donovan's type. Helen was a gorgeous, size zero blonde. Not an extra kilo on her.

Time passed tediously; every tick of the clock was a tick too long before the next. Sophie helped nurse Anji back to health, ever-present, calling, visiting, clearing out boxes and bottles, and making sure she didn't wither into darkness. Sophie showed up unannounced, changing sheets that had been on the bed for weeks and washing pajamas that hadn't left Anji's body for days.

Anji only paid attention to the messages on the pizza boxes. They were the only thing she looked forward to. She evolved to finishing the pizza pie before ordering the next one. She refrigerated leftovers, although she didn't always heat the slices she ate. She appreciated she could get several meals from one box of pizza. It required less effort.

AUGUST 6, 2004

Sophie and her then boyfriend invited a few people over for dinner and a movie at their house. Anji hadn't wanted to attend, but Sophie insisted. "They're Mark's college buddies and you would be here to keep me company."

Anji went but didn't partake in the general conversation. After dessert, they set up *Tristan and Isolde* in the living room. At some point, tears began to spill down Anji's cheeks. Sophie handed her a tissue when Tristan watched Isolde marry his father figure. By the time Tristan died in Isolde's arms, Anji was a mess of mascara, tears, and snot. She hiccupped uncontrollably, her body shaking so forcefully it looked as if she were having a seizure.

Sophie and Mark hauled Anji into the guest bedroom and away

from the guests. Mark closed the door behind them and Anji clung to Sophie with a continuing torrent of tears, willing her mouth to move and share what she'd been holding inside, but sobs and chokes were the only sounds. When she finally stopped crying, the sun had risen. Sophie and Anji lay cuddled in bed and rose only when Mark brought them coffee in the bedroom.

The warm, comforting aroma awakened Anji's spirit. Anji told Sophie every detail, filling all the gaps she'd left out before. The tale burst from Anji like air from a popped balloon, fluttering nonstop every which way until there was nothing left but a limp reminder of its former self. Sophie took it in, listening quietly, letting it all pour out of Anji. For the first time in a long time, Anji felt lighter.

Sophie suggested Anji see a therapist. And she did. Anji talked about work and how hard it was to find a decent guy. She spoke about her parents and brother—anything other than Donovan. Eventually, she stopped going, unable to find the words to describe what was gone. Anji wondered why it was hard for her to find the words to express herself, ironic for someone dedicated to the art of written communication.

Anji did her best to obliterate Donovan from her life. If someone asked her about her love life, Anji said she hadn't seen anyone in a long time, as if those months with Donovan did not exist. As if omitting Donovan would lessen the hurt.

From that moment, Anji didn't utter his name. She rarely spoke of him and when she did, he was Older Guy, which was only to Sophie.

SEPTEMBER 4, 2004

Anji awoke realizing she hadn't walked in months. She got dressed and, with no direction in mind, she walked all day. She went all over the city. Her thighs itched, urging her to stop. Anji pressed on, the more her thighs itched, the more she walked. Sometimes the itch was so strong she felt like an entire ant colony had descended upon her. Still, she kept going, as if something beyond her was urging her on.

She did it again the following weekend and kept on doing it

until she rediscovered her love of walking. She made her way up to Harlem, down to Brooklyn, over to Queens, and anywhere her will would take her. She also walked into Central Park and found a calm place to sit and watch the crowds. She explored more and more of the park, and eventually came upon the rock that would become her special place.

Oddly, she didn't lose any weight, as Older Guy had wanted her to. He had called them kilos. She didn't lose any of those either. But she shed pain and darkness. And, eventually, she called her spirit back to her body. With every step she reclaimed one more piece, however tiny and however minute. What started as a broken shell grew back into a form she could recognize. Although some pieces never made their way back.

Walking helped her write. It unraveled her mental knots and produced the best writing of her career. She started seeing her job as a blessing, and finally decided she felt relieved she hadn't been fired all those months ago. She received more assignments. Anji pitched to Josh a "Lifestyle Experts in Your Area" series and he accepted. She traveled all around the country researching underground wellness communities. Wellness was a growing trend, and Anji interviewed every type of coach, guide, expert, practitioner, and guru she could find. She meditated with an ex-monk in Raleigh; completed a forty-day Kundalini yoga challenge in Los Angeles; and had her health birth chart read by an astrologist in Cheyenne.

Her dedication to *Really Living Magazine* wasn't out of a passion for her job, but to fill the void. She replaced Older Guy with ten-city itineraries, red-eye flights, and overnight bus rides. Coin laundromats and take-out meals in front of the TV in a hotel room became her faithful rituals.

Occasionally, she saw him featured in the news, and she realized she didn't hold a grudge against him. He was broken and she had held on hoping to reach his gentle, kind interior. She knew it was there. She had seen it in the softness of his gaze. If only he had allowed her love to envelop him, he would have found a safe haven for his hurt. But he had been the fog that eclipsed her sun.

Chapter Twenty-Two

DECEMBER 3, 2005

"WHY ARE YOU still hung up on that asshole?" Sophie asked.

Sophie and Anji had just sat down at a Blue Bottle Coffee on Clinton Street. It was a busy morning, as was the case on most Saturdays, and the buzzing atmosphere was a welcome distraction for Anji.

"I don't know . . . "

"Anji, you were with the guy for eight months and you still think about him. It's been eighteen months since you last saw him . . . why?" Her tone was gentle yet probing.

Anji felt an opening that morning—like she could finally speak about Older Guy again. "He made me feel like I was alive. Or seen. Or noticeable. Or worthy."

"But he treated you like shit. You disappeared. I didn't hear from you for weeks. If I didn't have the keys to your apartment, I would never have known that you were in such a deplorable state. Remember the time I walked in on you sitting on the toilet? The whole place stunk to high hell with actual shit and you sat there, catatonic, staring at nothing. I literally picked you up from the floor."

"I know . . . " Anji cringed at the memory.

"Then? What was it about that guy?"

Anji played with her coffee cup, deciding how to answer. "Sophie, he was my first love. I mean real love. And he showed me a world that I didn't think was possible for me. He seemed larger than life and being with him made me feel like I was attractive and deserving. I've always felt small and insignificant. The fact that he noticed me, helped me, loved me—"

"He didn't love you, my sweets. Throwing books at someone, belittling them, and making them feel fat and stupid is not love. It's abuse." Sophie's tone was stern, yet kind.

Anji played with her coffee cup again. "He loved me in his own way . . ."

Sophie gave her a pained expression. "Go on."

"He was lovely at the beginning. And he took me under his wing. He helped get me a job, and then I felt like he was grooming me, helping me to be and look better."

Sophie reached out and placed her hand over Anji's arm. "You are beautiful, Anji, and attractive, and you also command presence. It breaks my heart that you don't see it yourself. You don't need anyone to make you look or feel better. You are perfect just the way you are."

Anji gave her a small smile. "You say that because you love me."

"I say that because I mean it. That asshole didn't deserve you." Sophie's tone was soft.

"I know, Sophie. It was hard for me to see it then. I know it is time to let him go. He turned my life upside down."

"It is time for you to turn it right side up. Move on."

Anji nodded. They sat in silence for a while, and then she said, "If I have to be honest, it is me who I have to forgive. I think that's what hurts me most. He hurt me, but I also let him. I don't know why I kept on going back for more or why I hoped he would change. I thought I could heal him, and somehow he would see that and fall in love with me. I should have left sooner. Even Cynthia told me I should have left, and she had to know everything he did. I just took it, and I don't know why." Anji let tears stream down her cheeks. When she noticed an older woman looking at her, she wiped them away.

"My sweets, you see the best in people and you hope that they see themselves as you see them. But that is not the case. People are assholes and that's it. You've got to let them be who they are. But their actions have no bearing on you. You are not less or more because he couldn't help being who he is."

Anji stared at something out the window. Reflecting back on that time, Anji realized she had latched on to him because he had made her feel special, unique. He had helped her break away from the shell she'd grown up in. She had no longer felt like the ugly girl from her Colombian high school but rather like a woman who had blossomed into having sex appeal. She still wondered what it would have taken for her to be worth his while. She once spent $5,555 in MaxMara, hoping an upgrade to her wardrobe would make an impression. He never noticed.

"There is no point crying over spilt milk. I don't want you to get back into one of your quilt gloom sessions." Quilt gloom was a term Sophie had created that meant not wanting to get out of bed.

Anji smiled at Sophie. "Don't worry. I'm not getting back into quilt gloom."

"Can you forgive yourself?" Sophie asked.

"I know I will never let something like that happen to me again."

"Yes, but can you forgive yourself?"

"I don't know how . . . "

NOVEMBER 3, 2006

Sophie found a mold-topped dish in the fridge. "Can I throw this casserole out?"

Anji nodded. "What on earth is a casserole?"

"A cheesy baked dish usually with veggies, meats, pasta, potatoes, and such." Sophie still had a habit of checking on things in Anji's apartment. She had been inspecting the fridge.

Anji sat on the sofa, sipping a glass of Tempranillo. "Like mac and cheese?"

"Yeah, I guess. Where did this one come from?" Sophie closed the fridge, apparently finding nothing else that needed to be thrown out.

"My neighbor Lulu brought it over to introduce herself. She moved in last week." Anji had been in her apartment for five months to the date.

"Why didn't you eat it?" Sophie held her nose as she threw out the casserole in the trash.

Anji shrugged. "I didn't know what it was."

Having her own space, one that she owned, made Anji feel independent. She felt she had finally fulfilled her mother's wish. When Anji was seven years old, she sat under a mango tree reading a book. Her mother sat next to her and held on to her hand. "Anji, please promise me you will be independent."

"Hmm . . . " Anji didn't look up from her book.

"I mean it, *beti*. Don't depend on anyone. Have your own money. Don't be like me and the women in our family. You are smart and capable."

"Yes, mummy," Anji had said, still peering into her book.

"Anji, look me in the eye and promise." She squeezed Anji's hand.

Anji had been surprised by the intensity and sadness in her mother's eyes. She promised, unsure of what that meant. Yet, her mother's words had stayed with her, and she recalled them from time to time. She thought of them that afternoon. Anji couldn't think of a better way to be independent than to own the space in which she lived.

"I really like what you've done with the place. It feels very you," Sophie complimented, joining Anji on the sofa.

Anji treasured her little piece of heaven, feeling she was enveloped in a warm blanket every time she stepped into her home. Anji had furnished her apartment diligently, discarding her college IKEA furniture over time and replacing it with select pieces she had saved up for. She had decorated it with hand-made crafts from her travels: an antique iron pipe from Yangon, a pair of ceramic jaguars made by a great grandmother in Oaxaca, and a hand-sculpted sandalwood Ganesh made by a woodworker in Varanasi, before it became illegal to work with sandalwood.

Anji was thrilled she'd had a chance to fill the space with so many things that were her own. "Had I stayed with Older Guy, I would be living in a white and gray space."

"Sweet pea, you would have been forgotten." Sophie was matter-of-fact.

"Like all women. Aren't we all forgotten in some way?"

"Where is this coming from, sweets?"

"I just found out my mother loves peanuts. Everyone's favorites in the family are well known. I love a carrot pudding called *gajar halwa*, Sid loves these crispy fried dough rings soaked in syrup called *jalebi*, and my father loves the same *pakora* that you love so much. I'm twenty-six, and I just found out my mother's favorite nuts are peanuts, and that she prefers them roasted and salted in the shell." She realized it on a recent trip to India. Her uncle brought them home wrapped in newspaper. The delight on her mother's face surprised her. She had never known her mother was so fond of peanuts.

"It's because your mother is so generous and giving. She puts others above herself."

"Isn't that what all women do? I don't want to be that way—not anymore. I can think of only one time when I had the audacity to speak up." She had been fourteen years old at the time. Colombia was a Catholic country, which meant religious studies were part of the school curriculum. In Anji's school, they were clothed in the guise of "ethics." It irked Anji that the class was taught by a priest and the Bible was readily quoted.

She wouldn't have dared speak up had she not noticed there was a separate class for Jewish kids and a rabbi taught it. She had asked permission to use the restroom, and on her way back she noticed a couple of her classmates sitting in a different classroom and snooped from outside the door.

She had felt so slighted she burst into the principal's office, shocking everyone, including herself. "I'm not opposed to religious study, but I don't feel I should be obliged to learn Catholicism when the Jewish kids can learn Judaism."

The principal conceded and asked her to sit in the library during that period and research Hinduism. For the rest of the school year, she was to present him a weekly two-page essay on what she had learned. Anji had been so pleased with herself, she didn't care about the extra work.

"It was a pivotal moment for me. Until then, I hadn't truly understood my religion. There were no Hindu temples in Colombia, and my family only visited them during our yearly trips to India. The rest of the time, my parents confined their daily prayers and incense burning to the small altar at home."

She could barely identify the different statues that filled her parents' altar. Shiva rode a bull, Durga sat on a tiger, and Ganesh with his elephant head rode a mouse. Hanuman was the monkey god, and Krishna carried a flute. Lakshmi was the goddess of wealth and she stood on a lotus flower. It was through her research that she learned that Shiva was the Hindu god of life energy and represented the ideal of male. Durga was the Hindu goddess known as the mother protector and fighter of evil. Ganesh was the child of Shiva and Parvati. Hanuman represented strength and courage, and Krishna was an avatar of Vishnu.

"It pained me that I could more easily recite the *Ave Maria* or *Padre Nuestro* than any Sanskrit prayer," Anji said.

Sophie gave her a look of sympathy. "The Hail Mary and the Lord's Prayer are pretty well-known, I feel, especially growing up in a Catholic country."

The weekly essays she had submitted to the principal had helped Anji understand that mantras were not just about repeating words over and over to please deities, but they held spiritual powers. She learned that the repeated cycles of life and death in reincarnation were so that we could evolve and grow in each life and thus improve the sanctity of life. She came to understand that karma wasn't just about doing bad things that would come to bite you later in life, but karma was also about doing good, and was ultimately a matter of balance.

It awakened in Anji a desire to learn about other religions and spirituality. In her apartment, she had a small altar with Hindu deities as well as a Buddha, Virgen de Guadalupe, and an Egyptian ankh, among others. She burned incense to them every time she finished meditating. Her altar reflected the cross-cultures in her own life. As Anji gazed upon it, she wondered if her life was too amalgamated for others to comprehend—one person in particular.

"Sweet pea, I didn't mean to make you think about Older Guy," Sophie said, as if reading her mind.

"I know. I need to let him go. For so long, I held on to the deep connection we had at the beginning. He made me feel he knew things about me that I didn't even know about myself."

"The truth is that he didn't know you at all. He disrespected you."

Anji thought it was because of karmic retribution. She had to have done something bad in a previous life and the universe had found a way to balance things out. Somehow, she had deserved the disrespect.

Chapter Twenty-Three

FEBRUARY 24, 2019

AFTER THE SESSION with Margarita, Anji searched for a movie to watch. She wanted to release emotions and looked for sad movies that would make her cry. She started with *The Secretary*, and, although it showcased pain, it made Anji cringe rather than cry. She moved on to *Shakespeare in Love* but felt sad and not devastated.

Tristan & Isolde came up as a recommendation. She hesitated at first but then felt it was a sign. A few years before, Anji had been on vacation in Dublin. She had visited the sights listed in *111 Places in Dublin that You Shouldn't Miss*, and was filled with jitters when she saw that number fifty-two was Isolde's Tower & The Czech Inn. She set off from her hotel and walked twenty minutes past Trinity College to the Temple Bar area.

Isolde Tower wasn't distinctive. She had to refer back to the image in the book to make sure it was the right one. It was an unattractive apartment building. Her heart fell as she took in its blandness. Anji couldn't believe that one of the greatest love stories had been reduced to a dull set of metallic bars. It didn't even have a plaque.

Anji knew that watching the movie again would be cathartic. To commemorate the occasion, she ordered a pizza from East Village

Pizza and paired it with a bottle of wine. She was excited to see a message on the pizza box. It said, "It is looking lovely out there. As lovely as it is within."

Anji only shed a few tears while watching the movie. She didn't sob as she had expected. She felt as disappointed as she had been when she saw the Isolde Tower in Dublin. She knew then that she'd moved on. Finally.

FEBRUARY 26, 2019

Anji was at John F. Kennedy Airport with her head buried in Alice Hoffman's *The Dovekeepers*.

"Hello, angel," came a voice.

She recognized it immediately. When she looked up and saw no one, she thought her mind was playing tricks on her again, one of those voices she often heard.

"Back here."

She turned back, and sure enough, Donovan stood behind her, looking as beautiful and unapproachable as ever. He wore a black suit, white button shirt, and a pink handkerchief in his left breast pocket. He hadn't changed a bit, as if time had stood still. His bald head shimmered in the sun coming through the windows. It was so enticing she wanted to reach out and touch it.

"Where are you off to, angel?" His tone was soft.

She twisted from her waist to look back at him properly, "Madrid."

There was a sadness in his expression. "Work?"

"Yes." Anji looked at him carefully to see if she could decipher the source of sadness.

Donovan nodded, giving her the piercing look she recalled so well—the one that touched the deepest recesses of her soul. "Did I make a mistake?"

"A mistake?" Anji raised her voice hoping he would take the hint that he needed to raise his.

"Did I give up my soulmate?"

Anji took a moment to take that in. She wasn't sure she had heard correctly. "Your . . . your soulmate?"

His eyes were firmly locked on her. "You."

Anji felt as if the last ounce of breath left her. "Me? . . . Your soulmate?"

"Aren't you, angel? You're the only one who's ever truly seen me." He placed his hand on his heart.

"There you are, honey," Helen exclaimed, as she walked over. Anji recognized her instantly, having seen so many photos of her over the years. She appeared to be as young as Anji remembered. Time had also stood still with her. She wore a white, skintight body suit, showing her flawless figure. Her long blonde hair was held back in a tight ponytail. She had oversized sunglasses and bright red lipstick, the kind Anji would never be able to pull off. *Puta* red is what Anji and Sophie had called that shade. Whore red.

Donovan gave Helen a quick glance saying, "I'm coming, dear." He turned back to Anji, an air of loneliness coming over him.

"You didn't make a mistake," Anji said, more to herself than to him. She understood his longing to be cuddled in bed while someone stroked his back. His desire to be fed hot chicken soup while someone read to him something from the Brothers Grimm. But she also knew that role wasn't for her.

"Are you certain?" he pleaded.

"I'm certain." And she was. As much as she had wanted to be the one for him once, she no longer felt the need. A soulmate wasn't meant to bring this much hurt.

Helen reached Donovan and latched her arm around his elbow. She looked around. "Who are you talking to?"

He looked in another direction and didn't answer.

Anji scanned Helen's face, searching for something. She noticed Helen's earrings. Long teardrop pearls, the size of a thumb, with a diamond encrusted bow on the top.

"Anyone I know?" Helen asked, looking up at him. Donovan shook his head, and she continued, "That's all right, then."

Anji turned back and stared at the wall in front of her. She had been called a soulmate, once again. But not lonely dove. The two words eluded her. She reached for the Lemurian seed crystal in her handbag. She held on to it and felt wetness on her cheeks. The tears she'd searched for over the weekend made their way down her face.

FEBRUARY 28, 2019

"Would you have left him if he hadn't left you?" Margarita's voice was soft, nurturing.

Anji sighed. "No."

They sat in silence, letting the heaviness of the admission sink in. Anji was back at Margarita's office at Divya in Madrid. Margarita wore the largest ruby pendant Anji had ever seen. She wondered where she sourced her crystals.

"Why are you here?" Margarita asked.

Anji was taken aback. "To figure out what's happening to me?"

"Anji, my dear, this isn't a trick question. Why are you working with me?"

Anji felt every person she had been with kept a piece of her, and every relationship left her with less of herself. Perhaps one of them had taken the piece that held the key to her soulmate. She hoped she could get it back. "So that I can figure out how to make myself whole again."

"You are whole. There is nothing broken or missing inside you. It's only you who doesn't see it."

Anji looked at Margarita, and although she wanted to believe her, she wasn't convinced. "Interesting . . . "

"Have you considered that he might have been a soulmate for you, but not the *let's live forever* type. Rather, a karmic soulmate that wrecked your life to provide you the opportunity of a lesson you were meant to learn."

Anji felt a wave of crystalline energy wash over her. She knew that what Margarita said was true.

Sensing Anji agreed, Margarita asked, "What did you learn from Donovan?"

"How not to love . . . " Anji still wasn't comfortable talking about him.

"The universe brings people into our lives to help us grow as souls, even when they hurt us. How did you grow from Donovan?"

Anji couldn't think of what to say. Donovan was commandeering and expected Anji to twist to his desires. Anji had watched her mother bend to her father, but she hadn't realized it consciously. She hadn't realized that her mother had evaporated into the background, and that she was there, ever-present, indispensable, effusive with nurturing, never asking for anything in return.

Strangely though, it was Donovan's strong masculinity that had drawn her in. Anji might not have been conscious about it, but she was drawn to the male persona. Donovan had a big life. She loved being a part of it. She liked dressing up and going to events, even when Donovan introduced her as his protégé. She liked getting noticed and being part of society, even if no one was aware of her true relationship with him. He took charge and it supported her notion that men were supposed to take control and that life revolved around men.

"He was the first real relationship I'd had. I often felt he was my savior. I didn't know he hadn't been faithful until after the relationship ended. He called me his soulmate but, ironically, I felt I amounted to nothing for him. He didn't give me a second thought. He was cruel and disrespectful. Sometimes I feel it is some kind of karmic retribution."

"Anji, the universe doesn't send us difficult situations so that we suffer. We are not meant to suffer. We are put in situations that push us away from who we are so that we make our way back. What Donovan took away from you is what you most need to give yourself, so that you can see yourself, once again, as whole."

"I need to learn to love myself for who I am?" Anji realized the absurdity of the question as soon as she uttered it.

Margarita sensed it. "Is that really a question?"

Anji smiled. "No, Margarita. I really need to learn to love myself for who I am."

"I want you to think of some things. Who are you in a relationship? Who do you want to be? What is true love to you?"

Anji sat in silence as she pondered the questions. She knew she wouldn't come up with answers right away.

Margarita spoke instead. "Before we end the session, I want to circle back to your psychic abilities. It's clear you're a clairvoyant—you receive visions. From what you have shared, I'm certain that you are also clairaudient—you hear psychic messages. These are skills you can learn to hone and use them to be of service to yourself and others."

"Of service?"

"Yes. Of service means that you could learn to do the type of intuitive work that I do. It's something to think about, my dear."

"Interesting . . . For now, all I want is to focus on my healing."

"Fair enough. It's your choice. Consider the questions I asked you on relationships and love."

When Anji left the bhakti center, she went for a walk along the Paseo de Recoletos, joining the myriad of other pedestrians. She couldn't think of the answers to the questions. It was too soon.

Standing somewhere between the Plaza de Cibeles and the Plaza de Colón she took a breath. Something within her had shifted. She took another breath, this one so deep it filled every bronchiole. She hadn't realized she had been holding her breath for so many years. She stepped away from the main throng of people and stood still. In that moment, Anji forgave herself for staying with Donovan even when she knew she shouldn't have. She folded her body over her knees and let out the biggest exhale she had ever released.

When Anji returned to New York, she took the Van Cleef earrings to a pawn shop. She had worn them one time in Bermuda, and never again. She thought she would feel a thrill from getting rid of them, the anonymity of the next owner her greatest revenge. But when she stared at the $9,535 the pawn shop owner delivered into her hands, she felt flat. That was all she had been worth to him.

She hoped no one ever gave her another pair of Van Cleefs. Or any type of pearl earrings for that matter. If they did, it was clear where they'd end up. The pawnshop.

Chapter Twenty-Four

MARCH 2, 2019

ANJI WAS ON THE PHONE with Sid. It was his forty-fourth birthday and they were in the middle of an hour-long conversation—a rarity for them. Their usual weekly FaceTime chats were typically interrupted by his wife Meena, eight-year-old Radhia, and six-year-old Naitik. As a birthday treat, Meena had taken the kids out and gave Sid the afternoon to himself. They'd be back for a celebratory dinner.

Sid's life had turned out differently from Anji's. He was three years older and had studied computer science at Boston University and moved to London right after graduation. He met Meena five years after he had moved. They were friends for a year before they started dating, and they dated for six years before getting married. He was thirty-three at the time.

Dating for six years was a long relationship by Indian standards. But Sid was slow in making decisions. He considered things thoroughly, making pros and cons lists even in his sleep. He reviewed both sides meticulously to make sure he didn't miss anything. He not only considered the glass as half-empty, he had a plan in case the glass tipped over.

"I hate to tell you this, Anj, but time isn't on your side. I don't know how you feel about having kids, but you're going to run out of options soon." His expression was serious. His tone, matter-of-fact.

"I know," Anji said quietly. There wasn't much to say. Facts were facts.

"You can always adopt, of course, but I feel that you want to have your own children. Am I right?"

"I do." Anji hadn't admitted until then that she wanted her own children.

"What are you doing about it?" There was a hint of frustration in his voice.

"I've dated as much as I could," Anji said, defensively.

The gravity of her single status and advanced age slapped her in the face. It always did when she thought of her family. All her cousins were married, including the youngest, who was twenty-two. Anji was the only single one. It was a sobering thought. She tried not to let it plague her, but it was hard. The cousin had married in April 2016 and, at the wedding, every single person asked her when it would be her turn.

Anji had sat through so many *haldi* ceremonies, she should have been married long ago. *Haldi* was a purification ritual that used turmeric and other components in preparation for the wedding. It included a prayer in which the unmarried—usually younger—sisters sat with the bride. As the bride was purified, so were the sisters, increasing their chances of marriage. Anji had plenty of female cousins. For Hindus, cousins were considered the same as siblings. There was no word for cousin. Aunts and uncles were considered older or younger parents. *Mausi*, or mother's sister, meant little mother.

Anji believed that no matter how many times she was purified, her soul could not be cleansed. She had to learn to live with her single status.

Sid interrupted her thoughts. "Maybe it's time you change your strategy. I know you love living in New York, but I don't feel that city is good for you. Why can't you move to Madrid permanently?"

"Madrid?" Anji was surprised by the turn of the conversation.

"Madrid was at the top of my head because you were just there. It can be anywhere. The point is, you need a change of scenery, meet new people, and stop working so much."

"Interesting . . . " Anji couldn't fathom leaving New York. The city was part of her identity.

"You could move here, you know," Sid offered.

"That would mean quitting *Really Living Magazine*." The idea broke her heart.

"It isn't the only publication out there, Anji. There are plenty of journalism jobs. You can crash with us while you find a place to live. Meena and the kids would be chuffed."

Sid could be right. Anji was determined to run the course of this pursuit—wherever it took her. If it meant she had to leave New York, she would do it. Maybe she could turn into a psychic, like Margarita suggested.

Maybe, but not at that moment. First, she had to try making the best of her current situation. For now, she wouldn't think about moving. She would figure it out if and when the time came.

Margarita had explained that the power of spirituality was in the now, in focusing on the present rather than what was or what may come. She had said it was a choice. A choice to see beyond our illusions. A choice not to look back. A choice not to look ahead. A choice to look at the present—what was happening this instant.

Anji felt she had a choice. One was to keep herself safe and not take chances, not take risks, and stay afraid. Or she could take a chance and do what it took to figure out who her soulmate was. She would find him one way or another. She had faith, and that motivated her.

Yes, maybe Sid was right. Changing environments would give her a surge of new possibilities, a dynamic transformation that would surely lead to her soulmate.

"We want you to have a life, *beti*." Anji's mother's tone was concerned. Her parents had arrived in New York soon after Anji called Sid. They were staying with Anji for a week.

"Last I checked, I was alive and breathing," Anji said. Her mother's comment reminded Anji of her cousin Viruna who had visited in 2010.

"Can you do that?" Viruna had asked when Anji told her she owned her apartment.

Anji remembered wanting to say, "Yes. As if it weren't possible unless I had a man to my name." But she didn't. Instead, she was more conciliatory. "Yes, why not?"

"Oh . . . " Viruna had said. Her muted response suggested Viruna had figured out why Anji wasn't married. People were not meant to own a house, let alone have a life, until they had a husband.

Anji's mother wasn't as complacent. "Don't be smart with me. I'm trying to talk to you."

Anji sighed. "Okay, Mummy. I'm listening."

They were sitting in Anji's living room drinking *chai*. Her mother took a sip and when she put the cup down said, "We want you to be happy. We want you to get married and have children."

"Are you saying that I can't be happy unless I am married and have children?" Anji sounded defiant.

"Can you?" Her father chimed in, giving her a reality check.

"I'm happy now," Anji said softly.

"Are you really, beti? Can you say that for sure?" Her mother was persistent.

Anji had made progress with Margarita, but she still wasn't sure who her soulmate was. And that bothered her.

"We don't think you are," her father said.

"I'm happy with my job," she admitted to her parents. She debated whether to share the work she was doing with Margarita, but realized she wasn't ready.

Anji also didn't share with her parents that she'd been on dates. In the past, she didn't tell them about a boyfriend until she knew the relationship was going to last. Otherwise, they didn't know the specifics. They also didn't need to know about the hurt, the pain, and the heartache. She couldn't stand the disappointment in their eyes if they were to know about bruised shoulders and unaccounted days. Anji was grateful she had spared her parents from meeting Donovan.

"Your job isn't your life," her mother reasoned.

"I know . . . " Anji knew she had a life. She just didn't have the life they wanted for her. Or the life she wanted for herself. But she finally felt she was on her way there.

"We want you to have a happy home life, beti. We want you to feel rich and fulfilled. Not financial richness but the richness you get from having a husband and children."

"Your mother and I have been blessed to have you and your brother, and we want you to have the same," her father added.

"I understand. I want the same for myself, but it's not like I haven't been trying."

"We know, beta. Don't give up. Never give up," her father advised.

And there it was again. The conversation about not losing hope, like the universe was encouraging her not to give up. She might not have felt satisfied with the progress, but she hadn't given up, especially not since she'd started the work with Margarita. Anji wasn't sure what the outcome would be, but she was certain it was the right thing for her.

Anji considered the questions Margarita had posed in the last session. It occurred to her then that she didn't know the answers. Anji was expected to marry soon after graduating college. Respectable Indian women had a duty to get married and have a family. Anji was asked more frequently, "When will you marry?" than, "How are you?" as if her welfare didn't matter unless she had a husband to claim her. It made her feel invisible. Unworthy on her own merit.

The pressure of finding a husband was as persistent as a mosquito buzzing in her ear. She could hear it hovering but she couldn't see it. She started out trying different avenues and held on to the optimism she had learned in America. It was the hallmark of the country. Anji had learned that Americans tried as many candidates as possible from as many avenues as possible. If they found someone, they were lucky. If not, they would try again.

Anji had immersed herself in work, mostly because it helped her forget Frank, Donovan, and the others. She didn't want to dwell too much on what she wanted. She still believed she had a soulmate, but everything in her life pointed against it, and she didn't want to think about what that meant. She wanted to bury the feeling that something was wrong with her, hoping that if she ignored it, somehow it would disappear. She focused instead, on what she did well. She traveled her heart out.

Anji still needed to figure out what she wanted.

Chapter Twenty-Five

MARCH 2, 2019

AFTER SPEAKING WITH HER PARENTS, Anji went out for a walk. She had a lot she needed to process. Her parents stayed in to rest from the flight. She wandered up to Washington Square and ran into a Hare Krishna festival, which reminded her of a group she had known in Colombia.

Other than the Hare Krishna community in Cali, Anji's family was the only Hindu family she knew growing up. But Hindus didn't think highly of Hare Krishnas. It perplexed Anji because Hindu philosophy, in theory, accepted every form of religious practice. Most Hindu temples allowed entrance to everyone, regardless of their faith. But some were exclusive for Hindus, excluding even Hare Krishnas.

As she watched festival attendees singing and playing instruments around Washington Square, she considered the hypocrisy of it. Hindus believed that chanting songs of love and praise led to enlightenment. Why then, not the Hare Krishna way? It also bothered her that women weren't allowed to pray in temples when they are menstruating. Menstruation was considered dirty, yet life wouldn't exist without it.

When Anji was eleven years old, her parents finally decided to put their prejudice aside and visit the Hare Krishna temple in Cali. A small group of Hare Krishnas with ill-fitting yellow *saris* and *dhotis* welcomed Anji and her family with open arms. Anji had to admit that they seemed ridiculous to her—not their chants or missionary work—but Westerners in Indian clothing appeared more out of place to her than Indian people in Western clothing. She felt the urge to explain there was no need for them to dress up. After all, it wasn't Halloween.

Anji's family had felt homesick for India. There was no one in Cali they didn't have to explain themselves to; no one who didn't consider their clothing and habits as peculiar; and no one who didn't turn their noses up at the smells and intensity of the food. They longed for people who understood their view of the world and their religious beliefs. Anji's parents had a small altar at home with statues of their favored deities, but they yearned for a larger sacred space where they could celebrate rituals like *Diwali* that honored light over darkness, the coming of spring with splashes of color during *Holi*, and honor Ganesh during *Ganesh Chaturthi*, which was especially significant for Anji.

True to their generous spirit, the Hare Krishnas offered Anji and her family food. They had *dal, chawal*, and some type of *subji*—traditional Indian dishes of lentils, rice, and vegetables. But the food was terribly bland. Anji wondered how, despite their affinity for India, the Colombian Hare Krishnas had failed to incorporate one of the most distinctive aspects of Indian culture: the use of spices in food.

She remembered chewing the food slowly. When she swallowed, she heard a *gulp* as the dry bolus lumbered down her throat like a lump of coal. It was the only time in her life she had chewed her food the recommended thirty-two times, and it wasn't because she was concerned about her digestion. It was the only way she could avoid putting more food in her mouth.

The Hare Krishnas had a lot of questions. Many of them were encountering true Indians for the first time. To Anji, India was indescribable. The only way to understand it was to experience it. But this was cost-prohibitive for many of the Hare Krishnas, and Anji's family were the closest they were going to get to India. Anji's parents shared as much as they could.

Fortunately, it wasn't long before her mother said in soft-spoken Hindi that they should leave. Although these Hare Krishnas sang and chanted in Sanskrit, they didn't understand a word of Hindi. Anji's family left as graciously as they could. Her father politely promised to go back, although they knew they would not return.

After that, Anji's family fully embraced Colombian customs, keeping the Indian ones to private times. On December 7, *El Día de las Velitas*, a Catholic holiday marking the eve of Immaculate Conception, they lit candles all around their home alongside their neighbors. They attended the *cabalgatas* or horse-riding parades, as well as salsa music concerts, parties, food festivals, and other festivities during the *Feria de Cali* that took place after Christmas. The only events they skipped were the bull fights.

They learned to appreciate and eventually love Colombian food, reserved special nights for *sancocho de gallina* soup made from hen, plantains, and yucca, and for *ajiaco*, a corn, potato, and chicken stew. They snacked with crispy beef corn turnover *empanadas*. They made the best of the disparities in food and culture, immersing themselves separately in each. The only similarity between the two countries was the sheer variety of fruits. Colombians, however, turned every fruit into juice, made in either water or milk, and Indians ate their fruit at the end of a meal or as a snack.

Anji marveled at how much she had changed since she'd met those Colombian Hare Krishnas as a child. There were food stalls all around Washington Square with deliciously authentic food. The essence of New York City was a cornucopia of cultures. Anji realized she felt more at home in New York than in any other place she'd ever been. How could she ever leave?

She had found the sense of home she had longed for as a child in the city. All she had to do was make her way down Roosevelt Avenue in Jackson Heights to find Indian restaurants on one side and Colombian eateries on another. She could catch a Bollywood film and stock up on *garam masala* spice mix and deliciously toasted corn *arepas* on the same trip. It was emblematic that her two cultures had come together in that neighborhood, as if tailored-made for her.

Just then, someone thrust a flyer in her hands. She zeroed in on an image of a dove. Below it were handwritten words, "Forgive, forget, and open to love. Love is all there is."

And then, Anji's phone rang.

It was William. He was muttering and Anji moved away from the noise of the Hare Krishna festival to better hear him. He told her about his ongoing struggles at work. It was clear to Anji he had something important to tell her and that it didn't have anything to do with work, but she played along.

"I always thought you'd end up running a fish and chip joint instead of having a big corporate life. True joy is in the little things." As she spoke the words, Anji realized these were lessons she, too, needed to learn.

"Just like I always thought you would set up a tent in Time's Square to read people's fortunes."

Anji couldn't help but laugh. "Don't mock my burgeoning psychic skills."

"Okay, I won't. Have you found your suitable boy yet?" The mockery was still heavy in his voice.

Anji didn't expect the turn in conversation. *A Suitable Boy* by Vikram Seth was over 1,000 pages. She didn't think he had it in him to read a novel, much less one that long.

"You are impressed, aren't you?" he said proudly.

"Deeply. I didn't think Indian authors were in your repertoire."

"There's lots you don't know about me, Anj . . . So, tell me."

"Meeting Hare Krishnas hasn't increased my chances of finding a suitable boy," Anji said, trying to make light of the conversation.

"You've always had chances, but you don't see them."

Something about the statement rang true for Anji. "Maybe I need to go on a train journey . . . "

William laughed. "What on earth are you talking about?"

Anji explained that trains were featured in Bollywood movies, and Anji had often fantasized that she'd meet the man of her dreams as if it were a Bollywood love story. "I saw us boarding a train and locking eyes with one another. We'd know instantly we were meant for each other."

"And there would be dancing and shit?" William asked, continuing to laugh.

"Obviously. We'd start with a slow beat, shy and coy, as we got to know each other. But after a good ten seconds, which is all we'd need to know we were meant to be, our newfound passion would urge us to shake and gyrate our shoulders and hips as we moved from one end of the train to the other. This, of course, as we chugged along the Swiss Alps."

William was laughing loudly. "Anj, stop."

"Yes, I did just say the Swiss Alps. And if it sounds preposterous, it's because you haven't watched 1980s Bollywood movies. It was common to cut away from dramatic scenes in India to a song and dance staged in Europe."

"Anj, seriously stop. My stomach hurts."

They laughed for a while longer. As their chuckles faded, they descended into silence, a latent heaviness hung between them.

"You know those words in your vision—lonely dove—really seem to describe you. You are beautiful yet eternally on your own . . . "

Anji felt shivers and goosebumps ran all over her. William had used the two words she longed to hear. And she was shocked to hear him call her beautiful. "Yeah, something else I need to figure out how to fix. Will, I know you didn't call me to hear about my silly fancies. What's going on?"

"I asked Natalie to marry me." William rushed the words out.

"Wow. Congratulations!" Her voice came out in a higher pitch than she had expected, and she felt a tightness within.

"Anj, you don't have to pretend to be happy for me." His tone was flat.

"What are you talking about? I'm happy for you. Natalie is a nice woman. I like her." Anji hoped she conveyed the sincerity of her feelings.

A silence stretched out between them.

"This time I am asking for real. You'll come to the wedding, right?"

"Absolutely." Anji's voice was steadier.

"I'd love for you to be a groomsman, but I'm not sure how that would work . . . "

"Yes, it would be weird having me stand next to you at the altar. Don't worry. It is an honor you asked. Although I would feel more comfortable in a tux than a dress."

William snorted. "I'm sure you would. Simply knowing you'll be there makes me feel better."

"So, you already have a date?"

"Yes. October 5 at my parent's house in Long Island."

"Wow. Even the venue is set." That made it seem more real in Anji's mind than hearing that William had proposed.

"Natalie and my parents were planning this wedding long before I asked her."

"Interesting . . . "

Chapter Twenty-Six

MARCH 5, 2019

SHE FELT LIKE a rotisserie chicken turning slowly on a spit. She wore a full-length tunic. She looked up at the sky and was nearly blinded by the intensity of the sun. Sweat dripped down her back, and she used her sleeves to wipe the dampness that had accumulated on her face.

The sweat wasn't just from the heat. She was being chased. She had lost sight of her pursuer and was taking a moment to catch her breath. Her heart raced and her throat felt dry. She needed to keep an eye out.

She ran toward the entrance of the souk, 200 feet ahead, eager for the reprieve from the heat and the promise of a hiding place among the shops.

She looked behind her and caught a glimpse of someone coming after her. She took the first right as she entered the souk, going down an alley. She was caught in a web of scarves and textiles. She pushed them away but they seemed endless, attacking her like a swarm of grasshoppers. She turned to her left and was confronted by a putrid odor—the revolting and intoxicating smell of animal hides soaking in dyes. The heat, the odors, the sweat, the lack of air were overwhelming. She collapsed.

She felt herself fall. She didn't fall for long and when she hit the bottom it didn't hurt. She realized she was inside a wicker basket. When she rose, her head slammed into the firmly shut lid of the basket.

She slumped back from the shock, hitting the bottom. This thump still didn't hurt, even though she expected it to. She looked down, noticing that her tunic had been replaced with a belly dancer costume with tiny bells hanging from her waist belt. Her breath quickened as she gasped for air.

Just then a flute played. She liked the tune. She forgot her discomfort and her body began to move in sync with the music. She rose to her feet, like a cobra lured by a flute player. The basket lid fell away and she looked up at the bright blue sky. The sun was still shining, but not uncomfortably.

Her body undulated in ways she didn't know she was capable of, as if she were truly a snake. She loved it. She had never felt so free.

A crowd gathered around her, clapping and cheering. The flute player sat to the right of the basket. She recognized him.

She winked. He winked back.

———

Anji gazed out her bedroom window—she liked to sleep with her blinds up. It was dark out. Her clock read 3:33 a.m.

This vision clearly showed Nic, but she was unsure of what it was telling her. What did it mean for her to be chased in a souk, only to end up as a cobra rising up while Nic played the flute?

Perhaps she had needed Nic because he had balanced out what she had experienced with Donovan. Donovan had taken her to a dark place and Nic had helped to bring her back. Sort of. She knew that coming to terms with this relationship wasn't going to be as difficult as the others. She had to heal and forgive, but she had already made progress.

Just then Anji heard creaking noises from the walls in her apartment.

"Hello," she called out in jest.

"Hello," came back a soft whisper.

———

JUNE 6, 2012

Really Living Magazine had organized a team-building activity after work at a paint-and-sip studio on the Upper West Side. The last time Anji had painted she had been a child, and the thought of doing it while drinking seemed liberating.

Anji sat at a canvas on the front of the outermost row. As she set her things down, she noticed Nic on the stage. He was six-feet, two-inches with long dirty blond hair tied in a tight ponytail. He had thick hair—he used two hair-ties to secure his long mane. The hair on his face was longer than stubble, but not quite a beard. She wasn't sure if it was on purpose or if he hadn't bothered to shave. It gave him a rugged hobo look rather than that of a groomed hipster.

He wore a loose-fitting white button-down shirt that was open until the third button, revealing a hairless chest. It struck Anji that he was the opposite of Older Guy. Nic had all his hair on his head and Older Guy had all his hair on his chest. Nic wore four necklaces, each made of a different material: gold, silver, leather, and hemp. They seemed like four random choices, as if he couldn't decide which necklace suited him best, so he wore them all.

Nic noticed her noticing him. They made eye contact and smiled at each other. It was not a flirtatious smile but an acknowledgment that he was the instructor and she the student. Nic winked at her, a mischievous smile growing on his face. She looked away, her face growing hot.

Anji could tell Nic was not bothered about teaching; he was professional but disinterested. He spoke without enthusiasm. He taught them to paint a tree against the night sky with a full moon in the background and two owls perched on the tree's branches. Nic demonstrated with pre-set colors, although he allowed them to use different colors, if they chose.

He wandered around assisting people. He let Anji be, only approaching her at the end of the session.

"That is an unexpected choice of colors. Why did you pick yellows and pinks?" Nic asked. His face was so close to Anji's he could have licked her.

Anji pulled her face away. "I was in the mood for light, not night."

"It looks like an Easter painting."

Anji chuckled. "Yes, I guess the light blue on the sky looks pastel."

He smiled. "What are you going to do with it?"

Anji wasn't sure she would keep the painting. She kept her eyes on it instead of looking at Nic. "Umm . . . maybe I'll put it up in my bathroom."

Nic watched her. "Another interesting choice."

"That way it wouldn't be seen by everyone who comes over—just the select few who pee." Anji kept looking at the painting.

"Do you salsa dance?" Nic gave her a coy look, the mischievous smile creeping back.

She turned to him. The obvious answer was yes, she did a lot of Latin dancing, including salsa. But she no longer found the long lines and crowded spaces worth her while. And she found the ballroom-style salsa dancing in the US too choreographed to follow. She was more at ease with the relaxed style of Colombian salsa. "I'm not sure."

"Would you like to join me?"

Anji wondered if he was asking her exclusively or if he had been gathering a group of women to join him. She didn't know why she cared. "I'm sorry, I can't. I'm going out with these guys."

"You all work together or something?" Nic asked, the disappointment clear on his face.

"Yes, didn't you know? This is an employee event for *Really Living Magazine*."

"Another night, maybe?" Nic played with his necklaces.

"Maybe." Anji smiled but tried to appear nonchalant, certain she wouldn't hear from him again but flattered by the attention. They didn't exchange contact details.

Chapter Twenty-Seven

JULY 20, 2012

ANJI WAS ON the Upper West Side, walking up Broadway to Eightieth Street, just a few blocks away from the paint-and-sip. She was on her way to interview an energy healer for a piece she was writing for *Really Living Magazine*.

"Anjali!" someone called out.

She turned to find Nic waving from across the street. He was wearing the same outfit as the day they had met. She would later find out he always wore loose jeans, a generously sized button-down shirt, and the same four necklaces. The colors varied, but the outfit didn't. He ran across the street, wearing the same mischievous smile he'd had in class. "Hi, it's Nic. From the art class."

"Oh, yes . . . Nic. I'm sorry. It's been a while . . . " Anji had never been good at remembering people's names. She often wondered how she remembered her own.

"I know I have a forgettable face, but I have not forgotten you." He spoke casually, as if they had seen each other recently.

"I'm surprised you remembered my name."

"I've thought of you often, and the salsa dance you owe me."

His comment struck her as imposing—too close for comfort. "That's funny, I didn't think you were being serious."

"That hurts." Nic brought his hand up to his necklaces, running some of the beads through his fingers.

Anji remembered how she used to play with her necklace as a child. She always wore a necklace. Her parents put one on her in the hospital after she was born, and she had not been without one since. It was an indication that she belonged—first to her father's family and later to her husband's family, if she ever married. Anji felt naked if she forgot to wear a necklace. It felt like an extension of her.

"Let me start over." Nic ran his hand over his face, as if he were removing a mask. His expression was serious and he stood up straight, extending a hand to Anji. "Good afternoon, my name is Nic, and believe me, Anjali, I've thought of you every day since I met you last month. I looked you up on Facebook, and I thought of sending you a friend request, but I was afraid you wouldn't remember me. I was right. Now that I have formally introduced myself and shaken hands with you, I hope that when I send you a friend request, you will accept. I mean, you better, if we're going salsa dancing." He winked.

"I do remember you. I still have the painting. I'm sorry I didn't remember your name. I didn't think we would see each other again." Anji was surprised at her honesty.

"You're a corporate bigwig and probably don't want to be seen with a low life like me." His tone was mocking, but it was clear he wasn't joking.

"It's not like that at all." Anji's tone was soft and appeasing.

Nic smiled. "You owe me a dance."

"You're not letting that one go, huh?"

Nic nodded and then paused for a second. "How about now?"

"I'm on my way to interview someone," Anji explained.

Nic took a bow, like they do at the end of a theater show. "I will let you go for now, but you will say yes. I know you will. I'll knock your socks off when you do."

Anji smiled and continued on her way. She was flattered that he had thought of her. A notification of Nic's Facebook friend request came up before she reached the energy healer's office. He followed it with a message, reminding her of who he was and of their commitment to salsa dancing.

Anji turned off her phone and focused on the energy healer. When the interview was over, Nic was all she could think about.

She was tempted to reject the request and delete the message. As she settled on the subway, it occurred to her that she had not met someone so confident in while. He had a different quality to him.

She accepted his friend request, but didn't reply to the message, feeling an odd sense of satisfaction that she caused him a small disappointment—he wasn't completely getting his way. Strangely, although salsa dancing came up several more times, it was something they never did together.

SEPTEMBER 12, 2012

Anji had not heard from Nic for a few weeks and was surprised to see his message on Facebook.

Nic—11:35 am
Have dinner with me on Friday.

Anji—11:38 am
That's a question?

Nic—11:38 am
Yes.

Anji—11:38 am
It doesn't sound like one.

Nic—11:38 am
Sorry, I don't tend to be good with punctuation. Will you have dinner with me ... please?

Anji debated on what to do. She felt curious about what it would be like to date someone like Nic. He seemed free-spirited in a way that she wasn't. It intrigued her. She felt cautiously optimistic, like Nic might show her a side of life she wasn't familiar with.

Anji—11:40 am
Okay

Nic—11:40 am
Yes?
You said yes!
I'll see you Friday at 7:00 p.m.. I'll be waiting outside your office.
It will be unforgettable. I promise.

Sure enough, two days later, Nic was waiting for her. He was wearing the usual, but with black jeans and a pink top. The requisite four necklaces were partially covered by a weathered black leather jacket.

"Hello, my bunny," he greeted.

Anji cringed. "Hi Nic, isn't it too soon for nicknames?"

"It's perfect for you," he said smugly and embraced her in a hug so tight, Anji wasn't able to step out of it until he let her go.

"Where are we headed?" she asked, trying to collect herself.

"There you go wanting to control everything. Relax, bunny. You're not at work anymore." He rubbed her shoulders.

Anji pulled away. "Shall we?"

Nic offered her his forearm and she was reminded of Older Guy for a brief moment. They walked to Grand Central Station and took the Six train to the L, and the L to Eighth Avenue. Then it was a short walk through the West Village to Mexicana Mama.

It was a quaint place, and Anji was amazed by the smells. The tables were placed so close together, it gave the impression of being one large eight-top table instead of four two-top tables. It was hard for people to get in and out of their chairs. They waited forty minutes to be seated, but Anji thought it worthwhile. The food was delicious.

Nic and Anji chatted with ease. Nic shared that, other than art, he had a passion for food. He knew all the Michelin-starred restaurants in the city. Anji wasn't sure if he had actually eaten at any of them but didn't ask.

Ironically, he was picky about his food. He avoided meats and chicken and consumed mostly fish and shrimp—no other seafood. He wasn't a fan of fruits and vegetables and ate them because he had to.

"That's odd for someone who is such a foodie, isn't it?" Anji asked.

"I was born with discerning tastes. I don't believe we all have to like everything," Nic said matter-of-factly.

"How do you feel about Indian food?" Anji's tone was cautious.

"I haven't tried it, but now that I'm with you, bunny, I hope you'll cook for me." Nic smiled broadly, making him look like a schoolboy.

"I'm worried about you being so picky. What about Colombian food?"

"Another cuisine for you to prepare for me." Nic winked.

"Interesting . . . "

Nic's father had walked out when he was a baby, leaving his mother with him and his older brother. She was more interested in dating other men than taking care of her sons. Alfred and Nic practically raised themselves and they were inseparable. Although they were ten months apart, people thought they were twins. When they turned sixteen, they stole $5,000 in cash from their mother and, in youthful ignorance, thought themselves millionaires.

They wanted to see the world, starting with New York City. They arrived by bus and checked in at the first hotel in Times Square, thinking this was their road to life as kings. Money ran out quickly and they soon found themselves living on the streets.

Nic began drawing on scraps of paper, old newspapers, and anything he could get his hands on. Soon people noticed and paid him for it. He decided to make it his career. Alfred still wanted to see the world. The brothers split up, with Nic staying in New York, and Alfred hitchhiking to California. They had parted ways fifteen years ago and had visited each other only a few times.

Nic's career as an artist wasn't as lucrative as he'd hoped. He took on odd jobs, bussing tables, bartending, cleaning offices, operating toll booths, and working at the paint-and-sip.

"Why don't you pursue art as a formal career?" Anji asked.

"Formal careers aren't for me. The only reason I'm at the paint-and-sip is for access to art supplies. The owner lets me do my thing in the mornings when the studio isn't in use."

"So, it's a matter of convenience?" Anji tried her best to keep an open mind and not sound judgmental. After all, that's why she had agreed to go on a date with him.

"I love how well you understand me, bunny." Nic smiled brightly, his eyes sparkling.

Chapter Twenty-Eight

OCTOBER 1, 2012

NIC WAS WAITING for her outside of work. "Hello, bunny. Surprise!"

Anji stopped dead in her tracks. "What are you doing here?"

"Do I need a reason to see you?" His face was beaming.

"No, I guess not, but I hate to tell you, I'm on my way to the airport. I've got a late flight to San Francisco."

Nic couldn't hide his disappointment. "What? Now?"

"Yes, my colleagues are waiting." Anji pointed at two people standing next to a black town car.

Nic's face fell further still. "Oh. I thought we could have dinner together. I haven't seen you for two weeks."

"I'm sorry, Nic. It's sweet of you to come over." Anji felt guilty for disappointing him.

"There's no way you can squeeze in a quick dinner?" His expression of eagerness was lost.

Anji shook her head. "If we don't head out now, there is no way we'll make the flight."

"How long will you be gone for?"

"A couple of weeks."

"Work is more important." Nic's tone was flat. He looked like a kid who had dropped his ice cream cone on the floor.

"You're important, too." Anji reached up and gave him a quick kiss on the lips. "I'll let you know when I'm back."

She walked away, leaving Nic touching his hand to his lips, clearly dumbfounded.

OCTOBER 12, 2012

Nic was waiting for Anji at La Guardia Airport. It was Anji's turn to be dumbfounded. He held a sign with her name, like one of the many drivers waiting to pick up their clients, except that he had no car.

"How did you manage to know my flight details?" Anji asked as she hugged him.

"Bunny, I have my ways." Nic winked. He told her he had called the office and got the flight details from one of her colleagues who remembered him from the paint-and-sip.

Instead of going back to the city in the town car with Anji's colleagues, she and Nic took a cab back. Anji dropped off her bags at her apartment and they walked to B&H Dairy for a quick meal.

"Anji, you'll be so proud of me." Nic's smile showed all his teeth.

"Did you sell one of your pieces?"

"Pride doesn't always come from money," Nic chided. He paused briefly. "I stopped a woman from stealing today."

"At the paint-and-sip?" Anji asked, wondering why anyone other than Nic would want art supplies.

"No silly. At the beauty shop."

"You work at a beauty shop? I thought you worked at the paint-and-sip?"

Nic's reply was stern. "It's only once a week. Do you want to hear the story or not?"

He shared that he had long suspected a woman in her seventies of stealing. Someone realized that items went missing when she showed up, and Nic started watching her. He figured out her strategy was to pass gas, the foul smell effectively clearing out an area in the store. She picked up a product, pretended to look at it, and surreptitiously dropped it into her purse, leaving the store before anyone suspected.

That day, Nic followed her closely, undisturbed by the farting.

He caught her in the act and they called the police, forcing her to pay for the item or leave it.

"She was pretty scared. I'm sure she'll stop."

Anji was amused. Nic had a way of portraying the story that was theatrical and amusing. He shared other stories that kept her laughing. Some were genuinely funny, and others she found entertaining because of the way Nic told them.

Anji paid for dinner. She was grateful Nic had shown up at the airport. Before leaving the restaurant, Nic, who had a habit of biting his nails, pulled off a hangnail with his teeth, causing his finger to bleed. Anji wiped the blood and pulled out a band aid from her purse. She applied it to his finger, saying, "*Sana, sana, colita de rana, si no sana hoy sanará mañana.*"

"Please say that to me every night." Nic's tone was soft and coy.

"I'm not sure that's a good idea. It's a rhyme in Spanish that parents say to their kids when they're hurt. It translates to heal, heal, little tail of the frog. If you don't heal today, you'll heal tomorrow."

He closed his eyes. "Anything you say sounds divine."

OCTOBER 13, 2012

Anji woke up to an email from Nic timestamped at 1:21 a.m.

> Hi Anji,
> Tonight, was fantastic. Our goodnight kiss meant so much to me. I feel something I thought I would never feel. My heart is going to explode. I'm head over heels for you.
> Perhaps you haven't figured out that what we have could be BIG. I imagine some idiot filled your heart with doubt, and now you don't recognize true love even if it stares you in the face. If you don't give us a chance, you are giving up on your soulmate. We're soulmates. How else could I explain the intensity of my feelings?
> I've been more honest with you than with anyone else in my life. I want to be happy and it's with you.
> Don't doubt this. Don't doubt us. Let me show you how to love.
> What do you say, my bunny?

She thought about her response all day, and finally replied just before nine o'clock.

> Hi Nic,
> I had a good time last night, but it's too early to tell what we have.
> We come from such different worlds and we know very little about each other. You are special and unique. You have so much to offer.
> I'm not sure that we're soulmates. I feel it's too soon to tell. I don't feel that level of intensity yet.

Nic responded a few hours later.

> Anji, I understand. We have different upbringings and cultural backgrounds. Yet I feel like I've known you my whole life.
> Like you, I have been saving my love for the right person. I am facing the most important decision I will ever make. That is to open myself up to you and show you everything inside me.
> You've placed so many barricades up so that no one hurts you again. But do you know that the real you shines through every once in a while? I catch a glimpse in your eyes and it opens up all that life and love you hold inside.
> Can you deny feeling something when we shared that incredible kiss and you let yourself be vulnerable? That is a sign of soulmate love.
> We have coincided in time and space. We are meant to be. We are perfect for each other.
> Let me love you.

"I don't understand why you feel so strongly about me," Anji said, over the phone. Nic had called her a few moments after sending the email.

Anji felt overwhelmed. She had always wanted a soulmate, but Nic was moving too fast. She felt a connection between them but it wasn't what he felt. She wanted to feel free in a relationship and not be bogged down by declarations of love, especially not after only two dates.

"I can't explain it. It's bigger than me. It's bigger than you. You could give me a lifetime and I will not find the words to explain it. I trust this feeling more than anything I have ever trusted in my life. You should too." Nic sounded certain.

It disconcerted Anji. "Nic, I am not willing to make a commitment, but I want to get to know you better. Let's take things slow, with no expectations and no big declarations. If you are willing to do that, let's move forward at my pace."

Chapter Twenty-Nine

DECEMBER 3, 2012

ANJI WAS PROMOTED to lead journalist at *Really Living Magazine*. Her "Lifestyle Experts in Your Area" series that she had started in 2004 had developed a cult-like following. Eclectic specialists clamored to be featured; business boomed after Anji featured them. Anji was on the road so often, her relationship with Nic was practically long distance and they communicated mostly via text.

Nic—7:33 a.m.
I can't wait to hold you in my arms and feel the intensity that you bring into my life. Soon you will come to see we are soulmates.
Please don't ever regret that you've given me this chance.
I really, really love you.
PS—I quit my job at paint-and-sip

Anji—7:12 p.m.
Congratulations are in order. I'm happy you are taking control of your life and opening up to do art on your terms. I wish you all the best. XO

Nic—7:38 p.m.
Thank you for the good wishes. I don't know what I'm going to do next.
How's your trip going? Do you miss me?

Anji—11:20 p.m.
Sure, I miss you.
My trip is going well. I'm meeting a psychic in 10 minutes. It's late, but she only works at night. She says that is when the veil is the thinnest and this enhances her psychic connection.
I've got to splash water on my face and wake up.
xo

Nic—December 19, 6:25 a.m.
Tell me something you've never told anyone else. And be HONEST.

Anji—2:00 p.m.
Let's see . . . I buy People Magazine *so that I can do the crossword puzzle at the end. It makes me feel smart.*

Nic—4:55 p.m..
That's what you call a confession? You can do better than that.

Anji—7:17 p.m.
You first.

Nic—December 20, 6:52 a.m.
I dated a hooker.

Anji—7:48 am
You can't just say that and not tell me more.

Nic—8:05 a.m.
We met at the bar where she picked up clients. She picked me up and didn't charge me. We had a genuine connection. I didn't judge her and I didn't ask questions. She didn't judge me and she didn't ask questions. It worked.
Your turn.

Anji—8:08 a.m.
I like to dance in the dark . . . all by myself.

Nic—8:09 a.m.
It's official. You don't have secrets. EVERYBODY dances in the dark by themselves.

It didn't bother Anji that Nic had dated an escort. Had it been a different relationship, she would have felt jealous, wanting to know who she was, what he loved about her, how they managed to stay together, and why it ended. But with him, she felt like a spectator, accepting what he shared without comment or question. She wondered if he made up stories to get a reaction from her, to test the depths of her affections. If so, she knew it wasn't a game she was willing to play. She was sure she would always come up failing.

DECEMBER 31, 2012

Anji spent the holidays with her parents in Cali and flew back to NYC to celebrate New Year's with Nic. She rented a car and they drove up to the Catskills to spend a couple nights in a cabin Anji had rented, away from all the pomp and fuss that irritated Nic. They lay in bed and ate buckets of fried chicken they had picked up on the way.

They watched snow falling on the pine trees right outside their windows. Anji felt as if she were out in the forest but was grateful of the heat emanating from the fireplace in the room.

He slapped her tenderly on the belly and there was a jiggle. It echoed silently through her exposed midriff and was swallowed up under her tucked up white cotton t-shirt. There had never been a jiggle like that before, and the silent reverberation grew into an explosion in her ears.

He noticed it too. Their eyes met and he looked at her, searching. His gaze turned into something tender, easing her rising embarrassment. His growing embrace slowly melted her impulse to hide herself. It was okay, it seemed, that she had jiggled so loudly, and she felt herself relax, curious about how he'd handle this. Maybe he wouldn't chide her like others had before.

His search grew more intent, but she didn't know what he was looking for, although it was clear he was on the hunt. He lifted her t-shirt, studying her breasts. He caressed her just below her belly button.

"You're pregnant." His eyes grew big with wonder and delight. "You're pregnant," he confirmed softly.

"Bellies don't jiggle when you're pregnant," she said, the jiggle now dead as she pulled her shirt down and stood up as if lightning had struck.

"You haven't been pregnant—" he started.

"Neither have you," she shot back.

JANUARY 6, 2013

Sophie invited Anji and Nic for Sunday dinner. She still celebrated every New Year with Hoppin' John, which she prepared herself. It was the only time she cooked. She served the mix of rice, black eyed peas, and pork with a side of collard greens and biscuits with gravy. It was said that eating Hoppin' John around New Year's ensured prosperity for the next twelve months. Sophie was pregnant with Tasha and, given the struggles she'd had conceiving, she was particularly intent on keeping the only superstitious act from her Southern family traditions. She decided she would take no chances of any potential complications to her pregnancy. Anji hadn't dared to question Sophie, even though the tradition of Hoppin' John, as Anji understood it, wasn't related to conception.

Nic and Anji stopped at Grand Central Station to buy macaroons to take as dessert and, since it was a nice evening, they decided to walk to Sophie's place from there. On their way, Nic stopped at a food truck.

"What are you doing?" Anji was irritated.

"I'm hungry," he replied.

"But we are going to have dinner . . . "

"I can't wait." He looked at her with large puppy dog eyes.

"You better finish that before we get to the apartment, and it better not affect your appetite." Anji shook her head, hating that she sounded like a parent. She felt compelled to raise a shaking finger at him but refrained from doing so.

They walked in silence. Every time Anji looked at Nic, it seemed to her that he wasn't making a dent. He savored every bite of his sandwich, chewing slowly, and diligently licking sauce off of his fingers and the aluminized wrapper. He hadn't finished by the time they reached Sophie's apartment building. Anji was so frustrated, she didn't want to speak to him. Without saying a word, Anji went up to the apartment, leaving him on the street.

The holidays were barely over, and Sophie had already taken down all the Christmas lights and decorations. The apartment was back to its usual beauty. It was as impeccably styled as Sophie. Nothing was ever out of place, even when Anji dropped in unannounced. Anji had checked the baseboards once, for kicks, and didn't find a speck of dust.

Nic came up twenty minutes later and barely ate any of the food that was served. Anji and Nic hardly interacted with each other during the meal, each answering questions posed directly by Sophie or Tony.

After dinner, Anji and Nic stood outside the building.

"I can't believe you left me outside on my own," Nic said.

Anji glared at Nic. "I can't believe you bought a shawarma and didn't eat a bite of the dinner they served. Why couldn't you wait?"

"It's always about you, Anji." Nic raised his voice.

"My pregnant friend makes an effort to prepare dinner—"

"Sophie didn't lift a finger for that meal, and you know it. Neither did Tony. They showed up to the meal, just as we did."

"That may normally be the case, but this time, Sophie cooked herself. It was important to her. If you cared, you would be more compassionate." Anji's tone raised to match Nic's.

"Forgive me Oh Mighty Righteous One." Nic put his hands up in prayer position. His tone was mocking.

"I can't deal with this right now." Anji turned away.

"That's it then? You're just going to walk away?"

Anji looked back. "I'm about to turn thirty-five, and I feel like I'm the mother of a thirty-year-old man. I don't want to be a mother of an actual baby, and definitely not of a grown adult who throws tantrums."

"I don't throw tantrums." Nic's tone was heavy.

"I never thought I'd see an adult act that way."

"You're so aggravating Anji. I wish—"

"Let's drop it before we regret what comes next."

———————

That night, Nic didn't want to sleep in Anji's bedroom, claiming it was haunted. She had told him that she had heard a voice from her walls and he was spooked. He spent a listless night on the couch and left early in the morning.

Sophie called Anji after confirming she was on her own. "What was going on last night?"

"I'm sorry, Soph. I hope you're not offended that Nic didn't eat. He ate a shawarma as we walked over. I left him on the street so he could finish. He was full and didn't have your delicious dinner."

"I'm not worried about that. What's going on between you two?"

"I don't know . . . I'm tired of this. He gets on my nerves."

"He is your wrong half, my sweets."

Whenever a relationship was doomed and a breakup was inevitable, Sophie called the person the wrong half.

Anji felt conflicted. She admired that Nic expressed his feelings without reservation. She didn't feel she was good at that. She held back with self-restraint and doubt, more concerned with what others—particularly her family and close friends—would think.

She didn't understand how Nic could say "I love you" so easily. He uttered it as effortlessly as "thank you" or "good morning" or "hello," but she didn't think he knew the weight of those three words—the absoluteness. She was aware that he desperately wanted to belong to her. He desperately wanted her to belong to him. He thought that if she uttered those words back to him, he would be miraculously fulfilled. He wanted so badly to belong to something and to someone.

Despite what Sophie said, they stayed together. Nic hung on to hope and Anji to complacency. For her, it was easier for them to stay together than for her to find the energy to handle his disappointment at a breakup. There was also a part of her that hoped that with time she would find a way to love him.

Chapter Thirty

WILLIAM CALLED to wish her a happy Valentine's Day. Anji shared her struggles with Nic to get a male perspective from William.

Nic had told her that after he quit at the paint-and-sip, he hadn't found another job. When he didn't sleep over, he had couch surfed at friends' places. Anji knew his financial situation was strained even when they first met, and with the exception of their first date at Mexicana Mama, she covered all their expenses. But she hadn't realized he was in such a dire condition. It turned out he had gotten an eviction notice and was kicked out of his apartment.

"Is he going to contribute when he moves in? Utilities or mortgage?"

"I'm not sure . . . " Anji was not looking forward to having Nic in her space and preferred not to think about it.

"Have you talked to him about it?"

"I don't want money to be an issue between us." Anji couldn't understand what had motivated her to offer Nic to move in with her. But then again, he spent most nights with her so it didn't seem like a big transition.

"Move in with me," Anji had offered the moment she saw the look of desperation on Nic's face. Her stomach clenched mere seconds later, but it was too late.

"Yes! Yes! Yes!" Nic had jumped up with joy.

She had offered to pay the rent he owed so that it wouldn't affect his already poor credit. Anji hadn't asked what he had done with his money.

"So how much have you spent on him?" William asked.

"I don't know . . . "

"Anj, just tell me what you have covered so far."

She ran through the expenses that came to mind and William tallied them for her.

"Anj, that's nearly forty thousand dollars. Are you sure you want to continue being with this guy?" William didn't appear to be criticizing Anji, despite the firmness in his voice.

After she hung up the phone, she went out for a walk. It wasn't usual for her to walk at night, but she was left with a knot in her stomach. She power walked up to Gramercy Park and back. As she did, it occurred to her in all the times she had prepared food for Nic, she had never offered to make Indian or Colombian food. And he had never made anything for her.

When she got back to her apartment, she did something she hadn't done in a long time. She kneeled in front of her altar and prayed.

———————

FEBRUARY 15, 2013

Nic was supposed to have moved in with Anji the previous day, but he hadn't. Every time Anji spoke to Nic, his plans changed. He first said he would move in on February 1, then on the seventh, and finally on the fourteenth so they could celebrate Valentine's Day together. They didn't even see each other that day.

Nic's stories changed regularly, the excuses growing ever more preposterous. He suddenly needed to return furniture to relatives in New Jersey whom he had not previously mentioned. Friends he owed urgent favors to sprouted in Connecticut. Anji was irritated by his fickleness, but tried her best to be patient, reasoning that Nic was going through a difficult time and that he needed to tie up loose ends.

She was simultaneously relieved. Anji thought it ironic that Nic thought Anji didn't give him anything. He complained often about how little Anji contributed to the relationship. Yet she felt that she indulged him in all that he asked and more. She recognized she felt guilty that he loved her more than she loved him, and somehow, she felt the need to compensate.

"Maybe you shouldn't move in. Stay with your family until you sort things out," Anji said in a voicemail she left for Nic that night. She had called him several times that day but was unable to reach him.

At 9:55 p.m., the doorbell rang. When Anji opened the door, Nic was down on one knee.

"Marry me?"

"Are you crazy, Nic? Get up." She pulled him into her apartment before Lulu could notice.

"Why won't you marry me?" Nic whined.

"You haven't been able to move in. How can we jump from that to marriage?"

"I got you this ring." He scrambled in his pocket and pulled out a silver ring with four or five tiny diamond studs. "I know it's not much but it belonged to my grandmother."

Anji took a step back. "Nic, that is too much. I can't accept."

"Why Anji? Why am I not enough for you? We're soulmates." Nic continued to hold the ring out to her.

"We're not." Anji played with her sweaty hands. She was astounded at how easily she uttered the words. This time, there was no point sticking around. The certainty of her emotions sent strength up her spine. She felt herself stand tall.

Nic walked slowly toward the sofa, sat down, and held his head in his hands. After a few moments he looked up at her, his eyes filled with tears.

"Nic, I'm sorry. I'm really, really sorry," Anji said.

There was nothing else to say. He got up and left.

Anji was swept by a wave of peace as she closed the door behind him.

JULY 19, 2013

Nic texted Anji a few months later.
Nic—6:43 p.m.

If your outer layer is made of steel, you'll survive. If it is pure scum, it will crack with the first punch, and when that happens, I will climb into you and take what you owe me!

Anji—7:01 p.m.
I'm not sure what to make of that ... Are you okay?

Nic—9:57 p.m.
I'm perfectly well.
Are you finally convinced that I'm a good person, or are you going to continue to point out my every imperfection?

Nic—10:27 p.m.
My father died. Funeral is tomorrow.

Anji—10:28 p.m.
I am so sorry for your loss.

The next morning, Anji made her way to Port Authority and took a bus to Ridgefield, NJ where the funeral was taking place. She'd gotten the details from Nic in further texts. She didn't mind the nearly thirty-minute ride. She felt it was important to show her support to Nic. She didn't ask Nic how he had found his father.

Anji fidgeted nervously as she waited to pay her respects. She watched the woman in front of her, standing in front of the casket. The woman's face twitched in disgust and she spat on Nic's father's face. Apparently, Nic's father had been a bigamist. While still married to Nic's mother, he had set up a whole other family in New Jersey, a mere ten miles away from where Nic had spent most of his life.

As Anji watched the woman, it occurred to her that he must have done something more egregious than set up a second family. When Anji walked up to the casket, she saw the path the spit had left down Nic's father's left cheek. She considered wiping it off, but when she looked around no one seemed bothered, so she moved along, wondering how many other people Nic's father had lied to.

She caught sight of Nic. She wished she had the courage to spit in his face. Not then, of course. His dad had just died. But another time. It surprised her to realize that she had that urge.

Nic walked toward her. "Hello, bunny. Thanks for coming."

Anji's insides turned but she pushed away her feelings and tried to sound sympathetic. "I had to come."

Nic hugged her, holding on a little too hard for her comfort. "Is merlot still your favorite?"

"Your father just died." Anji shook her head in disbelief.

Nic looked pleadingly.

Anji sighed. "Merlot is my least favorite."

Nic looked at her closely. "Do you have someone to share that wine with?"

"I am not dating at the moment." Anji felt her body grow tense.

"You don't have to understand me. Just love me as I am. How I loved you."

Her stomach clenched. "Seriously? We're moving from merlot to love?"

"Are you still mad at me?" Nic sounded like a five-year-old.

Anji looked at the other people, wanting to leave the funeral. They stood awkwardly in silence.

"You are my soulmate, regardless—"

"This isn't the time or place for this conversation," Anji said solemnly.

"Anji, I don't want to disappear from your life. You lifted me up and then you let me free fall."

Anji didn't respond.

"I miss watching you sleep." Nic's tone was soft, complacent.

Anji quieted her growing irritation. "Nic, I care about you, and I'd like for us to be friends. But, that's it. I am no longer in love with you."

Nic played with his necklaces and looked down at the floor. "I don't think you ever were."

"I am sorry for your loss."

"Really? That's all." Tears welled up in his eyes.

Anji said softly, "Yes, Nic. That's all."

"It's always so easy for you." He was angry but he kept his voice down.

"It can be easy for you, too."

Anji left, no longer wanting to spit in his face.

Chapter Thirty-One

MARCH 9, 2019

"I HATED THAT Needy Boy called you *bunny*. I cringed every time he said it. Thankfully, he never met your parents. I couldn't see him doing well with all this," Sophie said.

Sophie was at Anji's place for an Indian meal. Anji's parents loved spending time with Sophie. Tony and Tasha were spending the day with his parents. Anji had also invited William, but he had plans with Natalie. Anji suggested he bring her, and he confessed Natalie wasn't a fan of Indian food. Anji had also asked Lulu, but she was preparing for a trip to Egypt with Steve.

Her parents had cooked Sophie's favorites. Onions dipped into chickpea flour batter and fried into crispy *pakoras* to start, *chole* or chickpeas cooked in a spicy gravy that was paired with deep fried bready *bhaturas* as the main course, and *kheer* rice pudding as dessert. After the meal, Anji's parents went to Murray Hill to shop for Indian tea and spices, which were not readily available in Cali. Murray Hill was known as Curry Hill for its assortment of Pakistani and Indian shops and restaurants.

Sophie put down her *masala chai*. "He was truly your lapsus brutus. What did you even see in him?"

"Nic was fun-loving and spontaneous. He was less traditional and that appealed to me. I wanted to be in a relationship where life didn't revolve around the man, and at first it seemed as if that's what I had with Nic. I enjoyed being in charge, at first. I was in control in the relationship, and I was happy to provide. That is until Needy Boy took it too far. That's when I realized I wanted something that was more equal."

Dating Nic went against every cultural and societal rule, but Anji felt a sense of liberation—a further break from tradition. No respectable unmarried Indian woman would live with an unmarried man. Anji hadn't seemed to care. She had pushed the boundaries of her traditional environment, tested the other extreme, and realized she needed to settle in a balanced relationship or equal partnership. "I can't believe I considered living with him. My parents would have had a legitimate reason to label me as the black sheep of the family."

Sophie dropped a piece of *gulab jamun* back into the syrup. She did not have a sweet tooth, but that afternoon, even after eating the kheer, Sophie wanted something else that was sweet to eat with the chai, and had asked for gulab jamuns, which Anji usually had on hand. Anji kept cans of the fried syrup-soaked doughy balls especially for occasions like these.

"Are you okay?" Anji asked, wondering if Sophie had gone into shock from over-consuming her quota of sugar for the day.

"Yeah, sorry. Something just dawned on me . . . Do your parents know that I lived with Tony before we married?"

Anji was surprised Sophie worried about what her parents thought of her. "My parents don't think any less of you. Don't take this the wrong way but Indians have two sets of standards. One is exclusive for Indians, particularly Hindus, and it is super strict. The other is for everyone else. Our housekeeper in Cali had five children, each one from a different man. She had married none of them. My mother sympathized with her so much, she felt the woman's plight as if it were her own. But if I or one of my cousins even looked at a man, it would be the end of us."

"That's a relief, I guess." Sophie gobbled up the last piece of gulab jamun. "How much money did you end up spending on Nic?"

"Nearly forty thousand dollars . . . "

"Shit. Sweets, that's excessive by any standards."

"I lent him money on several occasions and I paid out what

he owed in rent. That's how it amounted to so much," Anji said, collecting her thoughts.

Thinking back, Anji realized Nic grew comfortable with her being the provider. It seemed that the more she covered his expenses, the less motivation he had to contribute.

"I'm so glad he is out of your life," Sophie said, reading her mind, as usual.

"You know, it wasn't until a piece of tooth fell out of my mouth one morning as I brushed my teeth that I realized I was also in physical pain. When my dentist touched my jaw, I nearly fell out of the dentist's chair. Turns out I had been grinding my teeth, chipping away at them night after night. With Frank I lost my hair and with Nic my teeth." Anji put her hands on her face, shivering at the recollection.

Sophie leaned forward, placing her hand on Anji's. "Just be grateful the relationship ended. But I do have to ask: how did you not realize how much you'd spent on him?"

"You know I don't pay attention to these things. If William hadn't added it up, I wouldn't have known."

Sophie glowered, letting go of Anji's hand. "I can't believe you told him about this but never told me. It's been *five* years!"

Anji was taken aback. "I don't hide anything from you Sophie. You know that."

"I just found out tonight and William has known all this time?" She sounded offended and incredulous.

"I wasn't purposefully hiding it from you . . . "

Sophie gave Anji a meaningful look. "That's not my point."

"Sophie, William is not closer to me than you are, and you know that." Anji wouldn't admit that William was less critical of her, and at times, she found it less daunting to share things with him.

Anji and Sophie sipped on their masala chai in silence. Anji then told Sophie about the recent conversation with William.

"You will definitely find a suitable boy, sweet pea. Although the suitable boy doesn't have to be one of the men from your fantasies. What were the Bollywood types you were obsessed with?" Sophie asked.

"There have been so many . . . Salman Khan, Shah Rukh Khan, Hrithik Roshan, John Abraham. I mean, I could go on, but that was a while ago. I haven't kept up with current celebrities."

"What about Latin American ones?"

"C'mon Sophie, I no longer have the same delusions of my youth," Anji said, playfully defensive, relieved that the tense moments had been swept away.

"I'm just teasing, sweet pea."

"Margarita would say it's not a coincidence that a suitable boy has come up twice."

"Not everything has to have an explanation."

Anji shot Sophie a sharp look. She was in no mood to continue the teasing.

"What do you think it means?" Sophie asked, appeasing her.

Anji took a moment to gather her thoughts. "I didn't feel attractive growing up, and I know my active imagination was a way for me to cope with feeling like an ugly duckling."

Sophie leaned toward Anji and placed her hand on Anji's thigh. "You are a gorgeous woman."

"It doesn't matter what I look like. What matters is how I feel, and I grew up feeling like I was an ugly duckling surrounded by a sea of beautiful and graceful swans. Ugly duckling is a misnomer. I was the unwanted second cousin of the ugly duckling, aka the pigeon, aka the rat of the sky."

"Anji—"

"Sophie, don't take this the wrong way, but I felt the same with you. You're gorgeous, and men and women like you alike. Heads turn when you walk into a room." Anji was surprised by her honesty. She hadn't planned on being this frank with Sophie. "I know this is something I carried from childhood. There are songs written about how *Caleñas*—women from Cali—are the most beautiful in the world. And it's true. My classmates were gorgeous."

"I'm sure you are exaggerating," Sophie said dismissively.

"Sofia Vergara's cousin was my neighbor; Fanny Lu was my brother's classmate; and Shakira attended our sister school in Barranquilla. One of my friends in college, who was from Barranquilla, went to school with her. I am not exaggerating. I did go to school with gorgeous women."

"Is that why it shocked you that William called you beautiful? You may not have looked like the women you grew up with, but you are beautiful. It shouldn't take William to validate that. You are the

one who needs to see yourself as that. Only you can validate yourself."
After a pause, Sophie asked, "What is a soulmate to you?"

Anji took a moment to consider this. "My perspective has changed. I know what it is not. It is not obsession. It is not hurt and damage. It is not what you can get from the other."

Sophie nodded. "You are saying soulmates show mutual respect for each other."

"That's right."

"That can exist in any relationship. I don't have to be with my soulmate to feel mutual love and respect."

"True. But let's take our friendship. I feel you are my soulmate—soul sister—and it is because I can be myself with you."

Sophie took a moment before she said, "That makes more sense. A soulmate is someone you share love and respect with, and someone you can be authentic with, showing all aspects of yourself—even the ones you are not proud of."

"Exactly."

They sat in silence sipping their chais.

Sophie spoke first. "You know you're not alone, right? There was a lot of pressure for me to look and act a particular way—short, silhouetted dresses, high heels, nails, makeup, and not a hair out of place. We had to play cool and comfortable in intolerably hot and humid climate. Charleston society is tough."

"Interesting . . . " Anji was aware that she had a tendency to think she was alone in the world, and it wasn't until she heard of someone who had a similar experience that she realized she wasn't so different. She let herself believe that she and Sophie were polar opposites and they weren't.

"And we have our own kind of arranged marriages. Society families have a tendency to marry into each other and it's not for love. Most likely it's for economic benefit," Sophie noted, as if reading her mind.

"Does Charleston have its version of matrimonial ads in its local newspaper?"

Sophie laughed out loud. "No, we don't. But we don't need them. The city is so small and society so tight, everyone knows everyone else's business. My mother was a debutante. She was presented to society at a ball to announce that she was an adult. She dressed in white and there was a big party, after which it was socially acceptable for her to have a boyfriend and marry."

Anji laughed. "My parents placed an ad for me in the *Times of India*. I still have clippings. I never told you because I was embarrassed. Up until I was thirty-five, my parents held on to the hope that I would call with the good news of my engagement. But the day didn't come and they realized I would soon be out of a marriageable age. My father couldn't stand that he didn't do all he could to ensure I was properly married. After all, it was one of his duties as a father."

JANUARY 1, 2014

"Beta, you know that all we want for you is your happiness," Anji's father said when they sat down. She was visiting her parents in Cali. It had been five months since she had seen Nic at his father's funeral.

"Yes, Papa, of course," she replied. Anji looked at her mother to get a hint about where this conversation was headed. Her mother smiled, revealing nothing.

"Your mother and I want to know what your plans are for marriage," her father stated as if it were a question.

"I hope to be married one day," Anji said, feeling her face grow hot.

"Do you have someone in your life? A relationship that you want to tell us about?" her mother asked.

"Not at this time." It had been nearly a year since Anji had ended her relationship with Nic. She would be thirty-six in two weeks.

"How do you feel about us looking for a suitable boy for you?" her father asked.

"What do you have in mind?"

"Your mother and I have exhausted all possibilities within the family. Your aunts and uncles know that you are of marriageable age, but none of them know of a husband for you. I've discussed this with your uncle Pankaj in Delhi, and he suggested that we put a matrimonial in the *Times of India*."

"An advertisement for a husband?" Anji couldn't imagine her single status being announced so publicly.

"Your name would not appear. We provide basic details and ask for the family to reach out. This is common practice in India." her father assured. Anji's father had posted an ad that said that a college-educated *NRI* female was looking for a suitable *thakur* boy, and to please send inquiries to astoi@hotmail.com. Her father thought he was clever when he came up with "astoi." It stood for Anji Sharma Times of India. He created the email account exclusively for matchmaking purposes.

"I don't have time for this," Anji exclaimed. She felt her stomach twist into a knot.

"Yes beti, we know, and we don't want to add more pressure. Your father will handle it all," her mother soothed.

"I'll handle the emails, review the information, and select good candidates. I will send your biodata only to those we vet. I will speak to the parents and the boy first. If I feel comfortable, I will pass the contact to you. Then it is in your hands," her father explained.

MARCH 9, 2019

"My father prepared my biodata. It had my photograph; height; weight; skin-tone (Indians prefer those with fair skin, which is ironic for a country made up of brown people); caste (same caste marriages preferred); religion (Hindu only please); hobbies (to appear well-rounded); education (downplaying it for women); current employment (to justify not paying a dowry); and personality characteristics (only the amenable ones). My father didn't want prospective candidates to know that I get really quiet when I'm mad, or that I am easily irritated when people ask too many questions, and that I grind my teeth when I'm stressed. He did want them to know that I like to cook, especially Indian food," Anji told Sophie.

"He ruled out teetotalers—how could I ever survive with a non-drinker? And they tried to rule out candidates who wanted marriage for a green card—I was a naturalized US citizen by then. They opted for candidates already living in the US. I waited for the guy to make contact and we would exchange a few messages. Eventually it would die off and I wouldn't hear from them again."

"Their loss." Sophie shook her head.

"At least my parents didn't waste time checking for the auspiciousness of our union. You know a friend of mine once had to marry a chicken because the Hindu horoscope said her first husband would die. Only after the chicken died, was she able to marry her actual husband."

Anji and Sophie laughed.

"In Charleston, the auspiciousness is based on the clout of family names and bank accounts."

They laughed again.

"I don't know what I would do without you Sophie. You've helped me through the most difficult times in my life. Like after Donovan. I was an absolute mess, and I wouldn't have gotten back on my feet if it weren't for you."

"You've done the same for me. You were there through all my ups and downs with IVF. You went to more doctor's appointments with me than Tony did. Remember the nurse who thought we were lesbians? You brought me back to life after my miscarriage. You came over every single day. I don't know what I would have done without you," Sophie said, wiping a tear.

The two friends hugged each other tightly, certain their friendship was the most stable relationship in each other's life.

Chapter Thirty-Two

MARCH 10, 2019

ANJI HAD A SESSION with Margarita over Skype and closed the door to her bedroom while her parents were in the kitchen frying *puris* and making *subji* for brunch. Anji's mouth watered in anticipation of the deep-fried doughy goodness and spicy vegetables. She would have to wait until after speaking with Margarita to indulge.

Every time she spoke to Margarita, she felt as if Margarita waved a wand over her, infusing her with magic motivation.

"What is this bringing up for you?" Margarita asked.

Anji knew there was no sense in delaying the inevitable. "What is it about me that doesn't make me a suitable woman for marriage? I feel it plagues my parents as well but for a different reason. They didn't say so, but I know they think I am being too picky."

"You have a responsibility to yourself, Anji. Not to your parents. I realize your upbringing makes this hard to accept. You do things for others out of love and generosity but don't carry guilt over not being how someone else wants you to be. You are only required to honor who you are."

Her parents' opinions weighed heavily in the decisions Anji made. She disappointed herself by disappointing them. It was a vicious cycle she didn't know how to get out of. "There has to be a reason this is coming up now."

Margarita wore a quartz point around her neck. It reminded Anji of her Lemurian seed crystal. Margarita's quartz was not a talisman, but yet another pendant in her collection. "It's a synchronicity. They occur when the universe aligns your inner guidance with outer guidance. It's like finding clues. They happen when you hear the same topic of conversation repeating itself, or when you think of something and hear someone say it. It's how the universe shows us we are connected, and how it sends messages that you're on the right path, to pay attention, or to look further."

"The synchronicity now being about my suitability? The word has been coming up a lot. Is that why? How do I know how to deal with it?" Anji asked.

"Pay attention to your feelings. Your inner knowing will alert you to the correct guidance."

"Maybe it's telling me that I need to let go of the idea that I will find a suitable boy?"

"I agree that the synchronicity is about feeling suitable and the universe is trying to alert you of a shift you need to make, but I believe that the shift you need to make is an internal one."

"That I am the one who needs to be suitable?"

"You are suitable, my dear. You need to *feel* suitable."

Anji allowed the statement to sink in. She knew Margarita was right. "Nic was someone I said yes to at the expense of myself. I stayed with him even though I didn't love him, even though he frustrated me, and even though I knew he was taking advantage of me financially. I realized this and still stayed with him, and I did so because I felt a sense of obligation," Anji reflected.

Margarita leaned toward the screen. "It seems you felt guilt. Guilt is not aligned with love."

"I thought I could help him. Give him stability to give up the odd jobs that distracted him from his art. It made me feel better about myself, like I was doing a noble act of some kind. I unconsciously hoped that helping him live a better life would help me live a better life."

Margarita nodded. "Guilt is something a lot of women carry. We tend to feel responsible for others."

"Especially Indian women. We feel guilt because it is our duty to care for our family. It's engrained in us as children. In releasing Nic, I had to accept that it wasn't my responsibility to help him or to give him what he wanted. The only responsibility that I had was to myself and honoring how I felt. The truth is that I never knew what he liked about me. I felt the same with Frank and Donovan. The difference is that I didn't wonder with Nic. I didn't care. It's only now that I question it."

Margarita's tone was grave. "My dear, you cannot display true generosity of spirit if you are unable to do it for yourself. You are as important as any other being and equally deserving of love and affection. But, if you are unable to love yourself, how can others love you? The universe will continue to send you men who are incapable of loving you until you learn to love yourself."

Anji sat back in her chair. "Are you saying I brought this upon myself?"

"In a way, yes, but not in the way you think. You deserve all the love this world has to give, and the universe wants you to see that. You are loving, lovable, and loved. You need to learn to give it to the right people and receive it from the right people."

Anji was sure she was never going to figure this out. "How do I do that?"

"Let's circle back. Why is it important for you to find a soulmate? How does this affect your view of relationships? What role do you play in a relationship? How can you be your own person and be in a relationship?"

"You've asked me these questions before." Anji reached for her Lemurian seed crystal and held it in her hand, hoping it would give her encouragement.

"And you haven't given me an answer yet, my dear." Margarita's tone was soft and gentle.

"I haven't thought about it much beyond the concept of a soulmate. Reflecting back, I can see that the men I dated were a way for me to test what I was looking for."

"What about Sophie? Didn't you say she was a type of soulmate for you?"

"With Sophie it's different. I don't have to try or test anything. We both know we will always be there for each other."

How is it then that she missed the mark with men? Anji didn't know if she wanted a traditional relationship as she saw in India and Colombia where masculine and feminine roles are well defined. Even Sophie had fallen into a traditional marriage. Tony was the provider and, although Sophie worked, her money was for herself. For most of the women she knew, their lives revolved around their husbands and children. But, Anji didn't know if she wanted a less traditional relationship where she was in charge. She had tried this with Nic, thinking it would enable her to be who she is and not lose herself. Yet, she felt she did anyway.

"My dear, you may not want to hear this. You are unclear about who you are, and so, it is hard for you to define what you want in a relationship. Once you disassociate yourself from your relationship status, you will get clarity on what you want."

Anji didn't think her relationship status was tied to her identity. "It's a strange contradiction. I want a relationship more than anything, but I am also afraid I will be erased in a relationship. It's a tug-of-war between my dreams and my reality. I guess that's why I feel so lost. For Indians, marriage is the answer and solution to everything. It's the only way someone would be happy. It's your life's purpose. Your husband is your soulmate. This was a given for me."

Anji once again recalled that she came to know her mother's preferences when she was a grown adult. In addition to peanuts, her mother loved *paan*. She liked chewing the betel leaves filled with areca nuts, lime, and spices after meals. How did Anji never know? It shook something in Anji, opening a crack and wedging itself inside. And it stuck. The moment. And the words. She wanted to make sure she wasn't tossed under a rug, or that someone in her family didn't know what her favorite foods were.

Margarita sensed Anji's uncertainty. "Your heart is the connection to your soul and to the universe. Don't decide with your head. Your head can fail you but your heart never will. Logic isn't always successful. Your intuition, on the other hand, is how you will find your way."

Margarita allowed Anji to sit in silence for a few moments, so that she could assimilate all that she'd shared.

"Let's get back to the voice in the wall," Margarita said, breaking the silence.

"What do you think the voice is?" Anji asked.

"It could be a number of things, my dear. Perhaps a departed one or what you may refer to as a ghost or a spirit—someone who has passed on and part of their soul or energy has remained behind. It could also be a higher being, such as an angel who guides, protects, or watches over you. This is part of the clairaudient ability that you can develop. What do you feel when you hear the voice?"

"I get scared, but not because it can hurt me. I feel scared because I don't know what it is."

"When you hear it next, envision yourself surrounded by white light and imagine the white light emanating from you to this other being. If you feel calm and ease, continue engaging with it. If you feel tightness or tension of any type, then ask it to go away."

Anji promised to give it a try. "I wonder if the voice has anything to do with my soulmate?"

"I don't believe so. I sense this is someone who has been with you a while."

Anji had been hearing the voice for many years, maybe as far back as when she'd moved into her apartment and possibly even when she was in college. She wondered if it was related to the blurred images she saw as a three-year-old. "Like a guardian angel?"

"I think this is something that will be clarified soon." Margarita smiled. "How do you feel knowing that Frank, Donovan, and Nic all called you their soulmate?"

"I know it is not a coincidence . . . "

"Perhaps what you are looking for is deeper than a soulmate."

Chapter Thirty-Three

MARCH 16, 2019

ANJI WALKED TO CENTRAL PARK, hoping that sitting on her rock to meditate would provide her clarity. She hoped that if she set the right intention, she would have a better result. There were people exercising, walking their dogs, or strolling nearby, but her immediate vicinity was clear. There was no one around the rock for at least ten feet. She hadn't visited the rock since she'd had the first vision in January. It was time to come back to it.

Margarita's words echoed in her head. What could be deeper than a soulmate? Anji took a deep breath. It was important for her to connect with her intuition. She struggled to quiet her mind. Usually, focusing on her breath kept her mind from running away with her thoughts, but it didn't work that day. She checked her surroundings and verified no one was pointing a finger at her or laughing out loud. No one was paying attention to her. She hadn't felt this self-conscious since she had first meditated on the rock years ago. She tried again.

She dwelled on how she'd held on to the concept of soulmates for much of her life, yet it was still so out of reach. She wanted nothing more than to find a man to love and who loved her back. She felt she had done her best in trying to find the right person to marry. She had dated—a lot. She had only had two big relationships in her life, one with Donovan and the other with Nic. The rest didn't last long enough to influence her in a significant way.

Reflecting back on her childhood dreams, she realized they were ludicrous and impractical. When she was fifteen and thought of her soulmate, it didn't occur to her that she wouldn't find him easily. It hadn't crossed her mind that he wouldn't be waiting. And waiting for whom? Little old her? Anji wanted someone who had lived a fulfilled life, someone who had traveled and seen the world and who knew what he wanted.

It also weighed on her that she was disappointing her family. As a respectable Indian girl, she was expected to do as her parents told her, and she hadn't done the two things her parents most wanted her to do: get married and have children. The two were inextricably linked.

Yet, Anji was certain that the lonely dove vision had to be an indication that her soulmate was on his way to her. It was a psychic message, a clairvoyant one. This had to be the reason she kept getting other dreams and visions. She felt she had to work through her past relationships to figure out who her true soulmate was.

Anji let herself daydream that she'd skip the pomp and fuss of Hindu weddings, skimming down to the most essential ceremony, the *Saat Phere*. Anji and her soulmate would circle around a fire seven times, each round signifying a vow for marriage. The first for nourishment, the second for health, the third for wealth, the fourth for strength, the fifth for progeny, the sixth for long life, and the seventh for friendship. Hindus believed that when they married, they did so for seven lives. Anji realized that if the same couple married one lifetime after another, it would result in an endless cycle of seven lives, so really it meant they'd marry that soul for eternity.

After the seven rounds, Anji's soulmate would place *sindur* on the top of her head, just a thin red line of vermillion at the parting of her hair, and their union would be complete. The sindur is how Anji showed her eternal connection to her soulmate—the Western equivalent of a ring.

All of a sudden, Anji received a download. A download was different from a vision. Margarita had explained that downloads were sudden knowings, a form of claircognizance. Instead of a vision infiltrating her meditation with images she could see in her mind's eye, Anji suddenly knew something she hadn't before, as if the information had been transferred into her through a hard drive connection with the universe. She didn't see anything. She simply knew it.

A twin flame was deeper than a soulmate. Anji had the certainty that the soulmate of her vision was her twin flame. She was surprised that, through this deep knowing, she knew that twin flames were mirror souls. Like yin and yang, dark and light, earth and sky. One did not exist without the other.

Twin flame love was true love, which meant having the ability to be their true selves without attempting to change the other. They brought out the best in each other. It was a true connection.

Just then, the tiger from her first session with Margarita appeared in her mind. There was no bench, but she could sense the Chinese man and Indian woman were nearby. They watched over the interaction Anji was about to have with the tiger.

In her mind, Anji asked if it was time for her to see the contents of the box. Her heart palpitated fast and her hands and feet were cold and clammy. She sensed the time had come. The tiger's big hungry eyes stared back at her. The brown and green in them told Anji this wasn't a look of hunger. Something in the twitch of the tiger's expression communicated to Anji that there was deep love. The tiger felt toward Anji as a mother would for a child. A surge of energy ran through Anji's body, like she had been elevated somehow.

The tiger was swept from her mind's view and the box appeared— the same lacquer box from the previous meditation. Anji drew in a sharp breath. She wondered if she was finally ready to see the contents. Before she could decide, the box opened up, revealing a strange symbol.

It was a triangle, and inside the triangle were two flames. Below the triangle, adjacent to the bottom line, was an infinity symbol. The box disappeared as quickly as it had appeared, and the only image that remained in her mind was that of the symbol.

Anji sat on the rock willing to receive more information but got nothing. After she was certain she wouldn't receive any more visions or downloads, she walked home, matching the speed of her feet to the reeling in her mind. She hadn't felt this type of clarity before and it lit her being. She reveled in the idea of her mysterious soulmate —twin flame—and felt certain of the depth of their connection.

When she reached her apartment, Anji saw an email from something called Spirit Galaxy. She was about to put it in the spam folder, until she noticed the words "twin flames" in one of the articles. She stopped breathing. She didn't remember subscribing, and it didn't seem linked to other newsletters she followed. It could be spam but the synchronicity was too great for her to ignore.

Her heart beat out of her chest. She clicked on the article that was titled, "Twin Flames Defined." She couldn't believe it. It explained that twin flame love was ancient and timeless; the oldest love stories ever told: in Hinduism, Shiva and Shakti, as well as Vishnu and Lakshmi in their avatars as Ram and Sita and Krishna and Radha; in Celtic tradition it was Cernunnos and Brigid; in Norse mythology it was Odin and Freya; and in Egypt it was Horus and Isis. They could be romantically entwined, like the archangels Faith and Michael and Hope and Gabriel. But not all twin flames were romantic, like Jesus and Mary Magdalene.

Some believed twin flames originated from one soul that had split into two. The two felt most themselves with each other. It was akin to the soul feeling whole. Anji didn't feel this theory made sense, wondering how a half soul could function fully in the world. Although it explained the loss she felt within, confirming that when she united with her twin flame, he would complete what was missing in her.

Where was he? She wanted to know every detail about her twin flame. What did he love most? Did he look forward to his day or would he rather roll over and go back to sleep? What helped him get through his workday? Was he a different person at work than at home? What made him despair? What was he afraid of? What lies did he tell? What brought him joy? When would he step forward? How long would she have to wait? Hadn't she already waited long enough? Couldn't he come to her soon?

Most importantly, who was he?

She wondered if she would ever get a chance to ask those questions. Faith would have her say yes and her instinct agreed, and that brought her comfort.

Chapter Thirty-Four

MARCH 17, 2019

ANJI HAD JUST FINISHED telling Sophie about her discovery of twin flames, and her uncertainty at how to approach figuring out who he was.

"Sweet pea, hiding behind your laptop isn't the answer. Don't spend so much time on dating sites this time. That didn't work, so do something different. You need to show yourself and meet people. You have better criteria now to pan for the gold," Sophie advised.

"You're right. I am my own person. I am a journalist, a friend, a daughter. I have a lot that I love. I have a family I love and who love me back. I have friends I love and who love me back. All I am missing is this."

She shared this during her session with Margarita later that day.

"I want to acknowledge how amazingly your psychic skills are unfolding. You've displayed several 'clairs.' First clairvoyance, then clairaudience, and now claircognizance. I wouldn't be surprised if you soon experience clairsentience. It's when you get psychic feelings."

"Interesting . . . " Anji felt chills and wondered what else would be revealed to her.

"The more you develop your skills, the more you will grow as a soul."

"For now, all I want is the skill to find my twin flame." Anji sounded almost petulant.

"Twin flames aren't my area of expertise," Margarita said. She closed her eyes for a moment as if she were receiving her own download. "I feel that learning about them is your journey, my dear. But I tell all my clients that they need to be clear on what type of person they are looking for so that the universe can deliver."

"I want a partner, a lover, and a friend. I am tired of superfluous connections."

"So, you want intimacy."

"Yes."

"Why is this important to you?"

"There is nothing that makes me feel lonelier than traveling alone. Sophie used to be my travel companion. We were great together, but we can't do that anymore because she can't stay away from Tasha for too long. And her budget is much different than mine." Sophie's tastes were extravagant, and Anji knew that if she'd fess up, Sophie would pay for everything without a second thought. Anji didn't want to risk their friendship over money. She had already learned that lesson.

"This isn't really about Sophie or travel, though, is it?"

Anji took a moment to collect her thoughts. "It's how I feel because I have to travel on my own. I already travel a lot for work, and when I go on vacation, I want to have someone to share that experience with. In the bigger picture, I want to have someone to share my life with."

"Can you think of a better example of the intimacy you are seeking?"

Margarita's astuteness never ceased to amaze Anji. She wondered if the crystals that adorned Margarita's neck enhanced her psychic abilities. That day, Margarita had a dark blue sodalite pendant on a silver necklace.

"I want to be with someone I feel comfortable sharing all my thoughts with, like I don't have to hold back or censor myself because I'm afraid of what they will think or how they will react," Anji said.

"We all have baggage, my dear. Relationships help us work through our issues with the other person."

"I will only get into a relationship if I feel it's balanced, supportive, trusting, and loving."

Margarita asked Anji to keep this in mind when she was dating. Anji was certain that she would. And, come hell or high water, Anji was determined to finally meet her twin flame.

MARCH 18, 2019

Really Living Magazine announced they were partnering with an online dating website, DateWell. It was designed to help wellness and mindfulness afficionados find like-minded romantic partners. The parallels between the philosophy of the dating website and the magazine played a role in the alliance.

Really Living Magazine wanted a few people from the team to try DateWell and report on it. Anji was one of the few remaining single people on the team and Josh wanted her to participate. Anji didn't have to write the story, but she would have to share her experience with the person who would. They both knew that dating stories weren't her forte.

Anji was impressed at how quickly the universe had provided her this opportunity. Maybe the tiger revealing the symbol was a message that she was finally going to meet her twin flame. She couldn't believe the synchronicity and didn't hesitate to set up a profile on DateWell. DateWell encouraged participants to share their mindfulness and wellness practices in their profiles and ask conscious questions of each other. While Anji appreciated the reference to users as conscious beings, it seemed elitist to her, wondering if there was such a thing as an unconscious question.

Otherwise, the site worked like most other dating platforms. If she liked someone, she hit the heart button. The other person received a notification of the hearting, encouraging them to click on her profile. If they hearted back, they were allowed to message each other.

Anji found it hard to filter through profiles. She didn't like making judgments on trivialities. Was playing video games code for slob and lazy? Could someone who had only been to Canada be considered a world-traveler? What if they didn't seem attractive to her but were kind, generous, charming, or compassionate? What if they were handsome but self-absorbed? Who knew?

It was hard to meet the right person, no matter how like-minded, through any dating platform. It still involved two people coming together in a meaningful way, and that was not easy. It had nothing to do with DateWell. That was reality. Anji didn't know how to come to terms with that and finding her twin flame.

Then she found Luigi's profile. He was attractive. An Italian with long, dark hair, he had light olive skin and green eyes—Anji's ideal combination in a man was dark hair, dark skin, and light-colored eyes. Luigi had practiced years of meditation, attended silent retreats, and candidly shared that he saw a psychotherapist. He stated he had done a lot of personal development. He knew what he wanted, he knew what he liked, and he did not hesitate to reach out for it.

Anji found his self-confidence extremely attractive. Every part of her urged her to heart him, and she followed her instinct without hesitation. She wondered if this was a sign that her clairsentient skills were developing.

Luigi hearted her back a couple of hours afterward. Then he sent her a message.

Luigi—8:57 p.m.
Hi beautiful, I find you extremely attractive, and it seems we have meditation, travel, and personal development in common. Tell me something about yourself.

Anji's heart skipped a beat. She did not want to seem too eager and decided to wait to respond.

Anji—March 19, 9:14 a.m.
Hi there, I find you attractive as well. I love dancing in the rain. How about you?

Luigi—9:14 a.m.
Naked in the rain?

Anji—9:14 a.m.
LOL. No, I'm not that kind of free-spirited dancer.

Luigi—9:14 a.m.
That's too bad.

Anji—9:14 a.m.
You didn't answer my question. Your turn.

Luigi—9:15 a.m.
How about we meet for a drink and I will tell you anything you want to know?

Anji would have preferred to chat with Luigi a bit longer before agreeing to meet in person, but she felt elated by the synchronicity. She didn't think for too long.

Anji—9:15 a.m.
Okay.

Luigi—9:15 a.m.
Excellent! Tonight 8 p.m. at the Standard?

Anji didn't know if she could deal with meeting him so soon. She felt extremely nervous. She wanted badly to make the best impression and had an irresistible urge to prove that she had an active social life, which meant she had to pretend to be busy that night. She wouldn't admit that her plan for the night was to binge watch season three of *The Crown* on Netflix while eating tacos al pastor from her favorite taco truck around the corner. She liked getting tacos from those guys because they did an excellent job of marinating the thinly sliced pork, their pineapple, onion, and cilantro were crispy and fresh, and they hand-made their corn tortillas fresh every day. She also needed time to get a waxing appointment with her favorite esthetician, who was usually on high demand. The earliest availability she had was on Thursday afternoon.

Anji—9:21 a.m.
How about Friday at 7:00 p.m. and not at the Standard. Too cliché don't you think?

Luigi-—9:21 a.m.
Fine. Friday, 7:00 p.m. at Please Don't Tell. St. Marks Place and 1st.

Anji— 9:21 a.m.
Oooh. Speakeasy. I like that. But PDT is hard to get into.

Luigi—9:22 a.m.
I'll make it happen.

Anji—9:23 a.m.
Great.

Luigi—9:23 a.m.
Dreaming about meeting you already.

Anji took a deep breath and calmed herself. She checked in with her gut and recognized this felt good. The butterflies in her stomach leaped at the attention. She couldn't help but wonder if this meant that Luigi was her twin flame.

Anji—9:25 a.m.
Great. See you Friday.

Chapter Thirty-Five

MARCH 22, 2019

LUIGI WAS WAITING for Anji. She liked a gentleman who didn't make her wait. He was standing outside Crif Dogs, the hot dog restaurant that housed the secret phone booth entrance to PDT. Anji recognized Luigi instantly. He looked even better in person than in his profile, something she didn't think was possible.

They walked through the phone booth and left the hot dog restaurant, entering a swanky, dark, wood-paneled bar. She loved the atmosphere at PDT. It was like a secret club but without the pretension of membership. Unfortunately, PDT was not a secret. It may have been once, but it wasn't anymore. It was a popular tourist attraction and wait times could last a couple of hours unless there was a reservation. People had to call nonstop to reach someone on the phone.

Anji and Luigi were shown to a table right away. She was impressed.

"You're stunning, baby. Your profile picture doesn't do you justice," he said as they sat down.

"Well, thank you." Anji was not comfortable accepting compliments, but she decided that this night would be different.

"Aren't you going to tell me I'm good-looking too?"

Luigi was extremely attractive. He had a full head of curly hair, but he cut it short, making it appear wavy. His eyebrows were full, but not in a dominating way. His eyes were a light greenish-brown. Some would call them hazel. He raised an eyebrow with an expression of naughtiness. His skin was smooth and tanned. She had to hold back from reaching out to touch him.

"You're quite forward, aren't you?" Anji laughed.

"Why pussyfoot around when you know what you want?"

"We're already talking about what we want?"

"Why not? Let's start with a drink. What do you want to drink, baby? You like unique cocktails, no?" Luigi's eyes rested on her chest. She was wearing a silk pink button-down blouse with the first three buttons undone. She wasn't showing cleavage, but that didn't stop him from staring.

"Today I am going with the Mezcal Mule." Anji returned the stare and noticed he had chest hairs peeking out of his striped, blue shirt.

"We'll make it two." Luigi smirked and looked directly into her eyes.

Luigi called over a waiter and ordered their drinks without losing eye contact. Anji felt the intensity of his gaze slowly unbutton her blouse.

She cleared her throat and shifted in her chair. "Where are you from, Luigi?"

Luigi cleared his throat as well. He told her he had been born and raised in Rome and moved to the United States to open his own restaurant. It had been a success, and he had opened a second location. He had hired a trustworthy manager and loosened the reins on managing operations. Otherwise, he wouldn't have been out on a date, especially on a Friday, which was his busiest night.

Luigi was thirty-six, five years younger than her, but Anji thought he had a mature outlook. He shared how the combination of meditation, psychotherapy, and self-development had brought him clarity and focus to run his restaurants. It also allowed him to be introspective and recognize what he needed for his self-interest and that of his restaurants.

"Why don't you have a strong Italian accent?"

"I worked really hard to get rid of it. I wanted people to understand me, and an Italian accent can be hard to follow. Also, when I came to

New York, I didn't want to be branded as an outsider. I spent a lot of time in the kitchens imitating how my guys spoke, and eventually I picked it up. I don't speak like an American, but I speak more clearly." Luigi used his hands when he spoke, waving them every which way. Several times, Anji thought he was going to strike one of the passing waiters, but he didn't.

"I can understand that. I used to have a thicker Spanish or Latin accent, but it's morphed into something else from years of living here. People assume I am Canadian because they can't place my accent."

"I wouldn't think you were Canadian, but what do I know? I'm only from Italy. Enough about me. Tell me about you, baby." His impish expression made a comeback.

He leaned in and reached his left hand across the table. Anji had been playing with the coaster, and Luigi placed his hand next to hers, touching the tips of her fingers.

Anji smiled. "What do you want to know?"

"What was it like to grow up in Colombia?" Luigi touched each of her nails, as if he were painting the dark blue varnish over them once again.

Anji didn't move her hand. "I enjoyed it. I mean, it was different for me because we were one of the only Indian families there, but it was home."

He stopped playing with her nails and looked up. "Are you puritanical, like Indian women, or open and sexy, like Latin American women?"

Anji pulled her hand away, placing it on her lap. "Indians are known to be traditional, and perhaps as prudes. But that's a stereotype. You should know that Latin Americans are also traditional and can also be prudes. Both women are open and sexy. I would say I am a bit of both."

Luigi sat back, placing his hand at the edge of the table, as if he were trying to hold one down. He took a deep breath and let it out slowly. "Baby, what I want to know is: are you open sexually or are you reserved?"

Anji sat back in her chair, folding her arms across her chest. "I'm not ready to answer that."

"You want us to get to know each other better, and I already told you so much about me. It's time to get to the good stuff."

"Seriously? I haven't told you much about myself."

Luigi took a moment, and then nodded. "You're right. In the self-work I've done, I realized sexuality is important to me, and I am open and straightforward about it, especially when I see there is a chance for a relationship to move forward. I haven't had this type of chemistry with someone in the way I am connecting with you now since my last girlfriend, and that was three years ago. I'm sorry I let myself get carried away, baby. I'm not normally like this. You have brought this out in me."

Anji raised an eyebrow. "Oh, so you are saying it's my fault?"

"No, not at all. I just find you so attractive, baby. I cannot help myself." He gave her a charming smile.

Anji was flattered. It had been a long time since someone had found her attractive in that way. She wanted to free her butterflies so they could dance in her stomach.

He laughed heartily and leaned in again. He placed his left hand where it had been before, his expression hinting that she should do the same. Anji kept her hand on her lap.

"You were saying that Colombia was home for you. Do you still feel that way?" Luigi tapped the table with his finger.

"New York is home for me now. I still get nostalgic for all things Colombian, and when I want comfort food, sometimes I think of Colombian dishes, other times I think of Indian dishes, and at this point I think of American dishes."

"Really? For me it is always some kind of Italian dish—pasta or otherwise. What are your comforts?"

"*Arepas* are my favorite Colombian food, *parathas* my favorite Indian food, and grilled cheese sandwiches my favorite American food."

Luigi laughed. "Eclectic. Although all breads. Corn, whole wheat, and white, yes?"

Anji nodded and smiled. "True, and all delicious. But different. Arepas are corn cakes. Parathas are buttery and flaky whole wheat flat breads, and I don't need to explain a cheese sandwich."

Luigi laughed again. "Do you feel more American now or Colombian? Or maybe Indian?"

"I feel more American. I'm attached to India and Colombia, particularly when it comes to sports, the Olympics, World Cups, and things like that, but I've lived here for so long that I can't help it. New York is home for me."

Luigi nodded, as if his experience had been the same. "How about community?"

When Anji moved to New York City, Colombians accepted her without question. She went to the Colombian student's association and no one thought she was Indian. All they wanted to know was the city she was from, but often she only had to speak for them to figure it out. She had a thick Caleña accent. When they found out she was Indian, they asked her if she did yoga and meditated. They were excited to tell her that they knew of Deepak Chopra.

Yet the Indians wanted to categorize her. Where was she from? And where did she really grow up? And when they learned, they were amazed. Indians were everywhere, yet they couldn't believe there was a family that had lived in Colombia. And they wanted to test how Indian she was. Was she religious? Did she dance classical *Bharatanatyam*? What language did she speak at home? Who were her other friends? Could she cook Indian food? What dishes could she make? How often did she eat Indian food? Was she vegetarian?

"I'm not like other immigrants. I feel different, so I make up my own community."

"I'll make a community with you." Luigi's tone was warm.

Anji thought Luigi to be sincere, and she felt cushioned in warmth.

The evening continued much like that, although their hands didn't touch again. They realized they both started their days meditating. Luigi was more disciplined than Anji. He meditated for a full hour each morning, waking up at 5:00 a.m. He ran for thirty minutes and did yoga for another twenty. He was at work by seven thirty. Anji was only waking up at that time. She meditated for twenty minutes, got ready, and was at work by nine fifteen.

When they said goodbye, Luigi kissed her on the cheek. Anji was elated. She had not had a date like that in a long time. He was attentive, he listened, and he made her feel desirable. She was certain the universe was pointing her in the right direction.

Chapter Thirty-Six

APRIL 26, 2019

LUIGI INVITED ANJI to one of his restaurants. It was a small place in the East Village called *Olio e Salvia,* or Olive and Sage. He named it for his love of sage oil. His grandmother, who was near and dear to his heart, swore by it for all types of ailments.

It was near the corner of Avenue A and Second Street in the basement of a four-story building. Luigi took advantage of the darkness in designing the space. It had dark wood floors and dark wooden tables with half-booths. The booth walls were tall, rising at least two feet above most people's heads. They had black leather upholstery dotted with round, golden studs. The chairs on the non-booth side were also upholstered in black leather and gold studs.

Inadvertently, Anji had dressed to match the decor of the restaurant. She wore black jeans, a black silk button-down top, a black leather jacket, and black knee-high booths. Had she known she would blend in with the furniture she would have chosen to wear more color. The only thing that stood out was her bright red lipstick, the kind she had called *puta* red when she was in college. Ever since running into Donovan and seeing Helen wearing the lipstick, she had decided to try it. The intense red highlighted the fullness of her lips. They appeared lush, like cherries ripe on the tree.

Luigi was sitting at the table when she arrived. He was on the booth side, reviewing documents. He barely noticed her at first, but when he realized she was pulling back a chair, he asked her to sit next to him in the booth. He put his papers away, while Anji stood half-frozen. She didn't like couples that sat next to each other at tables. She didn't understand why they needed to be that close and wondered if it was worth the neck pain. She would rather be able to look at her partner face-to-face.

"Baby, I haven't been with you all week. Just sit next to me," Luigi said, reading her mind. They had gone out on several dates since first meeting.

Anji sighed and slid into the booth. Luigi pulled her closer and kissed her briefly on the cheek. "Did you miss me?"

"Sure, I guess." Anji giggled. She chided herself for sounding like a schoolgirl.

"I missed you." Luigi stared at her lips, and bit down on his. "I don't like PDA at my restaurant. Doesn't set the right message."

Their table was in the middle of the restaurant with a direct view of the kitchen, which was semi-open. There was a glassed window that allowed diners a peek inside, although only the top racks and cooks' hats and faces were clearly visible.

Anji shied at the sudden intimacy. She looked up at the black chandeliers. They seemed like small spiral staircases with bulbs sticking out of each step. The bulbs were so dim they barely emitted any light. The light in the restaurant came from small lanterns on each table.

A server presented them with an antipasto of roasted peppers, fresh mozzarella, prosciutto, sopressata, and a variety of olives. Anji soon realized they would not be ordering. Luigi had asked the chef to prepare a variety of items. Some were from the menu; others were new preparations the chef wanted Luigi to try. Plates of food were served one after another without stop. An endless stream of waiters and bussers dropped fresh dishes and picked up empty, cold ones.

To Anji, it felt like Thanksgiving, if she had a large Italian family to celebrate it with. It wasn't a far cry from what her grandmother's house in India would be like if the entire family got together, all thirty-three aunts, uncles, and cousins, and shared a meal. There would have been a ton of small dishes and everyone clamoring to get their share. It would be far more chaotic than this. This was just two people eating for twenty.

Anji couldn't remember eating so much food in one sitting. They had stuffed artichokes, *cacio e pepe*, *gnocchi* and sage, eggplant *rollatini*, chicken *cacciatore*, *spezzatino*, and so much more. They were small dishes, which at first seemed manageable, but there were so many Anji couldn't make enough room for them. She was tempted by the crunchy layers and almond filling of the *sfogliatella* served at the end, but she was sure that one more bite would burst her stomach open. She only made space for the closing limoncello shot.

It wasn't just the food that was served in excess. Every two dishes or so, a new glass of wine appeared in front of her, prompting her to finish the previous one. Anji felt unable to move on to one glass without finishing the previous. She didn't like to waste any type of wine.

Team members from the restaurant sat with them at different times throughout the feast. The first person showed up a couple of minutes after the antipasto, and after that Anji and Luigi were hardly alone. It was evident they were curious about Anji. They also took advantage of Luigi's light mood, which apparently wasn't common.

Toward the end, Chef Gino joined them at the table. The kitchen had closed by then, and the restaurant was nearly empty, except for a few tables. Gino was burly and bald, yet Anji felt like he could cradle someone into the warmest bear hug. His laugh was hearty and strong.

"*Ciao bella*, aren't you a delight for the eyes?" he exclaimed as he sat down on one of the chairs. His eyes sparkled.

"Thank you." Anji giggled loudly as she nursed the limoncello. She loved hearing a greeting that called her beautiful.

"Why are you with this guy?" His head pointed in the direction of Luigi as he asked. "You should be with a man, man."

"A man, man? What do you mean?" Anji couldn't help herself and giggled again. She considered that she might have been more drunk than she realized.

"Someone you can grab hold of—I have plenty you can grab." Gino let out a rumbling laugh but quieted down when he looked at Luigi's furrowed brow.

The three of them walked out of the restaurant together after it closed. Gino said goodbye and walked away. Anji thought Luigi was going to walk her home, but he kissed her, hailed a cab, and sent her on her way.

Chapter Thirty-Seven

APRIL 27, 2019

ANJI WOKE UP with a dismal feeling in her body. Yet, she felt elated when she thought of Luigi. Visions of them getting married in the Italian countryside played in her head. Her bright red *sari* contrasting beautifully against the Barolo vineyards in the morning sun. The gold embroidery in the red silk shimmering brightly against the Nebbiolo grapes.

The fantasies made Anji's head spin, and before the memory of last night's wines and limoncello made her hurl, she got out of bed to make coffee. She drank it thick and black. Even the thought of milk made her feel nauseated. She had two Alka-Seltzers and felt better only after she burped a couple of times. She felt her stomach settle.

She reached for her phone and texted Luigi.

I had a great time last night. Thank you so much for inviting me to your restaurant. Your team was delightful!

Luigi's iPhone had read notifications, so she knew he had read it, but she did not hear from him. Anji grabbed her phone every time she received a notification, expecting to see his name come up, only to be disappointed. In the month they had dated, this was the first

time she had to wait to get a response from him. She couldn't figure
out if it was a sign that Luigi wasn't her twin flame, or if this was some
type of test the universe was sending her.

Anji called Sophie who assured her that Anji had nothing to worry
about. If Luigi was Anji's twin flame, nothing would keep them apart.

Luigi called in the evening the next day. "Hi, baby, did you miss
me?"

"Yes. Did you miss me?" Anji bit her nail, surprising herself by
asking the question.

"I did eventually . . . I needed some distance after the scene you
pulled." Luigi's tone was flat.

"The scene? What are you talking about?" Anji felt herself get
warm.

"With you slobbering like that? If I didn't like your pretty face,
this would be over. But there is something about you. I can't get you
out of my mind."

Sweat beaded around her neck and forehead. Much of the night
was fuzzy. She could have done something embarrassing and not
remember. "I am sorry . . . I know I was drunk, but slobbering?"

"Did you like the kiss we had?" His tone was dry.

"I don't know. I don't remember." Had they even kissed? She
couldn't recall.

"I don't give bad kisses, baby. It was the worst kiss I have ever
had. You were awful."

Anji's heart sank. "The worst? Really?"

Luigi breathed out heavily. He continued with a conciliatory
tone, "That's okay. As I said, you have a pretty face. I can't deny you
were fun. The staff liked you. So, I'm giving you a second chance."

Anji held her breath. "A second chance? I'm not sure if I should
be flattered or insulted."

They were quiet for a few moments.

"How about you make it up to me?" Luigi finally asked.

"Make it up to you?" Anji was incredulous.

"Yes, baby. Make it up to me."

"I'm not sure what you think I owe you?"

"Come on, baby. We could have had such a great night if it
weren't for how you ended it. You have to take responsibility for the
mess you were."

Anji felt the nausea of Saturday morning swirl back up. She thought carefully about how to respond. "I'm grateful that you invited me to your restaurant. The food and company were wonderful. If I can do something to show my appreciation for that, that's fine, but I don't feel I need to make something up to you."

"Gino would probably agree with you. Maybe you should have gone home with Gino."

"Why are you even bringing him up?" Anji was growing in irritation. What did Gino have to do with them?

Luigi sighed loudly. "Fine, whatever. Let's move on from this." He paused for a moment, his voice softer. "I need you to do something for me. You can't say no."

Anji couldn't shake off the tension in her body. She had broken out in a sweat. "You're making me even more nervous. What do I have to do?"

"Just say you'll do it, baby." His tone had turned flirtatious.

"How can I say I'll do it without knowing what you're asking?"

"Trust me. Just say yes," Luigi said, his tone gentle.

Anji's jaw clenched. "I won't until you tell me what this is about."

Luigi sighed again. "Okay fine. We'll have it your way—this demanding nature of yours is attractive, baby. I wonder in what other ways you like to push your weight around?"

Anji knew Luigi was trying to be conciliatory and fun, but she wasn't having it. "Get to the point, Luigi."

"I need you to suck my cock."

Anji felt the world go still. "I'm sorry. Did you just ask me to suck your cock?"

"Yes, baby." Luigi was serious.

Anji fell silent in disbelief. She took a few moments to collect herself.

Luigi spoke first. "I like you, baby, and I want this relationship to move forward. I can't handle all this dating bullshit without knowing if we're sexually compatible."

"Shouldn't we talk about this *after* going through more dating BS?"

"That's my point. Sex is an important part of my life. The only way for me to know if you and I are sexually compatible is by having you suck my cock. I can't get hard any other way."

Anji was amazed at the casual tone of the conversation, as if Luigi were asking her to come over for coffee.

"No one has ever asked me that," Anji admitted. She was having a hard time accepting that this conversation was actually happening.

They were both quiet again.

"Well, baby, are you willing to do it?" Luigi broke the silence.

"To suck your cock?" Anji felt that repeating the words made it easier for her to assimilate the conversation. His honesty was strangely refreshing, and she couldn't deny the logic in his explanation. She wasn't used to rationality in a relationship. "I appreciate your directness. But this isn't something I am willing to engage in at this point."

"Answer this. Do you explore your own sexuality?"

"How is that relevant?"

"Sexuality is important in any relationship. I need you to liberate yourself a little, to be open, to be willing to explore. Life is more fun when you play with yourself."

"Right, but you're asking me to play with you," Anji pointed out.

"And what's wrong with that, baby? Let's have some fun and see if there is a future in this."

"That's the problem. What you need to determine if there is a future in this relationship is fundamentally different from what I need. You want to have sex now and date later, and I want to date now and have sex later."

"What's the problem, baby? We would have sex eventually, so let's skip all the fuss and get to it."

Anji paced in her apartment. She felt she had been turning in circles. "I felt this relationship had potential. I felt this was going somewhere."

Luigi's volume went up a few notches. "I can't believe we are going back and forth on this . . . Listen, baby, I am being patient with you because I really like you. If you want to move forward, then you must come over and do this for me. I've got to be at the restaurant at eight o'clock, which gives us an hour. Why don't you put on some sexy lingerie so I have something nice to look at and get your beautiful ass over here."

Anji stopped moving. "Wait. You only have an hour?"

"Yes, come over quick."

"Seriously? That's it?"

"Yes, and we get to spend some special time together."

"Look, I am not into this. I've stayed on the phone with you because I felt we had something special. But it's clear we don't."

"Baby, I understand you're scared. Take a few days to think about it. I will wait for you. I don't want to waste more time. If you want to be together then let's do this."

Anji was speechless.

"One last thing before you go, baby. Send me some sexy pictures," Luigi commanded.

"Sexy pictures?"

"Haven't you ever sent sexy pictures to a boyfriend?"

"Actually, no."

"There is always a first time, baby. Take a photo of your tits, your pussy, and your ass, and send them to me."

Anji laughed. "That's really what you want me to do?"

"Yes. Preferably without your face."

"Wow . . . Okay . . . You just wait for that." Anji hoped Luigi caught her sarcasm. She hung up the phone and sat on her sofa, unable to find the will to move. His audacity shocked her.

Anji had wanted badly for the relationship to workout. But the message couldn't have been clearer. Luigi was not her twin flame.

Anji did not contact Luigi again, nor did she hear from him. She told Josh that she thought *Really Living Magazine* should partner with DateWell, despite what had happened with Luigi. Luigi was responsible for his own behavior.

Chapter Thirty-Eight

MAY 5, 2019

"I DON'T UNDERSTAND why women who are strong, independent, and successful get into relationships with men who are clearly not right? There is a voice that warns us from deep within not to get involved, but that voice is so silent it is virtually inaudible."

Margarita raised an eyebrow. "The voice is neither silent nor inaudible. It might be quiet, but it seems to me that you're deflecting. What is this really about, my dear?"

"My mind keeps on turning, wondering how I could have gotten it so wrong with Luigi. The tiger showed me the twin flame symbol and I thought it meant that meeting my twin flame was imminent." Anji reached for her Lemurian seed crystal, hoping it would comfort her.

"The universe doesn't work with our sense of timing. You may be meeting your twin flame imminently, but that doesn't mean that it will happen right away or that it will be the next man that crosses your path."

Anji knew Margarita was right. She had gone back to wondering what was wrong with her. Why couldn't she hold on to anyone? Why could no one hold on to her? She had been so desperate to find her twin flame, that she let herself believe Luigi was the one. "I jumped into these relationships with both feet, ignoring my inner warnings. I was convinced I was making the right choice. Somehow, I felt I needed to prove the inner voice wrong. It didn't work out. I know how it happened with the previous relationships, but I thought I'd learned my lessons. With Luigi, I felt all the signs were pointing to him being the one. I don't understand what I missed. Finding my twin flame seems out of my reach."

"Is it possible you are so desperate to find him that you're letting your ego take over instead of your heart? Can you tell the difference, Anji?" On that Skype session, Margarita wore a pearl necklace with no pendants.

"I think I can. I assumed I was developing the clairsentient skills you mentioned, but this wasn't about feelings. I let my ego get the best of me. When my ego is leading me, I feel closed, bitter, angry, or frustrated. It's as if I were in competition with myself. When my heart is leading me, I feel peace, joy, and openness."

"That's right. Did you follow your inner guidance with Luigi?"

"I thought I did. I had butterflies in my stomach from the time I started getting his messages on DateWell, and they continued during our first few dates. I thought that was an indication that things were going well."

"How did you feel as the interactions with Luigi continued?"

"I felt a pit in my stomach. The butterflies had flown away." Anji sat back in her chair. She hadn't realized she had felt that way until that moment. Instead of honoring her feelings, she had dismissed them.

"And you stopped seeing him. To me that means you acted according to your instincts. You are being too hard on yourself. You did well in ending things with Luigi, but my dear, where you need to grow is in trusting yourself." Margarita's voice was soft and soothing. "How have you grown from this?"

"Since you and I started working together, I have learned so much. Frank's memory helped me interpret signs and synchronicities. I know it means the universe is with me, that I am supported and guided. Donovan helped me recognize how I want to be treated in a relationship."

"It was a call for you to love herself, my dear."

"Right. Nic was my lapsus brutus."

Margarita laughed. "It doesn't matter. He happened. And he happened for a reason."

"To consider what I want out of a marriage. And Luigi helped me interpret the twin flame download I got. I can see how far I've come, but I still cannot make sense of what is happening to me."

"Have you considered what it means to have a true connection? It seems to me that is the purpose of a twin flame. I want you to think about what you are looking for in your twin flame—such as a life-long relationship that is loving and trusting. Get crystal clear on that. Then, wait for the universe to deliver as you watch out for the signs. But don't let yourself be influenced by everything you read. Learn to evaluate your circumstances instead of allowing yourself to be pulled by them."

———————

After the session, Anji walked to her rock in Central Park. She dragged her feet. Her thoughts moved around sluggishly, not at her usual buzzing speed. When she sat on her rock, she had a hard time clearing the muck. She realized Margarita was right. Despite fantasizing about beaches, fields, and trains, she hadn't considered the qualities she sought in a partner—in a twin flame.

She headed home after accepting that meditation on her rock wasn't helping. Anji paced from one side of her apartment to another. She felt claustrophobic. She threw a jacket on, grabbed her keys, and went for a walk. Meditating on her rock might not have done anything but walking always helped her process.

She walked for an hour before realizing that all she had done was mull further but gained no clarity. The same old thoughts continued to plague her. She headed back to her apartment and settled herself in her living room. She realized that wouldn't work either. She got up and sat on her meditation cushion. She grabbed a blanket and placed it around her legs, hoping that feeling warm and cocooned would help.

The symbol that had come into her vision before once again appeared in her mind's eye. There was no tiger and no box. It was just the symbol hanging in a dark void: the triangle, the two flames in the middle, and the infinity symbol underneath the triangle. This time she saw the image enclosed in a circle. She felt herself get warmer and butterflies fluttered energetically throughout her core.

But she had been here before, certain she would get an answer, and had drifted into muddy waters. She needed to make sure she remained clear, without letting her ego and her desperation get in the way. Calm and steady. She focused on her breathing—in and out, in and out—and she felt herself surrender. Anji couldn't see her, but she felt the presence of the tiger's large brown-green eyes watching, making sure Anji was safe and centered.

Anji's vision turned dark, as if a black screen had been pulled over her mind. She steadied herself and took a few more deep breaths to make sure she remained calm.

Information started to trickle in. It came in short messages, like tweets from the universe. They helped clarify what the symbol stood for. Each flame inside the triangle represented one twin. That made sense to her since there were two flames and they stood at the heart of the symbol.

Each circle of the infinity symbol represented one twin flame and the two circles joining together meant that they would have an eternal connection. The triangle was also a symbol for twin flames. The left corner of the triangle was the Divine Masculine, the right corner of the triangle was the Divine Feminine, and the top was their ideal relationship. The triangle represented that a twin flame relationship was the perfect balance of masculine and feminine energies.

Anji learned that the circle that enclosed them was a sign that all of this was divinely orchestrated, divinely supported. There was nothing she needed to do other than follow the signs that the universe presented her. Rather than run around mindlessly, desperately seeking her twin flame, she needed to pay attention because he was on his way to her. More than that. He was already there. She just had to open her eyes to see him.

Chapter Thirty-Nine

MAY 11, 2019

ANJI STARED OUT into the park. Her body was on the earth plane, feeling the heat of the rock. It was early in the morning, and a few joggers and bicyclists passed by. But there weren't many people—no one to distract her from being open to receive a clairvoyant message. She hoped her tiger would reveal more.

Anji felt a deep connection to her rock, stronger than she'd ever felt before. It was a mystical rock, and every time she came to it, she sat down as one person and stood up as another. So much of her transformed on this rock. It could not be a coincidence that she had received the clarity that she'd longed for while sitting there. She no longer believed in coincidences.

It was a sunny day. The nearing of the summer meant the evenings and mornings were still cool, but in the middle of the day it was warm. She wore a sweater. There was a gentle breeze, and she was soothed by the sound of the leaves rustling. It was perfect.

She knew she needed to channel the same energies that she'd had around her when she got the vision in January that showed her she had a twin flame. Back then it had come to her by surprise. She'd fallen asleep on the rock and hadn't expected to receive it. But on this day, she wanted to be open. She balanced her chakras and set an intention to keep her heart open so that she could receive guidance. She concentrated on her breath and placed her hands over her heart center, allowing words, images, or messages to come to her naturally.

For the first few moments, all she could hear were the noises around her. A mother called after her child, a group of friends laughed loudly, someone opened a plastic container of food, and there was a far-off cough. She struggled to concentrate, and the temptation to open her eyes won several times. She tried again, intent on finding her way.

She took a few deep breaths and heard the rustling of the leaves once again. She felt the trees nudging her to focus.

"No one is looking," they whispered.

Soon she lost sense of where she was or what was around her. All she heard was the beating of her heart. And then she received it—the vision that showed her twin flame.

———————————

Anji's body was ablaze with jitters and a tingling sensation. Her heart beat rapidly, and she heard the blood pumping in her ears. This time the vision was complete. She hadn't needed her tiger or a box to see it. Anji found the missing piece of the puzzle. Not only was the vision more detailed, but she knew exactly who her twin flame was. Those blue eyes had captivated her from the first moment she saw them. How could she not have figured it out sooner? She knew them so well.

She sat with the knowledge that it was William. It perplexed her. How could she not have seen it before? What had been holding her back from recognizing him? Why hadn't she been able to express the love she felt for him? It shocked her to hear the word love come up in her thoughts. Could it be? The voice got louder. Margarita had told her not to doubt, but her hands were sweaty and she felt cold sweat rising. She had to confirm William was her twin flame.

She sat on her rock a while longer. This time, she imagined a deep white light emanating from her heart center and spreading across every inch of her body. She could feel it pulsating throughout, filling her with lightness. Heart racing, she decided to start by asking questions about other areas in her life. She wanted to make sure that the visions were unfiltered. Accurate. Safe. She wanted to slow herself down. The tiger, Chinese man, and Indian woman were present, guarding and protecting her. They weren't the ones answering the questions. The answers seemed to come on their own.

"What do you want me to know about my career?" she asked in her head.

The answer came in a series of images. They appeared as in a dream, in her mind's eye, and she was swept up with a wave of understanding, knowing what the images meant without hearing words or sounds. It was a combination of clairvoyance and claircognizance. She saw herself typing away at her laptop. She knew that her writing career would continue as long as she found meaning and purpose in it. It reassured her.

"What do you want me to know about my health?"

She saw herself doing yoga, and knew it meant she should focus more on her practice. She wasn't consistent and often practiced like a chore, without intention. Like her meditations and spiritual practice, these too would improve with the right emphasis.

"What do you want me to know about my family?"

Anji saw her parents, Sid, Meena, Radhia, Naitik, and both sets of grandparents. They were standing in a circle, holding hands, surrounding her. She stood in the middle of the circle, looking at each of them. And then she saw him. William stood in the middle of the circle with her. He reached out and held both of her hands.

She was surprised. She was still gearing up to ask the question about her twin flame. And he wasn't part of her family. She thought it was a mistake. So, she asked the same question again. Once again, he came up. Her heart stopped and she was doused in sparkling energy.

Then she asked, "Is William my twin flame?"

She quickly rephrased it. Margarita had advised her to ask open ended questions so that she could get more information from her messages.

"Who is my twin flame?"

There he was, front and center, standing directly in front of her, holding her hands.

A wave of knowing swept over her.

———————

Anji felt a soaring within, as if the sun had exploded in the center of her being. A supernova that sent a billion pieces of galactic stardust all across her body. She should have been scorched, but she felt alight and alive. And she was in one piece. She had never felt so whole in her life. And free. She was sure she could take flight off the rock. She felt she was lifted into the ether by a thousand angels.

The world finally made sense. Anji saw all the connections that had eluded her before, and understood that everything that happened to her before had happened the way it did so that this moment could take place. It had all been so carefully orchestrated. A series of dominoes that cascaded to etch her life.

For the first time, Anji felt she was a part of something greater, bigger, and more meaningful than herself. She finally felt like she was part of the world. She walked home feeling that she had never felt so herself. Her feet felt like they floated on the sidewalk and she smiled the whole way. People made eye contact with her, and to her surprise, even the surly New Yorkers smiled back, confirming the love within her had been set ablaze. It was infectious.

Of course, it was William. It felt absurd that she hadn't realized it before. When she peered into his eyes, she knew there was a place for her. She belonged. She was home.

She had felt that way since they had beers eleven years ago. Once Anji got past her stereotypical judgments of him and they had started talking, she had felt as if she had known him her whole life. The bond between them was palpable then and it continued to be now.

How many times had they communicated with each other without uttering a word? How many looks had they exchanged that were full of meaning? When she looked at him—into his eyes—she felt she could read him like an open book. She often didn't need to explain herself to him. Over the years, many had asked her what was going on between them, assuming there had to be something deeper.

Despite their superficial distinctions, at their core, they mirrored each other's values. What was important to him, was important to her—love, connection, trust, loyalty, surrender, openness, truth, integrity, and honesty. They understood each other. She had never felt so comfortable with anyone else.

Anji had assumed that when she met her twin flame there would be fireworks or some type of cataclysmic experience. That's why she had a hard time discerning him. She had been friends with William for a long time before it was clear that they were twin flames. All this time, she hadn't been conscious of their soul connection, of her love for him. Now that she had recognized the dots that linked them, she couldn't deny it. Anji didn't have a doubt in her mind that he too couldn't deny the deep connection between them.

As she unlocked the door to her apartment, Lulu stepped out of her own with a gray-haired gentleman wearing a three-piece light blue suit. Lulu wore a long flowery dress and her long white hair was wrapped underneath a red hat with a small white veil that covered her forehead. She exuded youth, despite her age. Lulu introduced Anji to Steve. Anji was happy to finally meet him. He was gentle and soft-spoken, a perfect balance to Lulu's talkative and spirited nature. He looked to be at least twenty years younger than Lulu.

"Where are you lovebirds off to?" Anji asked.

"Met Opera," Steve said.

"*L'Elisir D'Amore*," Lulu added with a slight giggle.

Anji watched them walk away and could have sworn Lulu had a light skip in her step. "The Elixir of Love" seemed like the perfect opera for them to watch. Anji felt she could finally relate to the love that radiated between Lulu and Steve.

There was no other feeling that came close to its magnificence. Anji used to think that love came from her heart, but now that she felt it truly, it irradiated from every part of her being, including her eyelashes. The deadest parts of her, the ones she had once considered extinct, brightened with life. It was like discovering she was a billionaire on the day her house was foreclosed on.

When Anji closed the door behind her she realized there was only one problem. William was going to marry Natalie. In less than six months.

Chapter Forty

JULY 5, 2008

"WHAT IS LOVE?" William asked.

Anji was surprised by the question. After their photography class, they had eaten at Anji's favorite south Indian vegetarian restaurant, Saravanaa Bhavan, on Curry Hill on Lexington Avenue. Anji had discovered the place when she was a student at NYU, and it was rare that a month would go by without her stopping by for a meal. She wasn't a fan of eating Indian food in restaurants, feeling the food was too rich and heavy. It didn't taste like what she ate at home. But Saravanaa Bhavan was authentic and she craved their *dosas*. William had joined her that day. He had not had *dosas* before and when Anji explained they were thin crepes made from rice and lentils, he was curious to try them.

"Love? What do you mean?" she replied.

"It's a simple question," he said and smiled.

"Yes, but with a complicated answer." She was nursing another beer. Anji didn't particularly like beer, but when she was with him, it had become their drink of choice.

"Try." He stretched his arms and spread his palms but kept his eyes on her.

Anji smiled. "Love is a feeling. It's what we feel for other people.

It's the energy exchanged between two people who care for each other."

"Like between us."

Her heart was flooded by a tidal wave. "Yes, sure. There is definitely love between us."

He looked down at his beer.

"Why do you ask?" She tried to quiet the hammering in her insides.

William glanced up for a second and his eyes went back to his beer. "I feel love is responsibility. I used to think it was playful and brought joy, but I realize now that it brings pain and heaviness."

Love had also brought her pain. Anji played with the perspiration beads on the beer and the wetness in her hands. She felt hot around her neck. She started sweating. "What would you like love to be like?"

"Like this." He pointed back and forth between them. "You know? Easy."

Her heart stopped. "You mean like friendship?"

"Yes," he said, sighing deeply.

Her heart sank. She sighed as well. "And you don't think you can have that?"

He shook his head and looked up. "Why can't the women we love also be our friends? It's impossible. At least for me."

"I think it's possible. Why can you have a friendship with a woman you're not dating and not one with the woman you love? Loving relationships are about building a connection, and I think that can only be done through friendship."

He seemed unconvinced. "Is that what you want love to be like?"

"Yes. That is what we all should strive for. That is definitely what I want."

William shook his head again and gazed at her as if she were a child. His expression suggested that time would soon prove her wrong. "What would your ideal relationship be like?"

"I don't know. I've struggled with relationships. All I can tell you is that, even though my parents are okay with me having a boyfriend, I know I would be in my ideal relationship when I feel comfortable telling my parents about it."

"Your parents are strict?" He seemed relieved they had changed the topic.

"They aren't strict per se, but Indian culture doesn't allow it—women needing to be chaste and all. We wouldn't be able to live together, for instance, especially without a ring on my finger."

"I live with my girlfriend now."

Anji nodded. "What would your ideal relationship be like?"

The heaviness returned; the air grew thick. "I thought the relationship I have now was ideal. It started that way . . . "

Anji tried to clear the fog and changed the subject. "What would you do if money were no object?"

"I would travel the world and visit as many places as I could," he answered without hesitation. He relaxed back into his chair and continued, "I'd love to explore without a care in the world. I'd have no problem taking odd jobs here and there to make ends meet. I could stay in one place for months or weeks and move on when I got what I wanted. I would do that until I saw every single country in the world."

"That is quite a plan."

"My best friend Kevin and I used to talk about it often."

"And what happened?"

"He drowned in a rip current when we were eleven years old."

"Shit. I'm sorry."

"Sometimes I feel I should do it just to honor him, you know?"

"Maybe you should."

William sighed and his shoulders slumped. "We're not all as fortunate as you to love our jobs and have them pay for our travels, Anj. For some of us, our jobs are a means to pay the bills."

It was the first time he called her Anj, and she felt chills. "I know."

"What about you? What would you do if money were no object?" His tone was lighter.

"Are we going to do this?" she asked.

"What?" He raised an eyebrow.

Anji motioned her hands between them. "Ask the same question we've just been asked?"

"Why not? It works." He shrugged, smiling.

Anji didn't answer. She knew William had more to share. He had told her he was confused about love. He didn't know what he needed to do to meet the right person. He floated from woman to woman; some were better than others, but they did not work. He thought he was destined to be alone.

"What are you looking for in a relationship?" Anji asked.

"The impossible."

"Explain."

William thought about it for a few moments. "There's a sea of pretty faces, but that gets dull after a while. I wish it could be easy— that we would talk about anything. I'm looking for someone normal. A best friend."

"You aren't normal. You don't do well with normal."

He laughed. "I feel more myself with you than with anyone else."

MAY 11, 2019

Looking back, Anji recognized that was the day she fell in love with him. She didn't know why it wasn't clear to her back then. She wasn't ready, clearly. She wondered if William had also loved her since that summer.

She thought it was a sign. How could it not be? She felt the same. She was truly herself when she was with him. She could tell him anything—except of course how she felt about him. She was afraid to tell him that. She was an Indian woman, and men were supposed to chase after women. It wasn't appropriate for her to make the first move. But she couldn't forget that years ago, it was William who had called her lonely dove. He had done so again recently. He got her.

Chapter Forty-One

MAY 25, 2019

ANJI AND WILLIAM were soaked from the impromptu dip they had taken in the ocean. It was a warm day, and the beach and ocean were packed with people. William had asked her to come for the day. He would have asked her to spend the entire Memorial Day weekend at his parent's house in Long Island, but they had a full house. Both sides of the family—his and Natalie's—were consumed with wedding preparations, which was taking place in just four months' time. It was only Saturday and William was already itching to escape for a few hours. He'd picked up Anji at the train station and they drove to Robert Moses State Park, certain he wouldn't run into anyone he knew. And that they could hide amongst the multitude out on the beach.

Anji couldn't help but see the synchronicity of the events. She had the clarity of William as her twin flame only two weeks before, and now they were sitting at a beach, as they had in her first vision in January. It was clear an opportunity was unfolding for her, despite the scorching rays of the midday sun that contrasted sharply to the cozy warmth of the moon in her vision. Or that in her vision they had been the only two people on the beach.

They sat on a towel next to each other facing the ocean. Each had their knees bent and arms resting on top. Two beers sat between them. William was quiet, reflective. Anji could tell he was mauled by his own thoughts. She watched him as he stared into nothing. The heaviness sucked the life out of him. He caught her looking at him and smiled. He couldn't hide from her, and he knew.

"You can't talk to women," he said, as if responding to something she'd asked.

"*You* in general or do you mean me specifically?"

He smiled again. "I can't talk to her. I don't know how. She gets angry or teary. I can't stand tears. I give in to the demand and later have to come up with a reason to leave the house."

She nodded, as if she knew what that was like. "What happens to you? To what you want?"

He scoffed. "What is it that I want? I lost track . . . "

"You know you can still get out of it."

They sat in silence for a few moments. "How? It would kill her. I can't do that."

"What about you?"

He gave her a sideways glance. "You asked me that already."

Anji softened her tone. "You didn't answer."

They remained silent for a few minutes. Anji decided the moment had come. It was auspicious. "Do you remember it was you who called me lonely dove?"

William looked at her. "I don't."

"I didn't remember at first either. The memory came back to me in the last couple of weeks. I was sitting in Central Park, staring up at the trees. I saw a dove flying overhead. It perched on one of the branches of the tree and for a brief moment, I felt as if it had spoken to me. As soon as it took flight, I remembered the text you sent me."

Anji reminded William that he had texted her when he was on a trip to London. He had just broken up with Marie, the woman he'd been living with when Anji and William first met. Marie and William were traveling around Europe and broke up mid-way across Italy. He flew to London on his own and sent Anji a text message telling her he was in Regent's Park, lying on the grass, staring up at a tree.

William—August 22, 2009, 11:09 a.m.
I feel the tree is speaking to me—maybe it's an Ent

Anji—11:10 a.m.
You weirdo

William—11:11 a.m.
You lonely dove

The words had taken Anji's breath away. She couldn't believe that he had captured her essence so accurately in two short words.

Anji—11:15 a.m.
Ents aren't real, weirdo

William-—11:22 a.m.
You're still a lonely dove

Butterflies had gone to carnival in her stomach, boisterous, and interminable. Drunk with delight. She felt them again sitting with William in front of the ocean. They gave her courage.

"Hearing those words flipped things for me back then, but I ignored them and I went on with life. I've spent the past few months searching for someone to call me lonely dove and it turns out it was you. I never thought that you and I were a possibility. I've always felt you are out of my league."

William gave her a sideways glance again, his neck tense. He didn't respond.

"When I share this with you, where do you feel it?" She turned to face him, hoping he would look at her, but his eyes were focused on the sand.

"What do you mean, where do I feel it?"

"In your body. What do you feel in your body, and where?"

He placed his hand on his abdomen, just above his belly button. "Here," he said, staring down at his hand.

"How does it feel?"

"I don't know. I can't explain it."

"Like a warm sensation?" Anji heard the pitch in her voice going higher.

"Yes." William clearly didn't share her excitement.

"I'm going to tell you something and, as I say this to you, I want you to notice where you feel it in your body. This may sound crazy. Maybe it won't. I don't know. Regardless, I just want you to listen." She took a deep breath to calm herself down.

His muscles hardened and he seemed to shrink away from her, his eyes still intent on the grains of sand.

"Go with me on this." The gentleness of her voice helped ease some of the tension. He finally looked into her eyes.

"You and I do not just love each other; we are part of each other. Our souls have lived with one another for time eternal. When you called me lonely dove, that was your soul acknowledging to mine that we have been connected for far longer than we have been alive on this earth in this lifetime."

His neck tensed and Anji could see the veins bulge out. She knew she was talking about ethereal topics, and he was more grounded and disinclined to spirituality.

She wasn't surprised when he asked, "How do you know?"

She took a deep breath, searching for the right words, hoping not to lose him. "There has always been a strong connection between us, wouldn't you say?"

His gaze was still fixed on her. "Yes."

"We feel comfortable with each other."

"I feel more myself with you than with anyone else."

"You've said that to me before. And haven't you always felt like you've known me? Or known how I've been doing? Or like you could sense what was going on with me?"

"I feel I know you like the back of my hand."

"Which is strange if you think about it, because we've not spent a lot of time together."

He shook his head as if trying to shake something off. "What do you mean?"

"We have been friends for eleven years, but we've never spent longer than a meal or drinks together. We probably spent more time together when we were learning photography. It's not like Sophie and me. We were roommates—we've stayed at each other's houses, we've traveled together, and we still speak several times a week. I know every detail of her life. I don't mean that you didn't know what was going on with me or I didn't know what was going on with you. But we haven't had the same level of closeness."

William looked at Anji again. "I remember having great conversations with you."

"Yes. We've had honest and important conversations. We were real. We didn't talk about hypotheticals. And yet, you and I have not spent much time alone together." Anji didn't take her eyes off him. They sat one foot apart but the distance felt like a chasm.

"True. Although I feel that even in a crowded room, we made time for each other."

"You can't deny we have a deep bond, a profound connection. I've marveled at the intensity of what we share with each other, despite the fleeting moments or crowded venues in which we meet. We always understand each other. It's an inner knowing that only you and I have. At least, that's how I feel about you."

He closed his eyes. "I feel the same."

"I didn't recognize how deep our bond was until I heard those two words come out of your mouth."

William opened his eyes and looked at her. "Lonely dove?"

Anji felt the distance between them shrink. She spoke excitedly, as if the words would be lost if she didn't voice them right away. "When you said them, I also felt it, right here in my belly. It was overwhelming. I didn't understand how someone could know me so well and describe me so accurately with just two words. That was enough for me to recognize there was something there."

"That was a passing comment . . . " His voice was soft.

"All I know is that our souls wanted us to recognize each other, to experience that unity, long before we had any awareness. We've always felt that bond, that inner recognition of each other. We are an intimate part of each other, and that knowledge is so strong we sense things about one another without having to say a word."

"I always felt I knew you well. And I feel you understand me—better than anyone." William's eyes were alight, but his voice sounded tight.

"I feel the same."

They sat in silence, staring out to the ocean.

"But why haven't we seen it before?" he asked.

"We weren't ready. We weren't ready until now. We had to live our lives to prepare for this moment. We had to go through all of that to find ourselves here and now. No matter the circumstances, no matter the consequences, no matter the people we've been with, and no matter what we've lived through, we were meant to come together at this moment. In fact, we needed all those things to happen in order for us to come together.

"I know you don't believe in reincarnation, and you don't have to. I don't have any proof, but I have this sense—like a deep knowing. That's what all these visions have been about—to awaken that deep knowing. It told me that we've been spending lifetimes finding our way back to each other. That is what our lives' purpose is. That is all our souls want us to do. And we do it, time and time again. We're not just soulmates. We're twin flames." Once again, she spoke fast. Her voice was louder than she intended and her body felt hot, not because of the weather. A cool breeze swept through, as if on cue.

William was quiet. He was still looking at her. Neither of them had moved during the entire exchange. Anji was hugging her knees and he was as well, but where there was an openness to her, she could tell his body was rigid. The veins in his neck her taut. Yet, his eyes sparkled with such intensity they were like two bright stars.

"Anj, I'm getting married to Natalie." William's tone was flat, almost stern.

Anji shifted her body to face him. "I know we still need to figure out how we are going to be together, but believe me, the toughest part is over. We have the rest of our lives ahead of us. I'm not saying that we won't face difficulties or tough times, but when we do, they will feel lighter and they will be much easier to bear, simply because we have each other. We are in this together, whatever this is. From this point on, do not ever—not for one second, no matter what is going on in our lives or what is happening between us—doubt that I love you. I do love you. I always have and I always will." She couldn't believe she had finally told him how she felt. A rush of energy surged through her.

"Anj, I don't feel like you're listening . . . " His knuckles had turned white from grabbing onto his knees so tightly.

"It's hard for you to see us together. I know it. But think about it. Even though we're not the same, we are linked. You are grounded, stable, inflexible, controlling, cautious, unbelieving, and aloof. I am ethereal, ever-moving, ever-searching, adaptable, full of faith, connecting, and spontaneous. Twin flames fit like a glove on a hand. When we come together, we correspond perfectly, like pieces of a puzzle locking into place. We don't attempt to change the other. We want the best for each other and we bring out the best in each other. We are not perfect, and we may not even be perfect for each other. All of those are misunderstandings of what a true twin flame connection is. The truth is that there is no such thing as perfection, but there is such a thing as true love and true connection. Our relationship is eternal. When I'm with you, even when I say your name, William, I feel like I've come home."

He looked at her as if he was considering his words. He hadn't moved at all and his whole being was tense. "Anjali, I am flattered. Truly. I cannot begin to comprehend the intensity of what you have experienced. And you've gone through a lot. I can't imagine what all of that has been like. Much less what it has meant for you to make sense of it all. I'm in awe of you. And yes, I love spending time with you. But you have to listen to what I am saying. I love Natalie. I'm going to marry her."

Chapter Forty-Two

JUNE 21, 2019

ANJI WAS SURE her twin flame union with William was doomed because they'd had no relationship to begin with. They had always been just friends. Only friends. When they met, there had been no sparks on either side. No instant attraction. She had known him for over a decade before she had any clue that he meant something to her. Theirs was unlike any love story she'd ever seen, read, or heard about.

No matter how much she tried to stay away from William, she saw his name everywhere, which confused her. She didn't understand why his name kept coming up if they were not meant to be together, if he was marrying Natalie. Yet Anji drew breath from every new post of his on social media.

She struggled to not think of him, to not have him permeate every thought, every breath, every memory. She didn't want to but she couldn't stop herself. He was the last person she thought of when she fell asleep. And on many nights, she dreamed of him. She had visions of being pulled away, sometimes floating away, and then falling straight into his arms. Or she would look behind her and realized he had been there all along.

When she woke up in the morning, she wondered how he had slept. Anji made *masala chai,* imagining she was making it for William. She had made it for him only once, years ago, and he claimed he would have loved to wake up with tea like that every morning. Anji imagined pouring him a cup as she poured herself one.

Anji felt it was only natural that she had fallen in love with him. *Look at him,* she thought. *He is perfect.* Her life made sense because he was in it. All he needed to do was exist. That was it. That was all she needed to be consumed by him.

She imagined what it would be like if they were to run into each other. Where they had once spoken candidly there would now be a barrier, an unshakable underlying tension.

"Are you seeing anyone?" he would ask.

"No." She would answer simply. "No, I'm not," she would confirm. As if that explained things further. "I don't think I ever will," she would wish she could say. He had a way of getting the truth out of her without asking.

Until Anji thought of William, she couldn't breathe. Until she imagined him starting his day she couldn't get out of bed and start hers. Until she felt his arms holding her asleep, she couldn't fall asleep. Until she imagined speaking to him and filling his ears with her words, she couldn't imagine writing them down. Anji simply couldn't find a way to release William.

She wanted to tell him everything. She wanted to tell him what she was doing. She wanted to tell him what had happened in her day. How she had finally been able to roll the *parathas* she made for lunch into perfect circles—they came out exactly as she had wanted them to. What she liked at the new coffee shop she went to and the juicy conversation she eavesdropped on. Why sometimes she lied to her friends, pretending to be busy, when all she wanted was to binge watch a show on HBO. How some nights she preferred the pleasure of her own company because solitude brought her solace. How other nights she wondered why she didn't have more friends, because she would give anything to have a glass of wine and a good conversation instead of dealing with the loneliness of her reality.

Anji imagined William would care. More than that, she imagined he would want to know. She pictured him listening to everything she had to say, intent on knowing everything about her. All she could do was speak to the image in her head. That version listened no matter what she said or when she said it, and sometimes she could go on for hours. William would look her in the eye when she spoke, hanging on to her every word. He didn't say much. How could he? He was a vision, not an imaginary friend.

At moments, Anji was so sure the vision would become a reality, and it was only a matter of time. But when she couldn't stop glancing at her phone, and when time and time again, she saw no message from him, she faltered. Her heart hurt, and she wondered how many more times it would continue to hurt.

Anji read the book *Normal People* by Sally Rooney, and laughed when Connell said to Marianne, "I'm not a religious person but I do sometimes think God made you for me." Anji knew God had made William for her.

But she hadn't seen him or contacted him since the day at the beach. Anji no longer felt at ease, like she once did, to reach out to him. She didn't text him when she thought of something to share. She didn't arrange to meet him for brunch or drinks or a walk in the park. It was better to leave things unsaid. After all, she could only deal with one rejection at a time. Anji had to rise to the reality that William was wrapping Natalie in his arms.

Anji read about relationships—broken ones—hoping she would find a clue as to why he didn't love her. Quiet tears rolled down her face but she didn't get any closer to understanding. It only intensified the ache of emptiness within her. Most of the stories were about people who loved each other and no longer did, or couldn't find a way to get along, or didn't have the courage to be together. Maybe he did love her and was too shy? Or afraid he would get hurt?

Anji was comforted by the memory of the twinkle in his eyes and the openness that came over his being that day on the beach when she told him they were connected. She knew he heard her words and understood. She had seen his aura expand. Something about what she'd said resonated with him at a deep level. She had never seen his blue eyes sparkle so brightly.

In the past, when someone called her their soulmate, she had bolted. She couldn't blame William for having done the same, yet a part of her knew that he got a wave of understanding. Something came over him that opened him up. She didn't know what would come of it, but she knew it had happened. She felt a warm sensation in her solar plexus, as she had all along in this process. She knew it was a sign that she was being supported.

But wait, she remembered. She had told him she loved him. She told him everything with sordid details—way more than what he'd ever need to know. How could he feel shy after that? Of course, he didn't. He simply didn't feel the same way she did and he had said that to her. He'd told her plainly and clearly. Then she remembered the tightness she saw in him when she expressed herself at the beach.

No, hers was not a story of a broken relationship. Hers was a tale of unrequited love. There was nothing left to understand. She just had to bide her time. And that felt suffocating. The air closed in around her until she saw him, saw his name, or found a photograph reminder on her phone. Then she was able to gasp until the next time—a momentary reprieve.

Anji remembered a palm reading she'd had when on holiday in India.

"You will marry late," the palmist had said.

"I am already late according to Indian standards." She was thirty-three years old back then.

"You will marry late by any standards . . . You have already met the person you will marry. He is a friend but you don't see it yet. You will soon, or in fact, late. Maybe too late . . . " the palmist had said.

Back then, Anji had gone through her mental Rolodex of male friends. William hadn't come up because she had only thought of her single friends and he was dating someone then. At that moment, Anji hadn't been able to think of a possible single male friend.

She realized now that the palmist had meant it was William all along. And yes, it was definitely too late.

Anji considered leaving her beloved NYC, heeding Sid's recommendation and moving to London. Or Madrid. Maybe she would develop her psychic skills like Margarita wanted her to. The important thing was to create distance between William and her. It would be easier for her to handle not seeing him. They would be physically apart. There would be no excuse. No Natalie. Then she could handle not calling or texting or him.

Maybe if she hadn't opened up in such a way, if she had gone to the beach and listened instead of speaking. Then she wouldn't feel so mortified, and William would still be in her life, and she wouldn't need to leave the city.

Wasn't there another way for her to learn her lessons? Why could he not make his love story with her? How could he not see that their connection was far deeper than the one he had with Natalie? Why was he unable to see the strength of what they had?

Anji would stay sad and single while William got to live out his love story without her. So it was not the knowing that he existed that she had to accept. It was the knowing that he would never be hers. She would be the woman who never got to be with the love of her life. And she could finally justify the loneliness she would always carry—had always carried. Yes, no two words could describe her more accurately than lonely dove.

Chapter Forty-Three

JULY 7, 2019

"I CAN'T BELIEVE I opened myself up like that and he rejected me." Anji was finally ready to speak to Sophie.

Sophie nodded, not commenting, sensing that Anji needed to share more.

Anji had retreated at first, like she'd had in the past, but this time, she had come out of it without the need of pizza and wine. Anji walked to make sense of it all. She walked to and from work every day and went to her rock on Central Park every Saturday and Sunday to meditate.

She and Sophie were having brunch at Serendipity 3, something they hadn't done since they were in college.

"It's easier for me to pretend to be aloof than it is to show how I feel. Growing up in an Indian household, we're not socialized to show emotion. Quite the opposite. We're taught to hide what is really going on and only show happiness and success on the surface. I'm not blaming anyone for this, but it's part of the reason it's hard for me to express what I truly feel.

"I was so hurt by Donovan and ashamed by it. I've often asked myself how it was possible for me not to know that he was having a full-fledged relationship with another person while he was with me. I learned to hide my feelings even more. I can see that, even if I was remotely aware of having feelings for William, I pushed them away. I remember thinking there was no point. He was beautiful and I was just me. Why would he be attracted to me?

"Yet we had a connection even then, and we both felt it. I remember the looks, the unspoken understanding. Perhaps we accepted that connection, neither of us trying to make something of it. We accepted, enjoyed, and cherished the unexpected bond." Anji put away the Lemurian seed crystal she had been holding in her hand. It had truly become her talisman.

"That's beautiful Anji, don't you think? To have someone in your life that you can connect with at that deep level and feel seen and understood without making an effort." Sophie placed her hand on top of Anji's.

"Yes, but then, why aren't we together? Isn't the whole point of this for us to get together?"

"Is it really?"

"Why did the universe send me on this goose chase then?"

"My sweets, don't you think that the universe wanted you to experience this? Isn't there a chance that you were meant to have that conversation with William and tell him how you felt?"

"You mean it wasn't about us getting together but about me expressing emotions?"

"Isn't this what we've been talking about? Your difficulty in expressing emotions? I'm not the spiritual one, but even I can see that a huge lesson for you is to learn that it's okay to express how you feel. So what if William knows you are in love with him? My sweets, you've finally released these pent-up feelings. That must be liberating." Sophie held Anji's hand in hers.

Anji had to admit that she had felt a shift since speaking to William, like the energy around her was moving, like she had crossed a threshold of sorts. "I've never expressed myself in the way I did with William on the beach. It's the first time I've been so blatantly honest with someone about what I feel."

"And that is huge. Maybe you and William aren't meant to be together, but without meaning to, he has provided you a great life lesson."

Truth always managed to make its way to the surface, no matter how much she resisted it and sometimes when she didn't expect it. William didn't have to ask her what was going on, but she always found herself telling him things she wouldn't tell others. Like when she was in debt because of the money she had loaned Nic. Or that he was her twin flame. There was no way she could have not told him of her great revelation. It was the same with Sophie. She couldn't keep anything from her.

When they said goodbye, Anji hugged Sophie tightly.

"You always give the best hugs," Sophie noted.

"That's what I've always thought about you. I resisted hugs for so long but now I love them. I wish there was a National Day of Hugs where the only way to celebrate would be to hug seven people every hour of the day."

Sophie laughed and hugged her again.

Anji realized she had grown to love hugs because they were a wonderful way to connect with others. They conveyed love, acceptance, joy, sadness, compassion, sympathy, and so much more. Hugs broke down barriers and brought people closer together.

Anji made her way home leisurely, stopping at window fronts and slowly sipping from a take-away coffee cup. Something big was shifting in her. She connected with herself in a different way than she had ever been able to do before. Her solar plexus was on fire, her core was active, glowing. Her heart center was warm, as if love was spreading throughout her.

She felt she was stepping into a vortex—an awakening within.

———————

JULY 15, 2019

They were in different cities. Anji was on vacation in a large rental house with her parents. The phone rang. It sounded like a rotary phone, but when she looked around, she couldn't find one. There wasn't a rotary phone, but she found a cell phone. She picked up, surprised to see William's name appear on the screen.

"Hi," he said.

"Hi," she said back. She wasn't sure why he had called but she did not feel comfortable asking.

He didn't say anything.

"Are you there?" she asked, to be sure.

"Yes. I'm here."

Then, he was silent again.

Anji shrugged. She had things to do in this dream, and she carried on doing them. She played with Sid's children. She talked to her mother. She made tea for her father.

William stayed on the phone with her. He heard her move around the house and it didn't seem to bother him. He didn't say a word, and it didn't seem to bother her. Anji held the phone to her ear and carried on. She sensed he needed time, so she waited.

When he finally spoke, he was riding the subway. The rhythmic chugging of the train on tracks caught her attention. She had not realized he had also been moving around.

"Are you sure?" William asked.

Anji knew what he was asking. "Yes, I am sure," she said.

"You still believe it?"

"Yes."

"There is no doubt in your mind?"

"No."

William went back to his silence.

Anji woke up. Her heart soared, and the knowledge, the awareness, and the assurance sunk in. The feeling was so strong it penetrated her bones.

JULY 20, 2019

She was in her house. But it did not look like where she lived. This was a loft in the suburbs and not her one-bedroom apartment in the East Village.

In the middle of the kitchen there was a large square island with a wooden top covered with food. There was fresh produce and containers with various spices, grains, and flours.

She sat at the island, drinking coffee, when the doorbell rang. She opened the door and there he was.

"Hi," William said.

"Hi," she replied, holding the door open.

William entered. They looked at each other. He didn't say anything.

"You want some coffee? I just brewed a pot," she offered.

"Sure."

He sat on the same chair she had just occupied and, as she set out to prepare the coffee, he grabbed her by the waist and pulled her into his lap. They both faced the island.

"What are you doing?" she asked.

"Have you changed your mind?" he asked.

She twisted around to look back at him. "Changed my mind about what?"

"What you told me the other day."

"No."

"Even though I said no, you still feel the same?"

"Yes."

Just then, the doorbell rang again. She got up quickly.

It was a chef, and he was there to teach her how to cook. The chef started the lesson without skipping a beat. All the food set up on the island had been there for this class. The chef wasn't fazed to see William, as if he were meant to be there. William wasn't fazed either.

William grabbed her and had her sit on his lap again, but this time he turned her cheek and kissed her. And the chef did not stop teaching. He carried on as if kissing was a step in his recipe.

She pulled away giggling, and explained to the chef, "I'm so sorry, Earl. We haven't seen each other in a long time."

Then she turned to William and said, "Stop it. We can do this later."

He smiled back, amused at her discomfort.

That's when she woke up.

JULY 25, 2019

Anji woke up to the sound of the TV being turned on. It was the middle of the night and she was sure she hadn't left the TV on. She wouldn't have been able to fall asleep if she'd done that. The TV was in her living room, and she had fallen asleep on her bed. She listened to the voices blaring from the speakers to make sense of what was happening.

She heard the words, "Jesus! Jesus!"

They sounded different than the voice in the wall. She recognized it was Will Smith. She got out of bed to turn off the TV and saw it was 2:22 a.m.

She knew it was a message that she was not alone. She was guided, supported, and safe. Just then, she saw the Indian woman dressed in a white chiffon *sari* appear in front of her. Anji didn't feel afraid, as she would have thought. The image wasn't in her mind but directly in front of her. Anji could reach out to her. She recognized that this was the same entity, except that instead of appearing in her mind's eye, Anji could distinguish her clearly in front of her.

There was something about the woman in white that seemed familiar to Anji. Anji was swept with a feeling of peace and love. She felt strangely comforted. The words *devi* and *beta* popped into Anji's head. Goddess and child. Anji thought it strange. Her *dadi's* name was Devi, and she had passed away when her father was a young adult, before her parents had gotten married.

In that moment, Anji understood that the woman was her grandmother's spirit, and what she had thought had been the voice in the wall had been her grandmother trying to keep Anji safe.

Anji finally understood that her *dadi* Devi was her guardian angel. She cried but this time, it wasn't out of sadness. Rather, utter joy.

Chapter Forty-Four

JULY 27, 2019

"I DON'T THINK you liked any of the men you dated," Sophie said.

She and Anji were sipping margaritas and snacking on chips and guacamole. The summer sun was upon them, and they were sitting at the rooftop bar at the Americano Hotel in Chelsea.

Anji grew tense and her eyes narrowed. "Why do you say that?"

There was Sophie again with one of her eerily accurate insights. It made Anji feel foolish that Sophie understood more of Anji's life than Anji did herself. She hated Sophie for it. And she loved her for it too.

But Anji had evolved. Margarita had helped her dissolve some of those blocks and get in touch with her heart. With her soul. Anji took a deep breath and felt herself relax. She was open to having this conversation with Sophie. It seemed purposeful—a way for her to come full-circle, to tie up loose ends, to get closure.

"Name one thing you liked about Needy Boy," Sophie said, picking up on Anji's receptiveness.

Anji didn't answer. She couldn't think of anything she liked about Nic.

"What about Older Guy?"

"Donovan. We can call him Donovan now."

"Well?"

"Luigi was attractive," Anji said dismissively.

"I didn't ask about him, and I don't mean physical attributes." Sophie nearly rolled her eyes.

Anji was silent again. She knew she couldn't fool Sophie. Her mind drew a blank. She had been attracted to Donovan but, other than his charisma, she didn't know what had drawn her to him.

Sophie continued, "Even Frank. You were scared of him and yet considered being friends with him."

They were both silent.

"I like William," Anji said, knowing it was a copout.

"He's your twin flame." Sophie's tone was flat.

Anji smiled. Of course, Anji couldn't place William in the same category as the other men. She thought hard. She had to have liked them, but she struggled to identify what it was. She had to have liked something about them, otherwise why did she date them? What was it about them that attracted her? The men were all physically attractive but, as Sophie noted, it wasn't about that. Anji wasn't superficial.

"Didn't Margarita say that you thought you were unlikeable?" Sophie asked.

It was true. "But that's about me, not them."

"Don't you think that affected your choice of relationships?"

Maybe it had. Anji's life was filled with people who didn't like her. Few had liked her at school. They stuffed her locker with *chontaduros* and the stink of the orange palm fruit had lingered for months. They placed chewed up gum from a Bon Bon Bum on a chair so that it stuck to Anji's pants. She walked with it to the next class while everyone laughed at her.

"It's possible," Anji considered. "The first boy to call me pranked me. He made a fool out of me. Frank knew nothing of me yet wanted me desperately to make himself feel better. For Donovan, I was a gullible plaything who enabled him to feel powerful and in control. Nic wanted the life I provided. Luigi only wanted sex. None of these men actually liked me."

"Is that what you think, Anji? That people don't like you?"

Anji nodded and looked at the table. Her voice was soft, barely audible. "Even you. I kept on waiting for the moment you'd realize you didn't like me."

Sophie reached for Anji's hand. "I adore you, Anji. There isn't a single thing I dislike about you."

Anji placed her hand on top of Sophie's. The contact gave Anji the confidence to share what she'd held within for so many years. "I wasn't able to see that. I resisted our friendship at first. That's why I didn't go to Charleston on Thanksgiving with you in our freshman year. I thought that the more time you spent with me, the quicker you'd realize that I was not likable. I wanted to hold on to your friendship, but in trying to protect myself from you inevitably dismissing me, I thought I would push you away first."

"Please tell me you don't still believe that. You are a constant for me. I know countless people, but Anji, you are my one true friend. There is no one I feel more comfortable being myself with than you. I don't feel the same degree of comfort with Tony," Sophie said.

Sophie stood up, extending her arms toward Anji. Anji rose to meet the embrace. They clung on to each other for a few moments. Sophie knew things about Anji that Anji didn't know herself, just like Anji knew things about Sophie that Sophie didn't know herself. They were soulmates. They trusted each other implicitly. Sophie and Anji were destined to be in each other's life, their souls intertwined.

"You are my soul sister," Anji said, peering deeply into Sophie's eyes.

"You are my person," Sophie whispered in Anji's ear.

Anji felt the depth of those words sink into her as they sat back down. Sophie was the first person that made Anji feel there was a place for her. "You are my person too."

"But you feel that about other people?"

"Yes. I guess it's because I didn't fit in anywhere. I was an outsider—in India, Colombia, New York, or any place. I don't belong because I'm from somewhere else. Even my parents made me feel there was something wrong with me because I wasn't married, and Sid has always done what I was meant to do but haven't been able to. It's no coincidence that Sid's full name, Siddharth, means accomplished goal."

"It's more than identity, though, isn't it?"

Anji thought that was why her life had felt incomplete for so long. She thought others would bring her a sense of completion. No, not others. She thought her soulmate would complete her. She had gone on a quest to find her soulmate and didn't find him because they were all the wrong guy. They didn't complete her. They didn't give her a sense of purpose. They didn't feel like that one person her destiny was tied to.

"Yes, you're right, Sophie. I dated men I didn't like. Maybe I picked them because I was self-sabotaging."

"Do you think it's possible that you set out to do what you had expected to receive?" Sophie asked.

"In what way?"

"You dated men you didn't like because you wanted them to be deserving of love. Maybe you wanted to prove it was possible for people to not be likable and still be loved. In a twisted way, you saw yourself in them. You picked men who were obsessive, insecure, possessive, dominant, needy—unlikeable. You aren't any of those things, but you felt unlikeable. And if they deserved love, so must you. If you found a way to love these men, you could understand how to get someone to love you. Or if someone found a way to love them, someone would find a way to love you."

Sophie's words made sense to Anji. That might have been her unconscious reasoning, but it wasn't the full picture. "But I didn't want that kind of love back. I didn't want to be pitied. I wanted true love. I still felt I deserved a soulmate. I believed from a young age that everyone did, including me."

Anji realized that even after recognizing what Sophie was to her—her soul sister—she didn't feel complete. Anji had reasoned that she wasn't in love with Sophie. The love that Anji yearned for was the deep and intense connection that gave meaning to life. She wanted love that seeped into her being in a way that felt alchemic and transcendental. She wanted something pure and beautiful, based on mutual trust and respect. Anji and Sophie's love was pure and beautiful and based on mutual trust and respect, but it wasn't alchemical. It wasn't transcendental.

Anji didn't share that with Sophie. "When I found out about twin flames, I thought it would be the key to my salvation. I had been searching for a soulmate when I should have been searching for my twin flame. My *alma gemela*. My life was incomplete without my twin flame."

Anji didn't sense Sophie in the same way she sensed William. Anji could read Sophie—distinguish her moods, know what she was thinking, say or do what she needed to make her feel better—but she couldn't sense her at a deep level. Anji didn't know when Sophie spent sleepless nights, or when she was having a rough day. Or when she entered a room. Or when she was going to call. She didn't have psychic dreams with Sophie and she hadn't seen the lives they had shared together. She didn't feel she could rest with Sophie. Not in the way she did with William. Anji sensed William. She didn't just read him. She could feel him. William had been her answer.

"But even William didn't make you feel complete, did he?" Sophie asked.

"No, he didn't. When he said no to me, it crushed me. If he hadn't been able to complete me, then who would? I had to learn to complete myself."

"How do you feel now?"

"I thought that when I was with my twin flame—with William—I would have proof that I was deserving of love, that I was liked, that someone else liked me, and thus, that I could finally like myself. I now know that is not correct. I need to like myself in my own right."

Chapter Forty-Five

AUGUST 11, 2019

"ANJI, DO YOU KNOW the spiritual meaning of a dove?"

"Peace?"

Anji saw Margarita smile on her computer screen. "Yes, it's the universal symbol of peace. Also of innocence. A dove represents feminine energy, which is intuitive. It is about prophecies—not just future telling but trusting your inner knowing. It is associated with the Holy Spirit as well as the Shekinah. Doves are ubiquitous yet powerful symbols."

It was the last session between Anji and Margarita. Anji had realized that her downloads and meditations were giving her the insights and guidance she needed. After working with Margarita just shy of six months, Anji felt ready to continue her spiritual practice on her own. Margarita agreed. She had said Anji's psychic abilities would continue to flourish, and Anji could use them for herself and/ or for others. It was her choice.

"What do you make of it?" Margarita asked.

"The spiritual meaning of a dove makes sense. I've been on a journey to discover my intuition, and it all started with what seemed like a prophetic vision of William saying lonely dove."

"What do you think your biggest lesson has been?" Margarita wore a golden healer quartz that sparkled just then.

Anji thought about it for a few moments. "To stand up for myself. To trust in myself. To listen to my inner guidance."

"Not just that, my dear. It's to love yourself. It's to love yourself as God sees you, as the divine being of light that you are, a being loved with no conditions and no limitations. You are worthy of love, Anji. You must see that, you must feel that, you must embody that. Only then will you be able to receive love. Doves are also symbols of love. They represent many goddesses: Venus the Roman goddess of love, Aphrodite the Greek goddess of love, and Ishtar the Babylonian goddess of love and the moon. They are about embracing our inner goddess. They are not only about romantic love; they also represent self-love."

The sessions with Margarita had led Anji to have intense experiences. Anji had come to understand the meaning of what was presented to her without needing to wait for Margarita's interpretation. When Anji shared her experience with Margarita, it was like sharing a story with a friend, rather than asking for advice from a mentor.

The previous night, Anji had learned her *dadi* made the noises in the wall to get Anji's attention, wanting her to know she was not alone. Her grandmother, her guardian angel, had been with Anji always, making her presence known during some of Anji's most difficult times. She had been there when Anji had struggled with Frank, at the start of Anji's relationship with Donovan, heard her prayers asking Donovan to stop throwing books, encouraged her to go to Mt. Sinai to treat her shoulder, propelled her to start walking again, and warded off Nic. She had shown up now because Anji was finally receptive, finally paying attention.

Margarita's objective had been for Anji to function in the spiritual world on her own, and she felt she had achieved it. Margarita would be available for one-off sessions if needed, but she was certain Anji no longer needed to meet with her on a regular basis.

In parting she said, "My dear, be confident. Have confidence in who you are and what you feel, and do not doubt what comes to you. Spiritual work is for life. You'll never feel that you are finished. That is why we are here—to learn as much as we can and to expand our souls as much as we are able to grow them in this lifetime.

"My advice to you, Anji, is to not care so much about what others think or how they feel. Prioritize what you feel. I'm not telling you to be cold and uncaring. Quite the opposite. Care deeply about everything and everyone around you, but not at the expense of yourself. Care about yourself above anything and anyone else. Be yourself. Love yourself. Speak your truth. Be authentic. Be considerate with yourself. Only then will you be able to reach your full potential. I know this is what you most struggle with, but I ask you to consider something. God and the universe are divine. You are of God and of the universe. Thus, you are divine. You love God and the universe. Thus, by loving yourself, you are loving God and the universe.

"Allow for your voice to rise and your heart to open so that your true self can shine. That's how you will be your authentic self and how you will live your life's purpose."

Chapter Forty-Six

AUGUST 18, 2019

ANJI WALKED DOWN to the East River Park and onto the Williamsburg Bridge. The recent conversations with Sophie and Margarita weighed on her mind. She thought her life's journey was to love herself. She had to learn she was enough on her own.

In that moment, it dawned on her that it was Anji who didn't like Anji. Her issue was not just about feeling complete on her own. Her issue was that she had not loved herself. Her real life's journey was one of self-love. Self-worth to be exact.

She kneeled down to take in the significance of the lesson. She took a deep breath and shook her body out, as if she were dispelling negative energy, not caring about the passersby giving her strange looks.

As she continued on her walk, Anji was grateful that the Romani woman had led her to Margarita. The old woman had been right. She needed to clear a blockage to find true love. The key for Anji to find the love she so desperately searched for was to feel her own love inside. Anji finally understood why it was said that we can't love others until we learn to love ourselves. Anji had finally released her burdens and found true love, within herself.

She recognized she still had work to do, particularly with her boundaries. She struggled knowing where hers ended and others began and knew she would always need to consider if she was making a decision at her expense versus the expense of others.

Forgiveness was key, and that included forgiving herself. Anji knew that when she forgave herself, she accepted her circumstances and it was easier to let go of the past. It released her attachment to the past. It made her feel lighter and free.

Forgiveness of others released the bitterness she held on to and that also lightened her load. Forgiving others didn't mean she had to bring them back into her life. It simply meant she had let go of the hold they had over her and release the negative feelings she was attached to.

She had been carrying the energy of transformation and harnessing it since the beginning of the year—perhaps longer. In the usual love stories, there were big gestures, big sweeping moments, romantic declarations of love. She'd had hers in a way she didn't expect. That day on the beach with William was her big declaration. She'd told William everything, put it all on the table. She hadn't been able to do that before. What bigger transformation was there? What other way was there for her to harness her strengths and gifts?

The experience had cracked open the carcass of the person she used to be and allowed for the emergence of the person she was meant to be. She was more connected to herself than she had ever been before, and she was connected to the universe, open to all the beautiful magic it provided.

Margarita had asked her about opening her psychic abilities and using them to help others. Yet, Anji felt, in the deepest part of her, that this wasn't her journey. Her journey was to use her "clairs" to get clarity on herself. Yes, she was clairvoyant, claircognizant, clairsentient, and she might develop her skills further, but that didn't mean she needed to change her profession.

When Anji arrived at home, she felt relaxed and at ease, more so than she had ever felt before. She sat down to write a letter.

———————

Dear William,

I don't know if we all have twin flames. Maybe we all do. Maybe some of us don't.

I know you are my twin flame. It's why I laugh loudly with you, from the belly, and let out the occasional snort. It's why you let out your kid voice and say too many "ughs." It's why I told you about the time I stole matches from a grocery store, the only criminal act of my life, and explained how I ended up $40,000 in debt after Nic. It is why you told me you still mourn the death of your best friend, although he passed away when you were kids.

When I am with you, every empty space of my soul is complete, like I've suddenly found the missing pieces of the puzzle, making me whole.

You must think that's why they say that our romantic partners are our other halves. But that is far from the truth. Our twin flames don't "complete us." We are whole and complete on our own. But we feel whole because, when we are with our twin, we are our authentic selves and speak our truth. We recognize our perfection as they recognize their own. We recognize their perfection as they recognize ours. We feel at peace. We belong. We are home.

Twin flames have the deepest connections. But we also have free will. It was mine to acknowledge ours and follow you, and it was yours not to. I know that if we aren't together in this lifetime, there will be others. And in every lifetime, all we are meant to do is acknowledge each other, and hopefully in one of them we can be together. I guess for us, this just wasn't it.

Just when I thought I had figured it out, it turns out I had got it all wrong. You felt so right and I watched myself collapse. I felt cursed. Strangely, I couldn't cry. I was desolate, but I couldn't cry. "Lonely dove" couldn't be more apt.

Thinking about you making your life with Natalie hurt, mostly because I pictured you loving her and not loving me. But it is also what helped me understand you weren't going to be with me. You have found your joy. All I can do is accept it. And accept you as you are.

And with that knowing, I release you. This time it feels different because I have faith. I know I am going to be okay. I have seen my soulmate—my twin flame—and in a way, you have come to me. We experienced our time together.

I will be with you on your wedding day to wish you nothing but blessings on your life with Natalie. I will always love you and I will always be in your life. How could it be any other way?

Love,

Anji

Anji mailed the letter to William. She wanted to make sure it reached him before his wedding.

Chapter Forty-Seven

SEPTEMBER 1, 2019

ANJI LOOKED OUT onto Central Park, taking it in. It was the day before Labor Day and the energy of the festivity was palpable. Families gathered around their picnic blankets covered with food containers, a couple huddled on a bench sharing a bag of popcorn and a hotdog, and a jogger ran to the beat from his headphones. Anji sat in the lotus pose, no longer caring about onlookers. She'd gotten over caring about what others thought. Her back was straight and she tilted her head upwards to the sun. The morning rays kissed her skin and she soaked in its warmth. Anji looked up at the trees, the leaves rustled as a gentle breeze swept through.

Anji closed her eyes and took a few deep breaths. She entered her meditative state and connected with the universe. She finally felt that she'd filled all the spaces of her being. It was something she hadn't experienced for most of her life, but over the last few weeks she recognized it had always been there. She was the one who hadn't seen that there had never been a part of her that was missing. She also knew that she had to experience all she had in order to find herself again—to remember who she was. And she was grateful for it, seeing there was no other path for her to have taken.

Just then, she sensed something different—a shift in the air. She sat still to discern where it was coming from. She snapped open her eyes, as if an alarm had rung. Directly in front of her, at a distance, was a familiar looking figure. Anji peered more closely, leaning forward as if that would help. She couldn't believe it. It couldn't be him. Her mind had to be playing tricks on her. She saw William everywhere.

Her being constricted and she turned away, willing herself not to be disappointed. It had happened too often, and despite all the work she had done on herself, the thought of him still brought a weakness in her. Anji closed her eyes again and took a few deep breaths to calm herself, certain that when she opened her eyes she would see a stranger. She looked back at the same spot. There he was, closer now. It was definitely William.

He looked right at her. He smiled, knowing she had seen him. Anji had nowhere to hide. She debated how to react, and before she allowed herself to think, she waved. Immediately, she regretted the childishness of her reaction. To her surprise, he waved back.

She knew she had to calm herself down. She wasn't sure whether to stand or wait for him to approach her. It occurred to her that he could be heading in a different direction, although he was walking on the grass headed straight for her. He hadn't looked away, his gaze set on her. There were no coincidences. He wasn't there by mistake. She closed her eyes briefly and steadied herself. She realized she had no other option than to continue to sit on her rock and wait for him to reach her.

Anji saw William was carrying a brown paper bag in his left hand and wondered what it could be. She then remembered the pages she held in her hand. She had brought the second letter—the one she hadn't sent. Before she had left her apartment that morning, she had felt called to bring it with her. As usual, she didn't carry a handbag. Her iPhone, credit card, and ID were securely strapped in her armband. She'd temporarily taken out her AirPods for the meditation and tucked them in the pocket of her yoga pants where she kept her keys. There was no other place for the letter but her hand.

She wondered if she was meant to hand the letter over to William and if she had the courage to do it. Anji started to sweat, nervous energy releasing through the droplets trailing down her back. Her solar plexus was on fire and, despite the heat she felt, she shivered. Her skin woke up in goosebumps. God bumps.

The closer William got, the more pressure she felt to come up with explanations for the papers she held. Maybe she could tell him she was writing about the key to weight loss, except that she hadn't lost any, so he'd see right through that fib. Maybe she could say it was an article on being body positive. That, she could sell.

Her butt hurt. The hardness of her rock had not bothered her before, but in that moment, all she could think about was standing up and stretching her legs. Her discomfort suddenly reminded her that she needed to let go of the resistance and surrender to the moment. She let out a loud sigh and she wiggled in place to release the tension.

William was upon her. The sight of the radiance of his face, the ease of his gait, and warmth in his expressions froze her in place. "Hi."

"Hi," Anji squeaked. She cleared her throat. "This is a coincidence."

He gave her a half smile, slightly crooked on one end. "I thought you didn't believe in those . . . I knew you'd be here."

"How?" Anji's heart was speeding down a rollercoaster.

"Isn't this your rock?"

"How do you know?"

He let out a "hmph" and sat down beside her. He glanced at the papers in her hand. "Writing out your soulmate story?"

"Yes," Anji admitted. Of course, he knew. He always knew.

William set the brown bag in the space between them. "Who is it this time?"

"You." Anji sighed, glancing down at the brown bag that clearly had a bottle of wine. "It's always you."

He looked at her, and Anji handed him the letter saying, "It's the letter I was meant to send."

"Instead of the one you sent?" He took the pages but didn't lose eye contact with Anji. "All that you said to me the last time . . . "

"Yes?"

"You believe it?"

"Yes."

William's eyes were the brightest blue she had ever seen. "Truly believe it?"

"Yes, I do." Anji hung her head for a moment and looked

back at him. "William, you have to understand that those things I experienced are part of who I am. At first, I thought the visions came to me from an unknown and external source that I had no control over. But they were simply a deeper part of me that I hadn't known how to reach. Now I do."

William nodded, as if he understood. "So . . . there is no doubt in your mind?"

"No, William, there isn't. Those visions are how—"

"Anj, I don't doubt your insights and intuition. You've always been able to understand things in a deeper way than the rest of us. What I'm asking is if you're sure about how you feel about me?"

"You are my home."

William smiled. He nodded again, taking it all in. He looked out to the park and his eyes settled on Anji's manicured feet. She was wearing a dark purple color. Essie called it Luxedo. She stared down at her own feet. She hadn't realized she'd taken her shoes off. She kept her eyes locked on her toes.

He handed her the brown bag. "Open it."

There was a bottle of Cabernet, a bottle opener and two plastic cups. As she poured the wine, William unrolled the letter.

Dear William,

Fear has led me to believe that I won't be able to make sense of the world unless you're with me.

Fear has led me to believe I won't find myself unless you're there to show me the way.

Fear has led me to believe I won't feel beautiful unless I see myself through your eyes.

The light in your eyes lights my life. The beauty of your soul illuminates my path. When your hand reaches out to me, when your look meets mine, when your soul unites with mine, there is no other beauty in this world and nothing else that makes me feel like I've come home.

And that realization was all I needed. That was my confirmation that you are my twin flame. Seeing you so transparently was a sign.

Our purpose in this life was to find our way back to each other, and we did. I did what I needed to do. Now it is your turn. You need to sit with the information, process it, and think about it, as you do with everything. That's who you are.

How could it take us so long? How could it not? How else would we find ourselves here, recognizing our love has always been and will always be? We have travelled separately, yet I trust that our journeys will bring us back to each other.

Time is arbitrary. There is no such thing as too long or too short. Everything happens exactly as it is meant to and when it is meant to. It makes sense that you came into my life when you did, that we've dated all the people we have, that you got engaged, and that we waited this long to recognize what we are to each other. It wouldn't have worked any other way.

I have accepted that you may not come to terms with me as your twin flame. Of those, I am certain, there is only one. I can only be yours and you can only be mine. Yes, I know that whether or not you come back to me, I'm still me. I'm unbroken. You don't take anything from me and you don't give anything to me. You may enrich my life and add meaning to it, but I'm still whole and complete.

I thought that people broke me. They chipped away at me and kept a portion of me that was lost forever. But that is not the case.

It turns out I didn't need you or anyone else to tell me I was born with all my parts in place. I may have lost sight of that knowledge. It may have been like playing a game of hide and seek. But I have always been there, waiting to be noticed, recognized, to be venerated by my own eyes, my touch, my feel. Not yours. Not theirs. Mine. I have a feeling that you have seen all of me all along. It was my turn to do the same.

I pray you recognize your twin flame, for when you do, you will know what true love and true connections are. You will know you have reached home.

I'll always love you,
Anji

When she had written it, the honesty in the letter made her feel lighter. She hadn't sent it but she had felt compelled to express those feelings. At the time, it had felt enough. She tried to burn it over the kitchen sink and release it back into the universe. But she couldn't bring herself to do it. Something had urged her to hold on to it.

When William finished reading it, he looked at her. "Anj?"

"Yes?"

"Look at me."

She did. She couldn't discern any tension in him.

His body seemed at ease. There was nervousness in him, but his being was open and alive. "When we met that day at the beach, I didn't know what to think. You said some incredible things. Some rang true, and some seemed too far-fetched for me to comprehend. You made perfect sense and, at the same time, I couldn't believe my ears.

"I have loved you, yes, but as a friend. I didn't feel romantic inclinations. It was too weird to think of you that way, and I thought you connected too much to being called lonely dove. You and I are so different; I didn't feel we were compatible. I can't keep track of you. Are you Indian? Are you Latina? You are everything, and from everywhere. I'm never going to be from anywhere other than New York. You are complex and diverse. I'm just me."

"I know it seems—"

"Anj, please let me finish."

Anji nodded and let him continue.

His eyes continued to shine brightly. "Everyone I've been with has wanted something from me. They've loved me for what I've had, what I've offered, how I look, or how I made them feel. None of the women I've been with have seen me—the real me—the guy who would be content working at a surf shop. They wouldn't be with me if they knew that's all I wanted.

"I've felt I was deceiving them, making them believe I am someone I am not. I felt I owed them something, that I had to give them what they were after—my money, my status, my body. I did it, but I lost interest quickly. They are beautiful women, and I loved them at first. But how long could I keep that up? You're different. You see the dude beneath the suit. And still, you love me. Why? I don't know. Maybe I'll never know. I don't deserve you. You're smart, you're crazy, and you're gorgeous. Why would you want someone like me?"

Anji's heart exploded. "William, you are everything to me. There isn't a single thing about you I would have any other way."

William looked at her intently, as if he understood. "That is why I had to find you. I took a chance, guessing you would be here. I needed to see you in person. You told me that I would know who my soulmate is when I got in touch with the deepest part of myself and I envisioned someone to share it with. You said that person would be my soulmate—my twin flame. I know who I am. I know what I want. And I want to share it with you . . . not Natalie. I love her—don't get me wrong. She's beautiful, kind, and I enjoy spending time with her. But she's not the one I feel at home with."

Anji's body was shaking. She couldn't contain the light surging throughout it. "What about the wedding?"

"It's cancelled. Natalie threw the ring at my face and is making me return all of the gifts. She wants to take the honeymoon trip with her best friend and have me pay for it."

"How do you feel about that?"

William chuckled and shook his head. "I deserve it. And she deserves better than what I've done. I don't know why I resisted for so long. Part of me wondered what you wanted from me, and if I had it in me to give it to you. I thought you wanted my soul, but the more time I spent away from you, the more I realized you've always had it. It's when I'm with you that I make sense."

The view grew blurry as she hyper-focused on William's eyes. "Where does that leave us?"

He looked at her deeply. "I love you."

"I've always loved you," Anji said.

"I think I have too."

"You think?"

"I know."

William leaned in to kiss Anji. Her entire being was set ablaze as she felt the softness of his lips touch hers. She thought she couldn't hold herself up. He pulled her into him, as if he knew she needed to be supported. They smiled at each other in the momentary interruption and looked again into each other's eyes. When their lips touched again, Anji felt their bodies coming together in a cosmic harmony, their hearts coming together in a storm of energies. The feeling was so intense, she felt herself step out of time and felt her body leave her so that she could see that this moment was meant to be through forces far stronger than herself. Their union was inevitable, all the pieces of their journeys finally falling into a place, and their past, present, and future making sense.

After they broke away from what felt simultaneously like an eternity and a flash connection over a synapse, they both had to catch their breaths, sitting with their foreheads pressed against each other. Anji felt him reach into the depth of his being to pull out the truth of his emotions. He pulled back to look into her eyes. His face was shining, a face so familiar to her, she felt it had always been with her.

"I love you," he whispered. He had said the words a second time, but there was a depth to them that hadn't been there before.

She sensed his vulnerability. His blue eyes sparkled like a pair of polished diamonds. He peered deeply into her gaze, her silence casting a shadow over him.

Her hands reached for his cheeks and she kissed him. Hard. So hard their teeth touched. She looked at him again, and found him still searching, seeking in her eyes the assurance that he too was loved.

"I no longer feel like a lonely dove," Anji whispered. "A dove maybe, but not a lonely one."

Anji and William succumbed to each other's embrace. She kissed him one more time, softly, on the lips. She held on to him but sat back a little. Air rushed in between their bodies, blanketing their skins with goosebumps. God bumps.

No, she no longer was the lonely dove.

Epilogue

DECEMBER 29, 2019

A PLAYFUL SMILE spread over his face. Anji realized he'd sensed she was awake. William had awakened before her, and she wondered if he had been up all night, but then realized that their embrace brought him comfort, and sleep.

William lay quietly still, waiting for her to join him in his waking hours. The slight movement of her body made him peer down at her. Anji looked up at him. They both smiled, and giggled slightly, relishing the moment.

They lay awake in each other's arms. That's how it was most mornings, and most nights. Sometimes they talked. Mostly Anji talked and William listened. The cadence of her voice seemed to bring him comfort. She hoped that her courage to share the hidden parts of herself would give him hope that it would be okay when he did.

"In love there is no judgment, no criticism, and no darkness," she said, as if she knew what he had been thinking about.

William replied as if they had been having a conversation all along, "I heard your name repeatedly. Between the day at the beach and me coming to the park, I saw your name everywhere. I came across articles you'd published, people asked me about you, and I saw your posts on social media. I went for a run and heard a guy calling out 'Angie' to a woman. A lady at the airport made an announcement for an Anjali. The concierge at the Four Seasons had a name tag with your name. I felt I was going crazy . . . I couldn't get away from you. Coincidence? All of it?"

Anji smiled. "I don't think so."

William said he had rejected it at first. It had annoyed him. But gradually, he felt the repeated mentions of her name were a source of life, an encouragement. He needed to push her away until he was ready. And one day, he was. He'd started looking forward to his daily dose of her, and eventually he understood he couldn't live his life without her.

Anji explained that twin flame separation was part of the journey, where one entered a phase of denial because they didn't have the metaphysical backing to handle the experience of the union. Twin flames often didn't recognize each other at the same time. One freaked out and rejected the relationship because they were not ready to recognize they had found their twin. Anji was sure this was what had happened to William.

"I'm so sorry," he said.

Anji kissed him, the gentle touch of her lips reassured him. His body relaxed under hers, and as she caressed his cheek, he smiled and nodded. His eyes were intense, the blue receding under the increasing size of his irises, turning them dark, almost black. She could see the faith in his eyes.

He kissed her back, tenderly at first, and in her openness found the encouragement to rediscover that part of her he had always known. The intensity rose, and he pressed harder, the softness of his lips molding into hers, yet with the urgency of people reaching for oxygen masks in a falling airplane—as though their embrace were the only source of life.

They stopped to take a breath, and Anji pulled back. The love spell paused momentarily, allowing Anji to look into his soul again without losing herself in it. His face was glowing and the light from his eyes spread to the rest of his body. A star shining brightly. He was smiling.

"Where did you feel that?"

This time he knew what she was asking. "Here," he said, touching his solar plexus, just above his belly button.

She smiled back. "Me too."

Their souls twirled and danced, rejoicing at the recognition of their union. They had done it once again.

Glossary

aborrajada—A large fritter made out of plantains and cheese dipped in batter.

ajiaco—A stew made out of corn, chicken, and potatoes.

alma gemela—Soulmate; literal translation is twin soul.

amawat—Dried mango pulp in the form of fruit leather.

arepa—A corn cake made from precooked cornmeal.

Ave Maria—Hail Mary.

bella—Beautiful.

beti—Daughter.

beta—Son or child.

Bhagwan—God or lord.

Bharatanatyam—Indian classical dance.

bhatura—Deep fried bread.

bienvenida—Welcome.

Bollywood—The Indian equivalent of Hollywood; the Indian film center is in Bombay (aka Mumbai).

Brahma—The Hindu god of creation.

bruta (o)—Dumb female (male).

cabalgata—Cavalcade or horse parade.

cacciatore—A sauce made from onions, herbs, tomatoes, bell peppers, and wine.

cacio e pepe—Cheese and pepper; Italian pasta dish made with pecorino cheese and black pepper.

caleña—Woman from Cali.

ciao—A greeting.

chai—Tea.

chawal—Rice.

chontaduro—Palm fruit.

chironji—A small tree nut distinctive to India.

chole—Chickpeas cooked in a spicy gravy.

churro—Fried dough covered in cinnamon sugar.

chutney—Spicy relish used as a condiment, usually containing herbs, fruits, and spices.

dadi—Paternal grandmother.

dal—Lentils.

Devi—Goddess.

dhoti—Traditional Indian men's garb where a cotton cloth is wrapped around the legs.

Diwali—Also known as "Festival of Lights;" Hindu festival that honors the victory of good over evil. On the lunar calendar it typically falls in October or Novemeber.

dosa—a thin crepe made from a batter of finely ground fermented rice and black lentils.

Durga—Hindu goddess known as the mother protector and fighter of evil.

empanada—A fried turnover; the Colombian version uses corn flour dough.

exorcismo—Exorcism.

gajar—Carrot.

garam masala—A spice blend that typically contains black pepper, cardamom, cinnamon, cloves, coriander, cumin, fennel, mace, and nutmeg.

Ganesh—A Hindu god with elephant head known as the remover of obstacles.

Ganesh Chaturthi—Hindu festival that honors the birth of Ganesh.

ghee—Clarified butter.

gnocchi—Small dumpling made of semolina, wheat, egg, cheese, and potato.

grosella—Country gooseberry.

gulab jamun—Fried dough made from flour and milk that is soaked in syrup.

gur—Jaggery; an unrefined, natural cane sugar.

hai—An exclamation used to express surprise, horror, grief, or regret, such as, "Hai Bhagwan," or "Oh lord."

haldi—Turmeric.

halwa—A sweet, porridge-like dish made from cream of wheat.

Hanuman—Hindu Monkey god representing strength and courage.

Holi—also known as the *Festival of Colors*; Hindu festival that honors the coming of spring and abundance of harvest.

ishq—Love.

jalebi—Deep fried flour batter soaked in sugar syrup.

kajal—Kohl; an ancient eye cosmetic made of dark powder for lining eyes and eyelashes.

Kali—Hindu goddess of death and time; she removes the ego and releases souls from the cycle of life and death (reincarnation).

kheer—Rice pudding.

kichadi—a dish made of rice and lentils.

kirtan—narrating or re-telling; a form of chanting that expresses love or devotion to deities or spiritual concepts.

Krishna—Hindu god for love and compassion; he is an avatar of Vishnu.

kurti—Indian female blouse.

Lakshmi—Hindu goddess of wealth and prosperity.

mala—A string of beads used to enhance spiritual practice.

mandap—A covered structure used for Hindu weddings.

masala—A spice.

masala chai— A spicy Indian tea, usually served in milk; spices can vary and may include ginger, clove, fennel, cinnamon, and cardamom, among others.

mausi—Aunt; a mother's sister.

mehndi—Henna painting on hands and feet for women arranged for Hindu weddings and other special celebrations.

mithai—Indian sweets.

mohabbat—Love, romance.

necesitas—You need.

NRI—Non-resident Indian is a well-known acronym for those living outside of India.

paan—Betel leaf filled with areca nut, slaked lime, and assorted ingredients. It often includes a red paste that leaves a red hue in the mouth of the consumer. It is normally consumed after meals, although it can be consumed at any time. After it is chewed, it is spat out or, in some cases, swallowed.

Padre Nuestro—The Lord's Prayer.

pallu—The decorative end of a sari typically worn over the shoulder.

pakora—A fritter made out of vegetables dipped in chickpea flour.

paratha—Flatbread made with wheat flour and layers of ghee or butter.

Parvati—Hindu goddess representing the divine ideal of female; mother of Ganesh.

pasa—it happens.

preeti—Pleasure, kindness, love, grace.

prem—Love or unconditional love.

puri—Deep fried bread.

puta—Whore.

pyar—Love.

qué—What.

rani—Queen.

rollatini—A breaded eggplant dish covered in cheese and seasoning that is rolled up and baked.

roti—Wholewheat flatbread.

Saat Phere—Hindu marriage ceremony in which the groom walks with the bride, and together they walk around a fire seven times.

salchipapa—French fries and pan-fried hot dogs cut into pieces.

samosa—A pastry filled with potatoes and peas.

sancocho de gallina—A soup typical of Cali and Valle del Cauca, Colombia that is made out of hen, plantains, and yucca.

sari—Traditional Indian female garb where a long cloth is decoratively draped around the body.

sfogliatella—Italian pastry that looks like stacked leaves; it is shell-shaped and includes a filling.

Shiva—Hindu god of life energy; the destroyer; the divine ideal of male; father of Ganesh.

sindur—Vermillion; red pigment used by Indian women on their head to show they are married.

sooji—Cream of wheat.

sopressata—Italian salami.

souk—Bazaar.

spezzatino—Beef stew.

subji—Vegetable.

taco al pastor—Taco of thinly sliced marinated pork meat, pineapple, onions, and cilantro and served in a corn tortilla.

telenovela—Spanish language televised soap operas.

thakur—A family of the landowner caste.

torero—Bullfighter.

Vishnu—Hindu god regarded as the preserver; he reincarnated to earth in many forms, the most famous of which is Krishna; he asked Brahma to create the universe.

Acknowledgments

THANK YOU, universe for lovingly prodding me to follow my heart and my purpose. It took me a while but I got there. Thank you for every dove, Anjali, William, sign, and synchronicity you sent my way, and for all the people you put in my path at the exact moment I was ready.

Thank you to every single reader. It's for you that I write.

Thank you, Bernadette Da Silva Fava for seeing what I wasn't ready to see. You were the first person to say I was weird enough to be a writer. Thank you also for being the first person I was comfortable enough with to share my writing "secret."

Thank you, Michael Tall for saying the words that inspired the title.

Thank you, Marcy Neuman and Sara Wiseman for being my spiritual teachers and guiding my growth and evolution. Marcy, it was you perceiving the stories within that drew their cord to me for my spirit to pull them out. Sara, you helped me recognize that writing was greater than me and part of my connection to Source.

Thank you, Amy Beth Rojas Kantorczyk for being my first reader and leading me from having the bones on the page to adding flesh to the story. Thank you for the various other versions of this you read and for being one of the beta readers. Your encouragement made all the difference.

Thank you, Anne Cushwa for your generosity in being my first editor. Without you I wouldn't have gained the courage to persevere.

Thank you to all of those *at Elephant Journal* and the Elephant Academy for introducing me to the art and pleasure of writing.

Thank you, Joanne Fedler. Through all that you offer, you have quietly and perhaps unknowingly been guiding me on every step of this journey.

Thank you, Rebeka Karrant and Bev Pevlin for being my Monday evening writing buddies when this novel was just taking shape. Rebeka, especially, for continuing with our calls far beyond when the time was up, for helping me feel at ease with my inner guidance, and for being a voice of reason.

Thank you, Nailia Minnebaeva, Lisa Benson, Barbara De Villiers Matthews, and Helena Ameisen for being my muses of visibility with whom I shared the first tears of vulnerability in this new path I chose to take. Thank you, Lisa for always being so encouraging and taking the time to comment on every post. Thank you, Nailia for designing the first cover of *Lonely Dove*. I wasn't ready then for what you created but the vision that you put in place kept me going.

Thank you, Karen McDermott for giving me a spot at the retreat in Crom Castle. That experience provided me an opportunity to speak out loud about being a writer for the first time in my life. You also provided me with the first-ever printed copy of *Lonely Dove*. Having something tangible changed me.

Thank you, Annalisa Parent for asking the questions that led to the first version of the manuscript that I was willing to share. Thank you for letting me be a part of the Writing Gym. Thank you, members of the Writing Gym for your camaraderie and outspoken support.

Thank you, Aleena Pitisant and Bilquis Ahmed for your notes on earlier drafts that taught me how to be a better writer. Thank you for reading the novel a second time and being part of my beta reader group.

Thank you to my beta readers, Gin Carter, Stephanie Caunter, Elif Egeli Nisanci, Daanish Khan, and Qais Sultan. Your words of encouragement were a light to my soul.

Thank you, Kez Wickham St. George for seeing the potential in me and in the manuscript and taking me under your wing. You provided the spice that was missing.

Thank you, Jim Dempsey for showing up when I most needed you. More than an editor, I felt you were my partner. I wouldn't have continued if it weren't for you.

Thank you, Koehler Books and the whole team for making my dream a reality. Thank you, Miranda Dillon for taking a chance on me and my manuscript. Thank you, John Koehler for your humorous words of wisdom and your guidance. Thank you, Becky Hilliker for making the editing process seem like a breeze.

Thank you, Nieraj and Alesya for encouraging me to pursue my dreams.

Thank you, Papa for being my one and only buddy, and for encouraging me to do what makes me happy, no matter how challenging it was to accept it was different from what I was "supposed" to do.

Thank you, Mama for being my number one supporter. It doesn't matter what I do or how crazy my projects or ideas are, you are always there, cheering me on, rooting for me, liking me, and loving me. It is because of you that I read. When I was a child, seeing you read opened me up to the world of books. Reading was the magical spark that led me to writing. You are my eternal support and my best friend.

I couldn't have done this without any of you.